SOLDIER

OF THE HORSE

A novel by

ROBERT W. MACKAY

TouchWood
Editions

TouchWood Editions
www.touchwoodeditions.com

LIBRARY AND ARCHIVES CANADA CATALOGUING IN PUBLICATION
Mackay, Robert W. (Robert William), 1942–
Soldier of the horse / Robert W. Mackay.

Print format: ISBN 978-1-926741-24-6
Electronic monograph in PDF format: ISBN 978-1-926741-34-5
Electronic monograph in HTML forma: ISBN 978-1-926741-35-2

1. World War, 1914-1918—Fiction. I. Title.

PS8625.K397S65 2011   C813'.6   C2010-906349-X

Editor: Marlyn Horsdal
Proofreader: Sarah Weber
Design: Pete Kohut
Cover image: Alfred Munnings *A Canadian Trooper and his Horse* (Detail)
CWM 19710261-0460 Beaverbrook Collection of War Art © Canadian War Museum
Author photo: Patricia Sandberg

We gratefully acknowledge the financial support for our publishing activities
from the Government of Canada through the Canada Book Fund, Canada
Council for the Arts, and the province of British Columbia through the
British Columbia Arts Council and the Book Publishing Tax Credit.

The interior pages of this book have been printed on 100% post-consumer
recycled paper, processed chlorine free, and printed with vegetable-based inks.

1 2 3 4 5 14 13 12 11

PRINTED IN CANADA

Soldier of the Horse is dedicated to the memory of my father, Tom Mackay, who was there, and to all those veterans of Canada's armed forces who served with and after him.

CONTENTS

◆ ◆ ◆

A CAREER AT RISK

◆ ◆ ◆

Something was wrong. Tom Macrae couldn't hear the frogs ratcheting away by the Red River. They would quiet down if a creature entered their space: a dog, say, or a man. All was silent except for the even breathing of his younger brother, Alec, asleep in the other bed. Tom pushed back his covers and stood up, pulling on his trousers.

A scraping sound from outside the farmhouse made him stop and stand still, muscles tensing. Then came a stifled curse. He pulled on a shirt and half ran down the hall in his bare feet. He tapped on his parents' bedroom door.

"Dad," he said. "Dad. There's someone prowling around outside."

He eased the door open. His father, Bill, stopped snoring for a second, then started up again.

Tom crept down the stairs. There had been a series of burglaries in East Kildonan in the last few weeks of the autumn of 1914. As he passed the gun rack he picked up a bolt-action .22 rifle and carried it to the front door.

He crouched by the left side of the door, the rifle's stock in his left hand. A muffled whisper came from outside. He jerked the door open and darted out. There was a blinding flash, and the world went black.

As Tom swam up through layers of consciousness, a shimmering white light blinded him, and an ache in his head became a throb. He was lying on his right side, across his front steps. Through narrowed eyes he identified the blazing headlights of an automobile parked a few feet away, facing him. Its engine noise was muffled, as if his ears were full of cotton batting. The wooden steps dug into his upper arm. He tried to move but couldn't; his hands were bound behind him. He felt something run down his face and saw blood, scarlet in the white light, drip to the tread beneath him.

"He's awake." The voice came from his left. He cautiously turned his head to see a uniformed figure. A policeman. He heard a thud from behind him, as though something heavy had been slammed against a wall.

His dad's voice, low and intense, snarled, "Get your paws off me, you four-flushers."

"Let him through," said another voice. The speaker stood in front of Tom, a burly figure in a rumpled suit and bowler hat.

Bill Macrae came down the stairs and knelt in front of Tom. He helped his son sit up, then pulled out a handkerchief and mopped Tom's face. It came away bloody.

Tom's head was spinning, but he mumbled, "You okay, Dad? What did they do to you?"

"Never mind about me, son. What the hell goes on here?" Bill demanded.

"Where's that rifle?" asked the man in the bowler.

A uniformed man stepped forward. "Here, Inspector," he said, and handed him Tom's .22.

The inspector opened the bolt and, turning away, shook the rifle until a cartridge fell into his hand. He held the bullet up to the light, then dropped it into his pocket. "Resisting arrest. Armed. Loaded rifle. Threatening." He looked down at Tom. "Deeper and deeper, boyo. You'll do time for this."

A wave of nausea squeezed Tom's guts. He gritted his teeth, almost choked, and vomited. He leaned forward, spraying puke on his own feet and the policeman's shoes.

The inspector grimaced. "Get him out of here." He turned to leave. "Take him to the cells. Then we'll see." Two oversized policemen yanked Tom upright and pushed him into the back of the idling automobile.

◆ ◆ ◆

Tom Macrae, twenty-year-old student-at-law articled to Henry Zink of the Manitoba bar, sat in the ten-by-twelve-foot interview room in Winnipeg's Central Police Station and fingered the top of his head. The skin had split open in a three-pronged pattern, and the doctor summoned by the police had closed it with six stitches. He had a blinding headache and still felt nauseated, though his stomach had long since come up dry. A series of shivers racked his body.

He had been in this room before, with its greenish walls, its oiled, dark wooden floor, the reek of sweat and stale vomit. Zink had him sit in when clients were being interviewed by the police. It looked and felt very different from this side of the scarred wooden table.

Tom heard the bolt slide back. The inspector entered, followed by a constable who closed the door and leaned against it. They filled the room.

The inspector had taken off his hat but still wore the rumpled suit. Iron-grey hair cut short defined his large head. He pulled up a chair to sit opposite Tom and stared through low-lidded eyes, his hands folded on the table in front of him. "My name is Boyle. I've got some questions for you."

"I know who you are." Tom had seen Inspector Boyle cross-examined in court by Henry Zink. There was no love lost between the inspector and the legal community. He was reputed to invent evidence once he had made up his mind a suspect was guilty—or at least, guilty or not, deserved to go to jail.

"Good. Then you'll know I mean business." He unfolded his hands and bent forward across the table, his face inches from Tom's. "I've got you for resisting arrest, and assault with intent to injure. You came at us with a loaded rifle, mister."

What? Resisting arrest? Arrest for what? Tom tried to organize his thoughts. His head throbbed.

"I wasn't resisting arrest. I was in my own home! I thought you were burglars, trying to break in. But that was kind of stupid of me—burglars wouldn't stumble around the way you did."

3

Boyle's eyes never left Tom's face. "I'd keep a civil tone if I were in your shoes, Macrae." He paused. "Where's Jack Kravenko?" he demanded.

"Kravenko? Kravenko's in jail."

"No, my boy, you're the one in jail."

So Bloody Jack Kravenko was on the loose again. Bloody Jack, subject of no end of newspaper stories poking fun at the police, because it had taken them months to catch the bank robber and murderer. Henry Zink was Kravenko's lawyer; Zink was not popular with the police.

"Let's try another one. Where is Henry Zink?"

"He's at home, I assume. Where else would he be?"

"Think again, Macrae. He's not at home. And he's not in his office, either."

Boyle sat back in his chair, pulling a worn metal case from an inside suit pocket to produce a small cigar. After careful examination he bit off one end and spat it on the floor. He rummaged in a vest pocket for a match, which he ignited with his thumbnail. When the cigar glowed an angry red, he pulled it from his lips and blew a cloud of smoke across the table.

Tom watched Boyle the way a gopher watches a coyote. The inspector's face slowly hardened, as a thick layer of cigar smoke filled the air. Tom felt his pulse pounding in his head. The walls weaved in and out and he couldn't breathe. He needed out of there. What would Zink do in a situation like this?

"Am I under arrest?" he croaked, his mouth dry as a prairie wind in August.

"You're assisting with inquiries," Boyle smirked. "Where was Zink when you saw him last?"

"At his office."

"When?"

"Yesterday afternoon."

"Who was there?"

"Just Zink and me and John . . ."

"John who?"

4

Tom straightened up, clamping his mouth shut. Zink wouldn't let a client answer questions like this.

"Do you own a gun?"

Tom blinked. "Sure. You took it when you arrested me."

"I don't mean a rifle—I mean a handgun!" Boyle thundered, smacking his fist on the table in front of him.

"No, I don't own a handgun. I've had enough of this. I don't know what you're up to but I know my rights. Tell me what this is all about or let me out of here."

"You'll get out when I say so," Boyle growled, his face now a mottled red. "When did you last see Jack Kravenko?"

Tom didn't answer, and Boyle continued. "I'll tell you when you last saw him. Two days ago. Two days before he got away, that's when. You smuggled a gun in to him. Which he used to escape."

Tom's jaw dropped. Boyle puffed on his cigar, nodding. It was true that Tom, Zink, and John Evans had been in the jail, meeting with Kravenko to get instructions, two days earlier. Tom knew he had not smuggled in a gun or anything else, but the mention of one made him uneasy. He suddenly felt protective of Zink and Evans, concerned that they, too, would be unfairly targeted by Boyle.

Tom leaned back and folded his arms. "I'm finished answering questions."

Boyle lurched to his feet, knocking his chair over. He swayed forward, his weight on his straightened arms, knuckles on the scarred tabletop. "I'll just give you a chance to think that over, mister. One of your pals has given us a helpful statement. He'll get special consideration at trial. You'd be smart to do the same." He shook his head as if in sorrow, and turned to the door.

"What pal? What are you talking about?" Tom asked.

Boyle didn't even turn around. The constable yanked the door open. Boyle stomped out and the policeman followed, the door slamming behind him as the bolt rattled home.

An hour later the door opened and two policemen came in. They handcuffed Tom and clamped on leg irons with a half-inch-thick bar between his ankles, added a chain for good measure, and dragged him down the stairs to Courtroom One.

The chain that ran from his leg irons to the handcuffs was short, so Tom had to stoop as he stood in the dock. The cop had given the manacles an extra squeeze, and his hands were turning blue. Tom wondered how long it would take until they fell off, like a bullock's testicles tourniqued with a rubber band.

He flexed his wrists, and the pain that stabbed into his forearms made him collapse against the solid, stained wooden enclosure. He pulled himself back upright, as anger at the police rippled through his brain. What the hell was he, an articled student of the law, an apprentice lawyer for God's sake, doing in the prisoner's dock? He should be sitting at the counsel table.

Tom turned to see his mother, sitting beside his father in the front row. She tried to smile when she saw him looking and Tom's heart sank. His father handed her a handkerchief and she dabbed at her eyes. Isobel Macrae's strong face reflected the emotional scars from the loss of Tom's youngest brother, Ray, who had drowned two years before. Tom wished there was something he could do to ease her latest burden. Bill Macrae took his wife's hand and gave her a concerned glance.

Tom took in the small courtroom on the second floor of the police station from an unfamiliar angle. It looked like a church, complete with a choir stall for the jury and a bar to keep the rabble in the pews, but prayer was unlikely to affect these proceedings. He held out hope, though, that his standing in the community as an articled student would at least allow him his freedom while all this was sorted out.

"Order in court," intoned the clerk, as Judge Ezekiel Dansing entered the room and climbed to the bench. Good old Ezekiel. Tom had been in front of Dansing only once before. Henry Zink had produced a legal argument that gave the judge and jury no option but to acquit their client, and Tom, as Zink's articled student, had sat beside him at the counsel table, feeling smug. He didn't feel so smug now.

"Yes, Mr. Clerk?" said the judge. But his gimlet-eyed gaze was fixed on Tom.

The court clerk stood and read the charge. "That you, Thomas Henderson Macrae, did, on December first, nineteen hundred and fourteen, aid and abet the escape from jail of one Jack Kravenko, lawfully confined. How do you plead?"

Tom was about to croak, "Not guilty," when the door at the back of the courtroom banged open. John Evans, King's Counsel, partner in Winnipeg's largest and most prestigious law firm, strode down the centre aisle.

"Your Honour, I have not yet had a chance to meet with my client."

Tom felt as surprised as the judge looked.

Judge Dansing was not to be thrown off. "I'll take that as a 'Not guilty.' You can meet with him to your heart's content, because I am remanding the accused in custody for ten days."

Ten days! Tom's stomach heaved, and he felt a rush of blood to his face. He heard a gasp and turned to see his mother's hand at her mouth, her eyes wide. How could any judge, even Dansing, do this to him, to his family? He swung to face the bench but the judge was gone, and the cops dragged him down from the dock and out of the courtroom.

Minutes later, Tom was in a cell on the top floor of the police station. He sat on the lower bunk and gazed at the steel wall three feet in front of him, rubbing his wrists. The handcuffs and leg irons were gone but the pain remained. The pain, and the anger.

He looked around his iron box and felt a stab of claustrophobia. Stretching his arms, he easily touched the front and back walls—under six feet. Even less from side to side. Half of the front wall was a barred door and the other half a rusting metal plate. Two bunks, a toilet, and a wash basin were squeezed into the spartan, white space.

Steel-shod boots clicked on the wooden floor of the passage outside his cell, and Tom pushed his head against the bars on the door so he could look down the hall a few feet. A scuffling noise and muffled curses accompanied what Tom could now see were two policemen with a rumpled, unsteady figure between them. It was Henry Zink, the man to whom Tom owed his recent professional standing. Zink groaned and muttered. A miasma of sweat, cigar, and rye whiskey assailed Tom as he watched. The jailers pushed Zink into the adjoining cell and slammed the door behind him. Keys rattled as the lock clicked home.

"That you, Tom?" Zink rasped. Tom could hear him shuffling to the front of his cell.

The two men stood facing the wall opposite their cells, shoulder to shoulder but for the thin metal barrier between them.

"Henry, what's going on here? I've been charged with aiding and abetting Bloody Jack's escape. How did he get out?"

"I don't know much more than you do, Tommy-boy. The police are looking for Bernie Inkmann too."

So Inspector Boyle was casting a large net, hoping to land Inkmann, who did odd jobs for Zink and had once been Zink's student, the position now held by Tom. Boyle was out to arrest the entire legal crew.

"Have they charged you, Henry?"

"I think they're just holding me until they can interview everyone. Then I expect to be out of here." Zink's whiskey-soaked breath wafted into Tom's cell.

Tom gripped the bars on the door, his knuckles white. Why would Zink get out when he couldn't?

Zink lowered his voice and spoke again. "Here's the deal, Tom. The cops will charge Bernie Inkmann, just like they did you. They think you and Bernie worked the escape with Bloody Jack. Maybe he promised you a cut of his stolen loot. Now, I can help you with all this."

What? Tom thought. Where is this coming from? He couldn't get his mind around what Zink was saying. "I didn't do anything! What do you mean, you can help?"

"I'm going to get a clean bill of health from my friend Inspector Boyle, once I get to talk to him. I want you and Bernie to own up to smuggling in the gun and I'll work my tail off to get you both reduced sentences. You'll be out in no time and I'll make sure there's money in an account for you."

"Gun? What gun?"

"Oh, you know about the gun, don't you, Tom? The one you picked up and delivered—not that I'm saying where to. Hell, you can say you didn't know it was loaded, or Jack said he'd only use it to scare the guards, or something."

"That's the stupidest thing I've ever heard. I didn't smuggle in any gun." If Henry had his way, Tom would be in jail and Henry would be out, free as a bird. "You're as bad as Inspector Boyle, making things up." Tom tried unsuccessfully to stop his voice from shaking.

"Calm down, young Tom. Think it over. Once I'm on the outside I can do you a lot of good."

Any solidarity he had ever felt with Zink drained from Tom in a rush. "Just like you did a lot of good for Bloody Jack," he exploded. "What are you going to do—smuggle a gun in to me, too?"

"Don't get smart, Macrae. I'll deal with you, and I'll deal with anybody who goes against me." Zink's voice hardened. "Anyone thinks Henry Zink is done for is in for a big surprise."

Tom heard his boss back away in his cell and flop onto the bunk. Heavy breathing turned into loud snores. Tom stood at the bars for a long time, staring out.

◆　◆　◆

They came for him early next morning. Tom was dog-tired after a restless night, his six-foot frame cramped in the tiny cell. His life was spinning out of control and he didn't know how to stop it, his mental turmoil overshadowing the ongoing pain in his scalp where the policeman had walloped him.

The jailers handcuffed him, marched him down the stairs, and loaded him into a horse-drawn paddy wagon, which jolted ahead. Tom jammed himself into a corner so he wouldn't bounce around, shivering as the bare wooden bench sucked the warmth from his body. The wagon swayed and clattered through the chilly dawn; Tom could make out, through the small barred window, that they were going south on Main Street. When the driver called "Whoa," the wagon creaked to a stop and one of the cops pulled him out into the faint light, where Tom recognized the back of the main courthouse. He had no time to collect himself before his escort pushed him through a doorway marked POLICE ONLY and up a flight of stairs.

The policemen sat him down in an interview room where they removed the handcuffs, leaving him alone, and took up station just outside the open door. A few minutes later John Evans came in and shut the door behind him.

Tom straightened. Besides being a big-shot lawyer, Evans was the father of Ellen. Good lord, what must Ellen think when she heard about all this?

John Evans was a slim, immaculate figure in a three-piece suit. "Your father has asked me to advise you."

Tom wasn't sure he needed advice. What he needed was to turn back the clock, get out of this mess. "I really don't know what's going on."

"I think you may know more than you're letting on. But never mind that for now. I'm not comfortable acting for you. For personal reasons. And because nobody knows where the police investigation will go next." Evans paused. "I must attend to something right away, but I'll be back in a few minutes. You can decide if you want me to help you, or not." He turned on his heel and walked out.

This was a nightmare, a nightmare parallel to the one Tom sometimes dreamed in which he had to run from terrible danger but could move at only a tenth his normal speed. Like trying to run in water up to his waist. But this time he was up to his neck.

For years, Tom had looked forward to becoming a lawyer. His family had scrounged and saved so he could go to university. He looked up to lawyers—ironically, he had even looked up to Henry Zink. Zink had a colourful history, but what mattered to Tom was completing articles so he could be called to the bar. He wanted to share in the camaraderie and professionalism of the lawyers he had met; he wanted to help people, and he wanted to make money and gain the respect it would bring. But back in his cell, Zink was talking like a crook.

Tom was in big trouble, and John Evans, King's Counsel, wanted to "advise" him. But Tom knew Evans had some sort of problems of his own, in spite of the lawyer's position. What would be next—advice that Tom should plead guilty?

♦   ♦   ♦

Only a few weeks before, on the day Tom met John Evans for the first time, the Portage Avenue streetcar had bumped and rumbled west along the avenue of the same name. There was nobody in it but the driver, Tom, and a sixtyish, well-dressed woman who glared at him through tiny glasses perched on the end of her nose. A Union Jack brooch clung to her ample bosom. In her spare time she'd be knitting socks for the boys going overseas and no doubt was wondering why he, young and fit, wasn't with them.

He scanned the front page of the *Free Press*. The British government—and hence Canada—had declared war on Germany barely a month before. Now, in early September of 1914, the professional soldiers of the British Expeditionary Force and the French army had been staggered by the German army's rush through Belgium. British and French alike were struggling with Germans on the outskirts of Paris. In response to these doleful circumstances, Canadian recruiting offices had been overwhelmed with volunteers; the Canadian Expeditionary Force was mustering in Valcartier, Quebec, where it prepared to cross the Atlantic to save the Empire. Well, the Canadian army could do it without Tom. He was an articled student of the law with a fine career beckoning.

He left the newspaper on the streetcar when he got off and walked the three blocks south to John Evans's home on Wolseley Avenue. A whiff of burning leaves spiced the clear fall air; the elm trees that lined the street glowed green in the late afternoon sun. Winnipeg was the largest city in western Canada, the Gateway to the West. Located at the strategic junction of the Red and Assiniboine rivers, it boasted electric streetlights and the magnificent Walker Theatre, an opera house that rivalled anything in eastern Canada.

Tom was nervous about this, the first Evans garden party to which he had been invited. The parties were a fixture of the season, a must for up-and-coming young lawyers and other professionals, and many of Winnipeg's leading lights would be there. And with any luck, some eligible young women.

Tom walked up to the brass-studded door and banged the knocker. While he waited he took a quick look around at the expensive homes with their well-tended lawns. Two years earlier, while he was in university, he had worked for the summer installing sewers two blocks over. He was finished with crawling in muddy ditches and damn glad of it.

Steps echoed from inside the house and the door opened. An older man in grey striped trousers and a charcoal jacket stood to one side, his face neutral.

Tom stuck out his hand. "Tom Macrae, Mr. Evans. How do you do?"

The man ignored his hand. "I am the butler, sir. This way."

The butler turned away and Tom followed him in. He could feel his cheeks burning. Great start, Tom.

They walked through the house, dark after the brilliant outdoor light, and out to a back garden with an acre of lawn, scattered flowerbeds, and ornamental trees. The butler approached a dapper, elegant man in his fifties, speaking to a girl who looked to be in her late teens, and an elderly couple.

"Mr. Tom Macrae," the butler intoned.

The dapper man, who had a well-barbered head of grey hair and a thin mustache, gave Tom a cool smile and a hand to shake. "John Evans, Mr. Macrae. Welcome to our annual affair."

The other couple meandered off, but the girl stayed. She had a direct gaze, blue eyes, and a spray of freckles. She was tall, almost as tall as Tom, and her chestnut hair cascaded to her shoulders.

"Aren't you going to introduce us, Daddy?" she asked, as she linked her arm in her father's.

"Of course, my dear. This is Mr. Tom Macrae, an articled law student. He works for Henry Zink, one of our . . . more colourful criminal lawyers."

The girl made a small movement of her head and shifted her body slightly, the movement striking Tom as somewhere between the start of a curtsy and a royal nod. He reluctantly turned back to John Evans, who was still speaking. "Mr. Macrae, my daughter Ellen. She has been attending school in the east."

Tom took in Ellen's willowy, fashionable shape, draped in a demure blue dress that failed to hide her appealing figure.

"You work for Mr. Zink?" she asked. "Then you'll know all about Bloody Jack Kravenko. Have you met him?"

"Oh, I've met him right enough," Tom replied, and was about to let some titillating detail slip to keep Ellen's attention. His recent working days had been spent with Henry Zink and Kravenko, preparing for Bloody Jack's murder trial.

John Evans frowned and interrupted. "Now, I am sure Mr. Macrae doesn't want to talk about clients. And I see more guests have arrived. Come along, Ellen, and we'll say hello."

Evans guided Ellen away, but as he did so, she looked back at Tom with a quick, direct glance and a conspiratorial smile that made him feel lightheaded.

A punch bowl and sandwiches were set up on a table under the rustling leaves of a willow tree. Tom wandered over and helped himself to a glass of punch. It looked innocuous, a neutral yellowish liquid with pieces of fruit floating in it, but his first sip revealed a refreshing citrus tang, followed by a slight tingle. He refilled his glass, and turned as a tall, khaki-clad man marched up to stand next to him. Calf-high leather boots glistened below the uniform of a lieutenant in the Canadian army.

"I'm told you are Henry Zink's latest student," he said, in what to Tom sounded like a vaguely English accent, while ladling a measure of punch into a glass.

"I am."

"I'm Cedric Inkmann. You must know my brother Bernard."

"Of course." Tom knew the Inkmanns were well connected in Winnipeg—indeed, Canadian—society. Cedric was a larger version of his brother, who continued to work for Zink in some ill-defined role. "How long have you been in the army?"

"Years," Inkmann said. "In the militia. Now that war has been declared I'm on active duty. I work at Winnipeg Depot, on training staff. Bit of a challenge, teaching farm boys to march."

Tom noted another characteristic common to the Inkmann brothers: They never quite looked you in the eye when they spoke.

Tom had drained his second glass. He refilled it again, and looked around to see if there was anything interesting going on, such as any sign of Ellen Evans. He caught sight of her as she strolled with another girl on the far side of the lawn.

Cedric Inkmann interrupted Tom's thoughts. "You needn't waste your efforts there. She won't have time for the likes of you."

Tom felt a surge of anger at Inkmann's tone. The aristocratic accent didn't help. "You should mind your own business," he growled, temper flaring. He felt like smashing Inkmann in the face, but instead he placed his glass on the table, working hard to stop his hand from shaking, giving his anger time to dissipate. On his best behaviour, he turned and walked away.

Tom was his father's son. Bill Macrae was a hard-driving, hard-drinking prairie contractor; he would hire dozens of rambunctious teamsters and labourers for various projects, and didn't hesitate to maintain order with his fists or whatever tool came to hand. Sometimes Tom, as the boss's son, was sent to collect teamsters from back alleys in the North End where they were sleeping off the effects of a night's carousing. Still drunk or angry men sometimes took a swing at him and the fight would be on. But Tom reasoned that bare-knuckle brawling was not a requirement for a law career and might even interfere with it, so he did his best to avoid trouble.

He took a deep breath and contented himself by exploring the back of the Evans lawn, which looked out on the Assiniboine River. The sight of the grey-brown river, slowing to flow into the Red two miles downstream, calmed him until the punch bowl once again beckoned. Inkmann had moved on and was nowhere to be seen.

The sun had slipped down behind trees to the west, and some of the guests, as if responding to its pull, were leaving. Tom saw a group of young people, mostly men, around Ellen and her friend. One of the uniformed men was Bill Reagan, whom he knew from university.

He walked over and noticed that Bill stood face to face with Ellen, which puzzled him. Bill was several inches shorter than Tom.

Ellen said something to Bill that Tom didn't hear.

"Fort Garry Horse," Bill responded. "It's a reserve unit, but we're being brought up to full strength in order to be ready to go overseas as soon as possible. Cavalry."

"Cavalry?" Tom butted in. "The papers say there's no place for cavalry in modern warfare."

"Nonsense." Bill snorted as if he were a horse himself. "Mounted soldiers are very mobile." He added with a laugh, "And at least I'll go to war like a gentleman. On horseback."

"A gentleman? Guess that lets me out," Tom joked, and was rewarded by appreciative chuckles.

He saw that Bill was standing on a flat stone, one of several that bordered a flower bed. No wonder he was eyeball to eyeball with Ellen.

When he teetered a little, Tom reached up with his right hand, grasped the back of Bill's tunic and pulled him down off his perch. He put his arm around his friend's shoulders and grinned at Ellen.

"Now where did Bill go?" Ellen laughed. "I could have sworn I was just talking to him."

"Oh, Bill is right here. He always lands on his feet, even if he falls from a great height."

"And what about you, Tom Macrae? Do you always land on your feet?"

"Always. And I've got nowhere to go but up."

Ellen gave him a frank look and smiled. "You must tell me about it some day. But I see Daddy waving, and I have guests to say goodbye to. I do want to hear all about Bloody Jack Kravenko and Henry Zink, though."

She gave a little wave of her hand, which might have been an embrace, given its effect on Tom as he watched her walk away. He had felt lightheaded earlier; now he figured it was a miracle his feet remained on the ground.

Miss Ellen Evans wanted to see him again.

◆ ◆ ◆

Tom's reveries were interrupted by the sound of John Evans's voice out in the courthouse hall, talking to the policemen. Evans came back into the interview room, closed the door behind him, and sat across the table from Tom. His face was haggard, as if he, too, hadn't slept well.

"I'm willing to help in a limited fashion, but after today I have worries of my own."

"I don't want . . ."

Evans cut Tom off with a raised hand. "I'm going to bring you up to date, then you can decide what you want to do. As you know, Bloody Jack is on the run. He escaped using a gun smuggled in to him by persons unknown." Evans gave Tom a sharp glance. Tom was annoyed at the unspoken question, but at the same time he was amused at Evans's tone, which would have been more in keeping with an address to the House of

Lords. "Kravenko used the gun to subdue the guards. He locked them in a storage room and climbed to the roof. Once there, he let himself down the outside of the jail, but the rope, which had also been smuggled in, parted when he was halfway down."

Tom would have laughed aloud if he hadn't been in jail himself. Jack Kravenko, the scourge of the entire province of Manitoba, the man who had eluded and taunted the police for months, had taken a pratfall while escaping jail. Tom was almost afraid to ask. "What kind of gun did Bloody Jack have? Where did he get it?"

"I don't know. But I fear the worst."

"Meaning it was smuggled in by Henry Zink?"

"Precisely."

Tom's mind raced. Henry Zink, Bloody Jack's lawyer, had been arrested, presumably due to the jailbreak. Tom had been arrested, linked to the escape by the simple fact that he worked for Zink, but not only that: Tom, and others, had often met with Kravenko in his cell. And somehow a gun had ended up in Bloody Jack's possession.

"Unfortunately, for Kravenko and perhaps for others," Evans continued, "he appears to have been injured in the fall. Even so, he hobbled off and made good his escape, although he dropped the gun at the scene."

"What do you mean, unfortunate for him 'and perhaps for others'?" Tom asked. A thought flashed through his mind: too bad Jack hadn't broken his neck; it would save the government the hangman's fee. But that was no way for a student lawyer to think.

"What I mean, Mr. Macrae, is that if and when the police capture Kravenko, they will take a statement from him. Who knows what he will say in an effort to gain some advantage?" Evans gave Tom a searching glance. "And that could affect a lot of people. I must also tell you that your employer, Henry Zink, is under arrest."

"I know Henry was arrested. We shared accommodation last night." Tom mulled over what Evans had said. "Just a minute," he cried, relief in his voice. The words rushed out. "You. You were in the cell with Bloody

Jack and Zink and me before his escape. We all carried briefcases. I was the first to leave, and I took my briefcase with me." He stopped. He had been about to say that, for all he knew, Zink or Evans could have smuggled in the gun. He didn't trust Zink, but he did not want to come to the same conclusion about John Evans.

As if he read Tom's mind, Evans said, "I do recall you leaving, but for some reason you were not signed out. I was. So was Zink, later on. So I have corroboration that Henry was in with Bloody Jack, after I left. You don't have that corroboration. My evidence would help you, but that makes me a witness, so I can't act as your lawyer in any formal way."

Again Tom desperately cudgelled his memory. Why had he not signed out of the jail after the meeting with Evans, Zink, and Bloody Jack? And who knew what story Zink was concocting to clear his name while implicating Tom? His mind rocked with an image of himself once again behind bars.

"I've got to get out of this." His voice cracked. He felt like ramming his head against the wall.

Evans spoke quietly. "There is something we can do."

Tom looked at him.

"Judge Paterson of the appeal court has taken a personal interest in your case. I know him well and have arranged an interview with him." He pulled his watch out of his waistcoat pocket. "He's waiting for us now."

Tom had nothing to lose. Evans led the way out of the room and down the hall to the judge's chambers, policemen pacing behind them. He knocked on a door, and one of the constables put his hand on Tom's arm.

"Come," reverberated a muffled voice from inside.

Evans opened the door, and Tom and the policemen followed him in. Seated in front of a large desk was Tom's father, Bill, and behind the desk, in a tall, ornate chair, was Court of Appeal Justice George Paterson. Paterson had once been Bill's lawyer.

On the wall behind the judge was the Manitoba coat of arms;

paintings of buffalo and Native encampments were hung on the other three sides of the room.

Paterson nodded at the policemen. "That will be all, gentlemen." They left, shutting the door behind them with a barely audible click.

Paterson stood, not a tall man, but an imposing, portly figure in waistcoat, striped trousers, and wing collar, with his robe tossed casually across a side table. He held out his hand and Tom shook it, not knowing what to expect. The judge steered him and Evans to chairs, then returned to his own.

"This is rather unusual. I'm sure you're wondering why you're here," said Paterson, as Tom glanced from the judge to his father. "Your father and your counsel," he continued, nodding at Evans, "have brought me up to date on the charges you face. I'm discussing this with you, by the way, out of respect for your father and of course I know John Evans well. But if any aspect of this matter reaches the Court of Appeal I will excuse myself and leave the field to my brother judges. So much for the formalities. From what I understand, the police, in spite of the charges they have laid, do not have a strong case against you. Their theory is that you filed the serial numbers off a gun, then smuggled it in to Kravenko."

"I didn't smuggle any gun. Or file off any serial numbers."

"I'll take your word on that, for the sake of our present discussion," Paterson said, frowning. "I understand, however, that a Colt hammerless automatic, probably the weapon Kravenko used in his escape, was stolen from Ashdown's Hardware by persons unknown. I also understand," and he flashed a glance at Evans, "that it was delivered to Zink's office. And that you, Zink, and Mr. Evans here visited Kravenko in his cell some time after that."

Paterson went on to recount what Tom already knew from Evans. He added, "I have just learned that a court clerk, who had been working late and chanced by, was shot by Kravenko after he descended from the top floor of the jail. The clerk identified Bloody Jack as the man who shot him. I also know that Inspector Boyle, the officer in charge, wants to see you all in Stony Mountain. You should know that Zink is a dangerous man—and a very capable one. In order to save his own skin he's pointing the finger in all directions, but most specifically at you, Tom."

The mention of Stony Mountain sent a shiver up Tom's spine. An overnight cell in the police lockup was one thing. Stony Mountain Penitentiary was quite another.

Tom's father leaned forward and spoke. "Judge Paterson has a proposition for you."

Tom looked at the judge.

"Tom, your law career may be over. Inspector Boyle is convinced you were involved in the jailbreak and will hound you until he gets a conviction. Even if you avoid him and are not convicted of anything, I doubt that the Law Society would ever admit you. Dirt will stick to you as this fiasco unfolds, and the leaders of the Law Society are not known for their generosity in admitting men of doubtful character."

Tom felt blood rush to his face. He had been dragged into a courtroom and embarrassed, and that was bad enough. Now here was a judge of the highest court in the province implying he was a dupe or worse.

Paterson's gaze flicked across a framed photograph on the side table. "There is a way out. With honour, that will wipe the slate clean. The British Empire is in the utmost need of men in Europe. My own son . . ." He paused, and Tom looked more closely at the photograph—a young man in an officer's uniform. He glanced back at the judge, whose face had slackened as if it were dissolving. With a visible effort Paterson regained control of his voice, and Tom knew for a certainty, even as the judge spoke again, that Paterson junior would not be coming home from the war. "You can volunteer for the army. A short stint overseas and all will be forgotten. You can pick up again—go into business. Who knows, perhaps you'll get some satisfaction from serving your country and make a career of it."

Make a career of the army? Fat chance of that. But if he didn't take this way out, he'd be back in jail with Zink. He knew Zink was a bulldog, a tenacious fighter who never gave up. Tom doubted that his protestations of innocence could overcome whatever tale Zink concocted, and Boyle, the policeman, would just as soon lock up the lot of them.

Tom couldn't face more handcuffs, another jail cell. And there was another consideration: his mother, who was not well in any event, simply could not cope with her eldest son ensconced as a permanent guest of His Majesty.

A career in the law had been his ambition, and lawyers his heroes. His goal was slipping away, and his heroes had feet of clay. He felt as though he were drowning, and Judge Paterson was throwing him a life preserver. Tom looked the judge in the eye. The hell with the law and the hell with lawyers. Unlike the judge's son, he'd be back. But first things first.

"It's a deal," he said. "Just get me out of here."

THE RELUCTANT HORSEMAN

◆ ◆ ◆

Tom pulled at his starched white collar, and a trickle of sweat ran down his neck. He sat bolt upright on a wooden bench, his muscular frame in a blue serge suit, a stark contrast to the figures on either side of him. To his left was a lanky young man in denim and high-heeled riding boots, spurs, and a black Stetson. The one on his right wore low-heeled boots, riding breeches, and a buckskin coat. The hat was a giveaway—also a Stetson, but flat-brimmed.

Tom had shaken hands with them—Bruce Johanson, cowboy, and Gordon Ferguson, ex-North West Mounted Policeman—and now the three of them fidgeted in the off-green orderly room of Fort Osborne Barracks, Winnipeg.

A corporal, partially hidden behind a desk piled high with papers and buff-coloured files, stopped typing and ripped a form from the carriage. "Macrae," he said. Tom stood and walked to the desk. "Read this. Check it's accurate."

The form was on legal-size paper—did the army know how ironic that was?—and headed "Attestation Paper; Canadian Over-Seas Expeditionary Force." Next of kin, address, marital status. It would bind Tom to serve for at least a year, more if required, during the "war now existing between Great Britain and Germany," or "until legally discharged." He had to swear to be faithful and bear true allegiance to King George the Fifth, and to obey "all the Generals and Officers set over me."

He didn't really pay much attention. He would sign it whatever it said. He picked up a straight pen off the desk and dipped it into the corporal's inkpot.

"Just a minute, Macrae. We need an officer to witness." The corporal knocked on a door behind his desk.

A moment later it opened and a bulky man in khaki walked out. It was Cedric Inkmann. He looked at the form and then at Tom. "Well, well. Tom Macrae."

Tom kept his mouth shut.

"Read the oath aloud, Mr. Macrae."

He did so.

"Sign it in three places, Mr. Macrae."

He signed. In three places, beside the *X*s. In triplicate.

Inkmann signed as witness, picked up the papers. "Welcome to the Canadian army, Private."

"Thank you," said Tom, his voice neutral.

Inkmann kept his eyes on Tom. "Corporal," he said, "once you have cleaned up your paperwork and uniforms have been issued, kindly march Private Macrae to the parade square. Explain to him, while he doubles for ten minutes, that he must address officers as 'sir.'"

The corporal jumped to his feet. "Yes, sir!"

Tom wondered if the penitentiary might have been a better option.

Inkmann went back into his office and shut the door. The corporal sat and processed the next set of documents, the thick sandwich of paper and carbons grinding through his typewriter as he hammered on the keys. When Johanson and Ferguson were sworn in, they addressed Inkmann as "sir."

◆ , ◆ ◆

Uniforms were issued. The corporal sent Johanson and Ferguson off to barracks, and marched Tom to the parade square. It was at least as long as a football field, and those hundred yards witnessed his inauguration into all things military. He learned that "double" meant "run", that new army boots were painful to run in, and that corporals did not like to do extra work in order to punish enlisted men. Corporal Baker took out his pique on Tom. When he was finally dismissed he had blisters on both feet, and he limped off to barracks.

Next morning Tom was one of thirty men fallen in on the parade square where, standing at attention in three ranks, they were yelled at by Corporal Baker and an enthusiastic henchman with one chevron on his arms—a lance-corporal, Tom had learned. The mysteries of standing at attention, standing at ease, stepping off with the left foot, turning and wheeling were drummed into the recruits.

After an hour of this they were dismissed and ordered to gather around a sergeant who stood at one end of the square, watching. He was a tall, angular man with a scarred face who looked as though he had been through the wars. The campaign ribbons on his tunic removed all doubt.

"Has to be regular army," Ferguson, the ex-Mountie, muttered in his Scottish burr.

The sergeant's glare quieted the men in a hurry. "My name is Quartermain. I will be in charge of you while you are here in Winnipeg Depot. You have all volunteered for the army, and the army will make use of you. You will go overseas within weeks. You have a lot to learn. From now on you will be known as the 1st Reinforcement. You will join my regiment, Lord Strathcona's Horse, as fast as I can get you there. You can consider yourselves lucky to be posted to the army's top cavalry unit. Any questions?"

Hell, Tom thought. Now that he looked more closely, he saw that Quartermain wore spurs on his boots. On reflection, there *had* been a lot of horses and horsemen at the barracks, but it had never occurred to him he'd be in the cavalry.

When Tom was a boy, his mother had a small gelding called Charlie. She would have Tom's father hitch Charlie to her buggy so she could do her errands and take the kids for rides to town. Charlie was spoiled and hard to handle.

Once, when Tom was twelve, he was sent to the pasture to catch Charlie. Charlie didn't want to be caught and kept turning away, presenting his fat rump so Tom couldn't get a rope on him. Annoyed, Tom had grabbed Charlie's tail and given him a smack with the coiled rope. The horse promptly kicked Tom in the face with both hind hoofs. He never went near another horse without thinking about his broken nose and loosened teeth.

Sergeant Quartermain dismissed the men. Tom was still thinking about his broken nose and hurried off to talk to Corporal Baker in the orderly room.

"What do you mean, you don't want to ride horses? You're in the bloody cavalry, soldier," Baker bellowed at Tom, who stood at attention.

"Well, Corporal, couldn't I have some sort of different job, one where I don't have to ride?"

"Sure, Macrae. The army exists just so guys like you get to do whatever you want. But don't worry. If you can't ride, the sergeant will see you get sent to the infantry. All you have to do is fall off your horse a lot." He gave Tom a malevolent grin. "Think your feet are sore now? You'd enjoy the infantry. Now get out of my office and report to barracks along with the rest of the reinforcement."

Tom went. He would put up with the cavalry. He had only ever met one infantryman, and it still gave him the shakes to think about it.

◆　◆　◆

A couple of weeks after the Evans garden party, Tom had been working late one night doing research at the courthouse library. As had happened so often recently, he found himself picturing Ellen at the party, her ready smile and easy way of speaking distinguishing her from other girls he knew. Her tall and slender but generous figure flitted through his mind's eye, her obvious charms not at all hidden by the voluminous fashions of the day. On the spur of the moment he decided to try to meet her at the General Hospital where she volunteered, assisting in the treatment of wounded veterans. He walked up Notre Dame, turned north on Sherbrook, and in minutes reached the hospital.

The old building was gloomy at night, a frame structure with steps leading up from the sidewalk to double doors under a pillared porch. Inside, a woman behind a counter bent over some papers. Tom told her he had an urgent message for Ellen. She gave him a doubtful look but directed him to the top floor.

Tom hesitated but carried on, feeling like an interloper, seeking Ellen out here at her work. He had contrived to see her briefly once or twice since the garden party, always in the company of others, and had found out she had an older brother who was in the British army, but no other close relatives except her father.

He climbed the stairs and looked down a long, poorly lit hall that smelled of floor wax and disinfectant. At the far end a young woman in a white nurse's uniform appeared briefly before going through a doorway. Tom approached the door where he saw a name tag pinned to the door frame. Sergeant D. Grey. He peered in.

The nurse and Ellen were side by side, facing a bed, their backs to him. Ellen, wearing a white nurse's outfit, straightened a pillow as Tom cleared his throat, and they both turned.

"Tom!" Ellen exclaimed, her eyes widening. "What are you doing here?"

"I was in the area anyway, thought I'd see what you were up to."

Ellen flushed. The nurse had paused, a spoon halfway to their patient, who sat upright, propped in place with pillows.

"If you want dinner, you'll have to get in line," the man croaked. His eyes slowly turned toward Tom, then just as slowly slid back to the nurse.

"He shouldn't be up here," the nurse muttered.

"I'll be finished in a few minutes," Ellen said to Tom, sounding vaguely annoyed. "You can wait for me downstairs."

The nurse brought her spoon to the man's mouth. He opened it and swallowed. A big man, Tom saw: barrel-chested, with a drawn face and lifeless eyes, gowned from the neck down. He couldn't feed himself—he had no arms.

The horror of Grey's helplessness struck Tom like an unexpected blind-side tackle, and he got out of there fast. He thought he was going to vomit but made it to the street and sucked in some cool night air. In his mind he pictured the blood pounding in his arteries and veins, muscles working, air pumping in and out of his lungs. It made him feel a little better.

Poor, damned Sergeant Grey. Pitiful sod probably thought he was serving King and Country, saving the Empire On Which the Sun Never Set. Well, he had paid a high price. God help me if I ended up like that, Tom thought. I'd go mad. He shivered, and sat on the top step.

He wasn't there long before he heard the door open behind him. He turned and saw Ellen, now in a dark brown suit with a bright blue scarf. He jumped to his feet.

"Really, Tom, you shouldn't barge in when I'm volunteering." She wagged her finger at him, even as a bit of smile tugged at the corners of her mouth.

"I thought I'd see what you did with yourself besides attend garden parties." Tom immediately felt as though he'd pulled his hand off a hot stew pot and jammed it into the coals. This wasn't going well. He added in a conciliatory voice, "You did look pretty busy."

"I am pretty busy. And I can assure you it's not all garden parties. Daddy wants me to continue with university, but I'm spending more and more time helping out at the hospital. People say there will be many more wounded before the war is over. Anyway, let's not talk about that. You can walk me to my streetcar, as long as you're here." She took his arm.

Tom was thankful he had weathered that little storm, but he couldn't get the image of the armless man out of his mind. "I have to admit, you won't find me tending to the likes of Sergeant Grey."

"Then it's a good thing I'm here to do it, isn't it?"

They walked most of a block before Tom asked, "What happened to him, anyway?"

"The story I heard was that a grenade landed beside him and his men. Sometimes they have time to throw them back before they explode, but this one went off as he was reaching for it. He had awful wounds, and they had to amputate. Nobody knows what will become of him."

"Heaven help me if I'm ever fool enough to enlist. If I do, you have my permission to take me out and shoot me."

"That's a stupid thing to say, when good men are dying every day. Some things are worth fighting for. Underneath it all you're probably as patriotic as the rest of us."

Sure. But not to the point of getting myself blown up. Tom kept the thought to himself.

Ellen spoke. "Did you know my brother was injured in Belgium?"

"No! Is he going to be all right?"

"He has a broken back." She bit her lip. "They say he won't walk again."

Tom gaped at her. "When did this happen?"

"Just a month ago. He was in the militia here in Canada, but he was in England on business when the war broke out and he accepted a commission in the British regular force. He was injured in the first weeks of the war. They'll be shipping him home soon. I feel badly for his wife, and to make matters worse, she's pregnant, with the baby due any day. It should be a happy time for her, but I've never seen anyone so sad."

"That's terrible."

"I'm sure I will be able to help. It's important that we be cheerful around him, the same as I am with Sergeant Grey. But I don't have to spend my life with Sergeant Grey. A few hours a day is one thing—a lifetime is another." Ellen was quiet for a few steps, then seemed to shake herself out of her mood. "Now what about you? You'll become a lawyer when you finish your articles?"

"Absolutely. One more year to go."

"I don't know how you can defend someone you know is guilty."

"Well, the theory is, everyone deserves counsel, guilty or not. If you start acting only for the people you believe innocent, you're no longer a lawyer—you're doing the jury's job. Anyway, I'm not interested in defending criminals. They aren't usually nice people."

"Daddy mainly works for businessmen—banks and clients like that. But I worry about him. My mother died two years ago, and now that I'm back home to stay, I can see he's changed a lot. He misses her, I know, and he works too hard."

"Don't worry," Tom said. "When I get called to the bar, I'll set up an office and he can come work with me. He can do all the easy cases."

"Very generous," Ellen laughed.

As they strolled along Notre Dame, Ellen's streetcar rumbled up and squealed to a stop. She gave Tom a kiss on the cheek and ran up the steps.

Tom smiled and waved at her as the streetcar jerked and started away. He watched it fade from the illuminated circle of the streetlight and dwindle into the distance and, as the image of the streetcar faded, a vague feeling welled up within him. He wanted Ellen. Wanted to have her, wanted to be with her, no matter what it took. There was a spring in his step as he set off for home.

◆ ◆ ◆

"TRRROT—march," bellowed Sergeant Quartermain. Tom clucked his tongue and tickled Rusty with his spurs to pick up the pace. He was third in a line of thirty mounted recruits, sweating under the unseasonably hot prairie sun that beat down on the parade ground of Fort Osborne Barracks. Saddles and bridles gleamed. The troop of reinforcements had spent a week marching, cleaning and saddle-soaping tack, polishing leather and brass, and mucking out stables before they had been granted the privilege of mounting their horses.

Quartermain's peaked cap was pulled down so the brim was a finger's-breadth above his nose. He sat his charger, ramrod straight, double reins in his fists as the mounted recruits trotted by.

"Walk."

Just in time. Despite having ridden a lot as a child, Tom had not been on the back of a horse for a year; already his thighs and buttocks ached.

The sergeant spurred his horse into a canter, swinging in front of the troop and raising his hand. "Halt." Turning, he rode slowly back along the line of mounted privates. "Call that riding? You look like a bunch of backwoods clodhoppers. You," he bellowed, pointing his crop at Bruce Johanson, who was right in front of Tom. "Sit up in the saddle like you know what you're doing. Chin in. Back straight."

Tom sat, back arched, reins in both hands over the pommel of his saddle. Rusty, his sorrel gelding, tossed his head up and down. Tom tightened the reins, and Rusty stamped and pawed at the ground, his ears back. Tom knew that was a bad sign.

"Keep that animal under control, Macrae," growled Quartermain. "That'll do for today. When you're dismissed, trot once around the field and carry on to stables. Those not on duty tonight report to the guard post before proceeding off base. Dis—MISS."

Tom nudged Rusty into a trot and circled the field. Sergeant Quartermain sat on his horse, watching. Tom slowed to a walk, passing in front of the sergeant before leaving the field. At that moment Bruce Johanson pulled up beside him.

"I'm looking forward to doing some real riding," Bruce drawled. "All this spit and polish is getting on my nerves, but what can you expect from a backwoods clodhopper like me?"

Tom glanced at the sergeant, who stared back, expressionless. Bruce laughed, but Tom kept a straight face. If he were to survive in the cavalry, he didn't want to antagonize anybody, especially not a by-the-numbers veteran noncom like Quartermain. All very well for a carefree soul like Bruce Johanson, who could ride with the best of them. Bruce spurred ahead in the direction of the stables.

Tom was anxious to get away from the army for a few hours, but in the cavalry, the horse comes first. He took Rusty to his stall and unsaddled him, then shed his own tunic and walked the horse outside with a halter and lead rope to cool him down. The men in shirts and suspenders, the horses blowing and sweating, walked in a steady file around the paddock. Johanson had shown Tom how to press his hand behind Rusty's foreleg, against the barrel of his chest, to check the horse's body temperature. Once Rusty was cool Tom returned him to his stall, brushed him down, fed and watered him. He mucked out the stall and scattered some dry straw. After inspection by Sergeant Quartermain, Tom was finally able to leave, change into a clean shirt— the men had been issued two each—and head for the main gate. He had an overnight pass.

When Tom walked into the guardhouse at the main gate, the corporal on duty gave him the book to sign out, then peered at his signature. He consulted a note.

"Macrae," he said. "Guard officer wants to see you." He knocked on the door behind him, opened it, stuck his head in, and spoke to someone. Pushing the door fully open, he waved Tom into a small office.

Cedric Inkmann sat bolt upright behind a desk.

"Stand at attention when you're speaking to an officer," hissed the corporal from behind Tom.

"That will be all, Corporal."

As the corporal left, shutting the door behind him, Tom studied Inkmann, who now affected a mustache. His hands were folded, with his fingers laced in front of him on the desk.

"Private Macrae. You were quite the man about town. Things have changed since I saw you at the Evans garden party, what?"

Tom stayed silent. Inkmann had all the advantages now that they were both in uniform.

"I'm just wondering, Macrae, if the police are still talking to you about the Kravenko foul-up?"

"No, sir. I haven't heard from them since I enlisted."

"I find that passing strange, Private. I'm sure you read the papers as well as I do. My brother Bernard has been charged, along with your former employer, Henry Zink. A lawyer, helping a convicted murderer escape jail, for God's sake. Bernard tells me he had nothing to do with Kravenko's escape and maintains his innocence. He thinks—the police told him—that you were involved. How do you explain that he is rotting in custody and you're free as a bird, swanning around as a member of His Majesty's Canadian army?"

"It's not exactly what I'd like to be doing."

"Don't be flippant, Private," said Inkmann, and stood. He kicked back his chair and paced the width of the small room. Coming to an abrupt halt, he stared at Tom, his jaw muscles working. "One more time. Why is my brother in jail and you are not? What did you have to do with Kravenko's escape?"

"Nothing."

"Nothing, SIR!"

"Nothing, sir."

"My brother Bernard is not a well man, Private." Cedric's face softened a little. "Confinement is not good for him. Our mother and I hope and pray he will soon be released."

Tom didn't have much sympathy for Cedric. His brother Bernie was thick as thieves with Zink, and Tom's best guess was that Bernie had indeed had something to do with the jailbreak.

"I told the police everything I knew, which was very little. I can't help your brother. Sir."

Inkmann's thin mouth worked under the skimpy growth on his upper lip. He glanced at the door. Tom could hear muffled conversations as fellow recruits signed out and left the barracks.

"I know there is more to this and I will be watching you, Macrae. I am in a position to do so. I am no longer confined to duties in one Canadian posting—I have been seconded to British Army Intelligence. I will not let go of this."

"I don't care what you do. Sir."

Inkmann flushed red. "Carry on," he said at last.

Tom did his best parade-square about-turn, marched from the room, and went through the door to freedom. He didn't draw a deep breath until he was clear of the barracks. As he sat on a bench waiting for the streetcar, he thought back to the panicky days before his arrest and court appearance, to the last time he had seen Bernie Inkmann.

♦ ♦ ♦

To his surprise, the door to Zink's offices in the Builder's Exchange Building was locked when Tom tried to open it. Hearing muted voices inside, he knocked loudly. Footsteps approached, and the door was flung open by Bernie Inkmann, a dandy who wore a sharply creased three-button suit with a silk waistcoat, not what Tom would expect for an odd-job man, a graduated law student who had never managed to pass the bar exams.

Tom followed Bernie into Zink's inner sanctum, where the stale air reeked of cigars and whisky. A blue haze hovered close to the high ceiling. Besides Bernie, who now lounged against the single window's frame with a cigarette in his mouth, the room was populated by Heny Zink, of average height but built like an aging bull, large head adorned by two days' growth of stubble, and in the corner of the room, John Evans, looking out of place in the pedestrian surroundings. A free-standing ashtray overflowed to one side of Zink's desk, while a tumbler of amber liquid sat by his right hand.

"Tom," Zink grated, "John Evans has agreed to help us with the trial. Who knows, maybe he'll have more pull with their lordships in the Court of Appeal, if it comes to that."

Tom could see why Evans would be an asset on an appeal, but he didn't understand why he would agree to help Zink with a trial, let alone on a losing file like the Kravenko defence. He remembered that Evans had expressed reservations about Zink when he introduced Tom to Ellen at his party. It felt a little strange to be around the man, especially when he thought back to Ellen's kiss when he had escorted her to the streetcar.

Zink spoke from behind his desk. "So, Tom, after a whole day at the library, what does your research tell us?"

Tom addressed Evans, not knowing how much he had been told by Zink. "Our client at first denied all knowledge of the robbery, but he didn't stick with that very long, given his boasting to the newspapers about outsmarting the police, even while he was still on the run. Now he's changed his tune. He claims he was in on the robbery but it wasn't him that did the shooting." Tom hesitated. Zink was not a man who took bad news well. "I've been researching the issue, and I'm not getting anywhere at the library." He plunged ahead, ignoring Zink's fixed stare. "Once Kravenko admits he was part of the robbery scheme when the manager was shot and killed, he's guilty of murder even if he didn't actually pull the trigger."

"Jesus H. Christ," bellowed Zink. "I didn't say I wanted a goddamned student to tell me the law." His splotchy face got redder and he pounded his fist against his knee. Wiping spittle from the corner of his mouth, he raised his glass, drained it, then slammed it down on the table. "I'll tell you one thing for certain," he raved, glaring from Tom to Evans and back again. "I've defended eight murderers—alleged murderers—and they are all still walking around. Bloody Jack is not going to swing, and I don't give a damn what it takes."

Tom and the two lawyers huddled around Zink's cluttered desk and reviewed the case law Tom had brought from the courthouse library. There was nothing in the law that Tom figured was going to assist in Jack's defence. Maybe between Zink and John Evans they could weaken the Crown's case enough to reduce the charge, or at least get him a prison sentence and not the death penalty. It seemed like a long shot, though, given the facts of the case: a man who answered Jack's description had robbed the Plum Coulee bank and for good measure fired a shot from a revolver, instantly killing the manager. Witnesses told the police they recognized Jack Kravenko, who had lived in the town for some months.

Zink, with Tom in tow, had interviewed Jack many times while he was in custody. Jack was an intelligent, accomplished con man who could talk a bird off a branch in any of several languages, and he never wasted an opportunity to tell Zink and his jailers about the supposed fortune he had amassed during a life of crime. Tom sometimes wondered whether Henry Zink wasn't paying too much attention to Bloody Jack's yarns and not enough to legal arguments, however hopeless they might be.

Zink's foul mood got worse as the afternoon wore on and nobody came up with a firm strategy for Kravenko's defence. Zink sent Inkmann for another bottle of rye and some food. He had a legendary tolerance for booze, but he was overdoing it that day.

Zink tossed back the last of his whiskey. "What the hell's the hold up with Inkmann? I'm getting hungry," he growled. He kept repeating himself, mumbling incessantly about establishment judges, all of whom were against him. He blinked and glared at Evans. "I would have thought a senior partner in a big-time law firm would have something to contribute by now."

Tom had a sudden feeling of sympathy for John Evans, who was having to put up with Zink. It was one thing for Zink to bully Inkmann and rail against Tom, who needed his endorsement to advance his career, but Evans?

Zink looked malevolently around the room, red-rimmed eyes peering out from under hooded lids, and fixed his gaze on Tom. He seemed to come to some sort of conclusion. Oh-oh, Tom thought. "Something I want you to do for me. Go to this address. A man named Jake will give you a package. I need it now." He scribbled on a scrap of paper and pushed it at Tom, who was happy to scramble to his feet and escape the oppressive confines of the office.

As he strode up the sidewalk, Tom wondered for the hundredth time if he had made a mistake in working for Zink; his behaviour was more erratic with every hour as the Kravenko trial neared. The address on Zink's note was in the north end of town. Tom walked to Main, caught a streetcar a few blocks north, then alighted and made his way west to a seedy area of rundown, poorly maintained houses.

He didn't see a house number, but a process of elimination brought him to a one-storey clapboard building with a stable or shed of some kind in the back. In the growing darkness Tom picked his way through the overgrown front yard and rapped on the door. No lights were visible, so he knocked a second time, harder.

The door flew open and a scrawny man needing a shave stuck his head out. "Do I know you?"

"I work for Henry Zink. He said you had a parcel to be picked up."

"I was told it was for Bernie Inkmann. Who the hell are you?"

"Bernie's off somewhere else." Tom didn't like being a stand-in for Bernie, and he didn't like the looks of his questioner, who had a twitch that made his head shake every few seconds. "All I know is Henry asked me to pick something up. You can give it to me or you can explain to Henry."

"All right, all right." The man looked left and right, then sidled out through the door, closing it behind him. "Follow me." He led the way through a cluttered backyard to the ramshackle shed. Tom waited outside and the man reappeared, holding a box about the dimension of a shoebox, only shallower, perhaps the size of three dime novels stacked up, tied with stout string. He thrust the box at Tom, who took it and turned away.

"Tell Zink he owes me," the man muttered. Maybe he does, it occurred to Tom, but I don't, and the sooner I get out of here the better.

He retraced his steps, and once he was safely on the streetcar he drew a deep breath. He couldn't imagine what was in the box, which was heavy and solid-feeling. What the hell was Zink up to?

By the time he reached Zink's building the street was cold under the electric lights. He climbed the stairs and walked down the empty hall. Unlike the last time he had approached the office, the door was ajar. He could make out quiet voices, Zink's gravelly baritone reverberating.

"You'll do as you're damn well told. Unless of course you want to . . ." His voice trailed off.

Tom rattled the doorknob as he entered and closed the door behind him. As he walked into Zink's office, the great man himself was sitting, hunched over his desk, whiskey glass once again in hand, and John Evans was pacing the room. Bernie Inkmann, tie loosened, lounged in a chair across the desk from Zink.

Tom's boss turned in his swivel chair and held out a hand. Tom gave him the package. "He says you owe him."

Zink raised an eyebrow, bent to open a bottom drawer in his desk and dropped the box into it. He seemed buoyed by Tom's arrival, sitting straighter, looking pleased with himself. "Leave him to me," he said with a chuckle. Tom glanced at Evans, who looked as though he'd rather be anywhere else. Inkmann was cleaning his nails with a penknife. "We're talking to Kravenko again at nine o'clock tomorrow morning at the jail. Be there. He's getting restless, the jailers tell me."

Tom figured Zink had to be at least half drunk, judging by the condition of the rye bottle Bernie had supplied. Evans told Zink he had an evening engagement and picked up his hat.

"Leave, then, and you can go, too," he thrust his chin at Tom.

Tom silently followed John Evans down to the street, where the older man offered him a ride. Tom declined, as his home was in the opposite direction. Later, riding in the streetcar toward East Kildonan, he wondered what would happen next.

♦ ♦ ♦

So now, Tom was in the army, Zink and Bernie Inkmann were in jail, and John Evans was safe at home with the lovely Ellen. Once more, Tom was waiting for a streetcar, having survived another brush with Bernie's older and far more powerful brother. He'd be a lot happier if he never had to see Cedric again.

♦ ♦ ♦

Damn the army. Tom rolled out of his bunk before the last notes of reveille sounded and stumbled to the washroom. A quick shave, throw on uniform and boots, stumble off to the stables. Damn again—forgot his puttees. Run back, grab them, wind them from just below the knees down, long cotton strips wrapped to cover trousers and boot tops, *not* from the bottoms up, because that's how the despised infantry wore theirs. Feed and water Rusty. Clean his stall. Wash, line up at the mess hall for breakfast of porridge, eggs, bacon, and burned toast. Back to the stables, throw on Rusty's blanket and saddle. Off halter, on bridle. Lead him out; mount up. Fall in. Wait for Quartermain.

Tom and his fellow recruits had heard a lot about Lord Strathcona's Horse in the few days they had been in the army. The original regiment by that name had carried the imprint of Lord Strathcona, the man behind the Canadian Pacific Railway, who raised a regiment in the west to fight in the Boer War. In 1914, when the Canadian Expeditionary Force was first mustered in Valcartier, Quebec, to train and travel to Europe, the Strathconas, now a regular regiment in the Canadian army, along with the Royal Canadian Dragoons and part of the Royal Canadian Horse Artillery, had been the first to arrive. As regular force regiments, they were instrumental in setting up the camp and getting the volunteers into some semblance of order. The Straths had then shipped to England on board the ss *Bermudian*. Quartermain had been sent back, in spite of his vigorous objections, and was now the senior noncommissioned officer responsible for bringing the recruits up to Strathcona standards.

The men sat in their saddles, facing the rising sun. The horses pranced and tossed their heads, their pent-up energy mirrored by at least some of their young riders.

"So where's our bloody Sergeant Quartermain, then?" asked Bruce Johanson.

"Don't look now," Tom told him, "but he's been sitting his horse at the other end of the parade ground the whole time. God knows when he gets up."

"Maybe he doesn't sleep," said someone farther down the line.

Albert Nickerson, who had been roaring drunk when he came back to barracks at curfew the night before, belched loudly. "Let's just get this over with. If we do a bunch of trotting again, I'll be puking all over the parade ground. I should have gone to sick parade."

"What a bunch of whiners," Johanson, the former cowboy, threw in. "I'm just sick of trotting in circles. When the hell are we going to do some real riding?"

Tom's hands were steady on the reins, but he felt a quiver at the pit of his stomach. He had heard stories from other recruits about the equestrian skills of the Straths, and he didn't want to get bucked off Rusty and make a fool of himself. Or, heaven forbid, get banished to the infantry. He felt like telling his friend Johanson to pipe down and stop baiting the sergeant. Over the chatter of the men and the jangling of bits, he heard slow, controlled hoofbeats approaching from behind.

"Quiet in the ranks." Quartermain walked his big bay around the end of the line and slowly passed along in front. "Nice to see such keen riders so bright and early." He leaned forward in his saddle, peering intently at the men. "It beats me how young bucks like you lot can't grow a decent mustache."

Someone snickered. The instructors had ordered the reinforcements to grow mustaches, which were much the style in the regular army. The recruits had other priorities—they shaved clean before going off the base at night, then left their upper lips unshaved in the morning. Tom doubted that the barely discernible half-day growth fooled anyone.

"Well, maybe you can't grow facial hair. Can you ride, or is that too much to hope for?" Quartermain turned his horse to face Johanson. "So we have some riders here, do we?"

Johanson sat rigidly. "Yes, sir."

"Don't call me sir, Private. You call officers sir. I am a sergeant, and don't you bloody forget it." The way he said it left no doubt about the relative importance of officers and sergeants.

"Yes, Sergeant."

Quartermain backed his horse so they could all see him clearly. "Pay attention. Take your feet out of your stirrups. Cross your leathers." Suiting his actions to his words he reached down, pulled up his stirrups, and dropped them on opposite sides of the pommel of his saddle.

Tom kicked his boots free of his stirrups and followed Quartermain's example. Rusty danced sideways, bumping Johanson's horse, which tossed its head. Tom grabbed leather to steady himself.

"Let go of that saddle," Quartermain shouted. "Follow me. WALK—march!"

He turned his horse and started a slow walk around the perimeter of the parade square. Rusty and Tom followed. Tom felt shaky without stirrups but had no real problem at this pace. He could have sworn Rusty twisted his head to give him a once-over as they made the first turn to the left.

After the second turn Quartermain reined his horse to one side. "Carry on," he said as Tom went by.

"No stirrups—big deal," Johanson muttered from behind Tom.

Tom glanced at Quartermain to see if he had heard. The sergeant had a sardonic grin on his face. "TROT—march!" he ordered.

Tom brushed Rusty with his spurs so he'd increase the pace but kept the reins taut to hold him back from a canter. He began to bounce in the saddle, so he held on with his knees and thighs and cheated a bit by grabbing what he could of Rusty's close-clipped mane. Rusty turned at the next corner and followed the line of the fence.

As someone behind groaned with every bounce, Tom gritted his teeth and posted, lifting his rump off the saddle as best he could to ease the pain that was building in his thighs. There was a curse and a thump as a body hit the ground. Tom turned and saw Nickerson stumble to his feet, his horse pulling hard, trying to get away. Pale-faced, Nickerson fell again, flat on his belly, but he managed to keep a death-grip on the reins.

"Keep on, you men," shouted Quartermain. He looked at Nickerson. "You—who told you to dismount? Get back on your horse."

Tom kept going, inwardly furious with Johanson and the others in the troop who had been riding all their lives and made it look so easy. He could feel his breakfast sloshing around in his stomach, and within minutes the pain in his guts more than matched his burning thigh muscles. He was able to hang on, though, as two more riders hit the dirt. With each one Quartermain bellowed, "Who told you to dismount?"

Tom reached the stage where he was too tired and sore to grip the saddle with his legs anymore, but he was able to balance, and bounce, in a fashion that kept him—barely—in the saddle. As they rounded the paddock again Rusty came to the open gate that led to the stables. Without warning he plunged sideways, and Tom fell headlong over his withers. He hit the ground hard and gasped for air, his wind knocked out. Rusty ripped the reins from his hand and galloped off. A watching corporal slammed the gate shut before he got through it, and Rusty headed around the parade ground, kicking and bucking, stirrups flying. Tom stood up, doubled over, and tried to breathe, spitting dirt while the laughter of his troopmates rang in his ears.

Quartermain snorted. "God give me strength." He spurred his horse away, his stirrup leathers still crossed, and cantered after Rusty. He and his horse looked as if they were one being, centaur-like. The sergeant cornered Rusty, leaned to grasp the trailing reins, and led him back.

Without saying a word he brought his horse to a halt in front of Tom, who grasped Rusty's reins and pulled his head around so he could look him in the eyes. Rusty had no choice but to stand still and not jerk away. Still holding the reins taut Tom gripped the saddle with both hands, vaulted, and swung his right leg across Rusty's back. Pain shot through his thighs.

"Use your stirrups," Quartermain ordered. "Now, TROT." Tom got his feet into his stirrups and trotted after the boys. Quartermain might be a Limey son of a bitch, but the man could ride.

DOMESTIC AFFAIRS

♦ ♦ ♦

Determined to make use of whatever time he had left before boarding a train to start his journey to war, Tom had sent a note to Ellen with an invitation that she had, to his relief, accepted. In uniform, he arrived early at the restaurant in the Royal Alexandra Hotel adjacent to the Canadian Pacific Railway station. The maitre d' looked sideways at a mere private, but Tom slipped him a dollar and was led to a table for two by the window. A waiter pulled back his chair, and Tom eased himself down. His buttocks ached. A week of trotting with no stirrups was equestrian hell, but his body was hardening and the pain was less intense with each day.

Tom's uniform was brushed and pressed, his boots shined. He gave the waiter his cap to look after, thinking briefly of the lady on the streetcar who had looked down her nose at him, all those weeks ago. He would have her approval now, all right. But he was still mentally shaking his head at finding himself in uniform, his civilian life receding into the past.

He relaxed, revelling in the quiet background murmur of polite conversation, the muted scrape of silverware on china. The room, with its crystal chandeliers and golden-brown, embossed wallpaper, was oddly calming, though it catered to a higher stratum of society than he was used to. The startling contrast between life in barracks and lunch in the upper-class dining room made him wonder how much different the war zone would be from his present challenging but safe existence. That is, if he actually got to the war, a distant and hard-to-imagine circumstance.

The minutes dragged by. Tom's thoughts wandered, as they often did, to his family. He had four brothers and one sister—or, at least, he used to have; Ray had drowned in a canoeing accident on the Red River, and his mother had never recovered from it. She had lost weight and was constantly listless. His father all too often took refuge in the bottle. Tom would have given anything to have Ray back and his mother restored, but that was not how things worked. And now she had a fresh worry, with Tom in the army and destined to go overseas.

Tom looked out the window for the hundredth time. Would Ellen turn up at all? Suddenly she was there, on the opposite sidewalk, strolling with another young woman. Tom's reflective mood disappeared and he felt his heart race.

Tom saw her wave goodbye to her friend as she turned to cross the street. He lost sight of her as she approached the doorway, then found her again as she emerged into the room. As Tom stood, waved, then walked toward her, Ellen's face broke into a smile.

"Hello, Tom," she said. "My, you do look different."

"I feel different."

Tom held her chair as she sat. She looked good, a vivacious young woman, dressed for lunch out on a sunny Winnipeg Saturday, in a long green dress with a narrow waist and a tight jacket.

"Glad you could make it," he said, sounding stilted even to himself. His mouth felt dry.

"How could I not? A girl doesn't get to eat lunch in the Royal Alexandra with a handsome soldier every day of the week." She smiled again. "How are you?"

"Well, to tell the truth, a lot has happened recently. But I expect you know most of it."

"Daddy doesn't tell me very much," Ellen said. She glanced at his uniform. "He said joining the army wasn't your first choice, but I knew that. But what's going to happen with that awful Mr. Zink? Oh—I'm sorry—perhaps I shouldn't be asking you about that." She put her fingers over her mouth and blushed.

It occurred to Tom that she might think he *had* been involved in the jailbreak. "No harm in asking. I really don't know any more about it than what was in the papers."

Recent newspaper reports had confirmed that Bloody Jack was still on the loose. Cartoonists made merciless fun of the forces of law and order, given Jack's colourful history and dramatic jailbreak. If he had still been in custody, his trial, presumably with conviction, would be over by now. In the meantime Zink remained in jail, as did Bernie Inkmann and a third man, a jailer. Their plight made the army look pretty good to Tom, sore buttocks and all.

"Penny for them," said Ellen.

Tom came back to reality with a start. Wool-gathering was not going to impress a desirable young woman. "Sorry. I was just thinking how lucky I am to be sitting here having lunch with the most beautiful girl in town."

Ellen blushed again, much to Tom's delight. Maybe all was not lost— out of law, into the army, but life carried on.

Later, as she ate, Ellen remembered her talk with her father shortly after Tom was implicated in the jailbreak.

◆　◆　◆

Ellen had flushed as she put her teacup down in the exact centre of her saucer. "Really, Daddy. What are you thinking?"

Her father had questioned her about her relationship with Tom, much to her surprise. She had thought of him as hopelessly Victorian, not given to prying into intimate matters.

"I am thinking of you, my dear, as always. You have asked me to help young Macrae. I suspect you may have some feelings for him," he ventured, and glanced at his daughter. He pushed on. "I am prepared to assist him, on one condition. That you have nothing further to do with him."

"Father, you're being . . . ridiculous," Ellen blurted, and wondered at herself. She had never before used such a term in conversation with any man, let alone her father.

Evans frowned. "Perhaps I know you better than you know yourself," he huffed. "I mean what I say. I will do what I can for Mr. Macrae—for no charge, may I add—but only on the condition that you have nothing more to do with him. I don't like this mess he has gotten himself into, and I don't much care for his prospects."

Ellen caught herself slumping forward so she deliberately straightened her spine to her full height. Her hands were in her lap, hidden from her father's sight under the dining room table. She crossed her fingers the way she and her mother used to do when they played their game. If their fingers were crossed, they could tell a story with a fib in it, to see if the other player could figure out what was true and what was not. Even without her mother, Ellen still played the game in her mind. Her father had never been in on it. She uncrossed her fingers, flexed them, and picked up her teacup.

Ellen stalled for time while she considered her quandary. There was something solid and reassuring about Tom, above and beyond his rather exciting physical presence, his strong-looking but sensitive hands, his steady grey eyes. And, of course, he had been well on his way to a good career, until the Bloody Jack imbroglio. She didn't want to contradict her father, but after all, it was her life, not his. However, Tom needed her father's help.

"Very well," she said, meeting her father's worried gaze. "I won't encourage him."

He had given her a sharp look but said nothing.

◆   ◆   ◆

After lunch the young couple promenaded down Main Street toward the centre of town. Leaves crunched underfoot as they crossed the park in front of City Hall, past the statue of Queen Victoria. Tom took Ellen's hand as they navigated a bit of rough ground, and she didn't take it back.

"Do you think you'll be sent to England?" she asked.

"It's just a matter of time. We're training hard. If you can believe the rumours, they need reinforcements even at this stage, to bring the regiment up to full complement."

"There's a trickle of wounded men coming in already."

"There'll be a lot more," Tom said. The Canadian army was not yet on the continent, so any wounded soldiers Ellen was helping would have served in British units. The Battle of the Marne and then a bloodbath at Ypres in Belgium had left the professional British army in tatters.

"Some of the men I volunteer with are so pathetic, I don't see how they and their families can face their futures." Ellen stopped walking and clasped both his hands. "You won't get killed, will you? Or crippled?"

"Never thought of it. I've got some time to put in, that's all, and then I'll be back. In one piece." Tom believed what he said, hoping he wasn't tempting fate.

"You'd better," she said, and kissed him.

Her lips were sweet, her kiss almost chaste but with the promise of more to come. They walked on, chatting, smiling, nodding at passersby. It was a glorious fall day, the sky blue, the air clear and crisp. Tom felt on top of the world as they walked, hand in hand.

She asked about his family, and he told her about the early days of the Red River Settlement, long before Manitoba was a province. Family stories went back to the days when only the charity of the Indians and Metis had saved the settlers from starvation. His grandmother had been one of the first children born to the Highlanders in their new, often unforgiving land.

"So now you know all about me. Where did your people come from?"

"My mother and father grew up in Ontario and moved to Winnipeg when I was a little girl. I stayed with cousins in Toronto when I went to school there."

Too soon the sun dropped toward the western horizon. Ellen was due to meet her father at his office for the drive home, and Tom was apprehensive. The last time he had seen John Evans, the older man had shepherded him out the back door of the courthouse after the meeting with Judge Paterson. He didn't know how it had been managed, but the charges against him were dropped. "I'm not sure what your father thinks of me."

"Your name did come up. But don't worry. I'll have a chat with Daddy. He usually goes along with my . . . foibles, he calls them."

So that's what he was. A foible. A weakness, a fault. A black mood descended like a curtain in the night. "I wouldn't be a very good catch."

Ellen pulled him to a stop. She frowned at him and waited until he met her gaze. "You may be the least of my foibles," she said. "Don't be so sensitive, Tom. It was just a manner of speaking."

Then he felt silly. He was still off balance and edgy when they reached the McIntyre Block on Main Street and met Ellen's father as he came out of the lobby. In the short time Tom had known him, John Evans had aged. He looked careworn, the lines in his face more pronounced.

"Hello, sir," Tom said, as Ellen let go of his hand and stood beside her father.

"Good evening, Mr. Macrae." Evans and Tom shook hands.

Evans cocked his head and looked at Tom like a tailor sizing a customer. "A pleasant afternoon, I trust, Ellen?"

"Yes, Daddy. Mr. Macrae was telling me tall tales about Winnipeg before it became such a metropolis."

Evans raised his eyebrows. He didn't look amused. Tom doubted that a client had ever had lunch with his daughter, and obviously it bothered him. Or maybe it was just Tom who bothered him.

"It's fortunate that we meet now, Mr. Macrae," said Evans. "It is imperative that we speak as soon as possible. Can you come to my office at eight o'clock tomorrow morning?"

"Of course. I'll be there."

Evans nodded and turned to his daughter. "Come along, Ellen. Mrs. Connelly will have dinner waiting for us."

"Thank you for a delightful lunch," Ellen said, reaching to brush Tom's arm with her hand, lingering an instant when their fingers touched.

Surprised and pleased at the display of affection, Tom's hand tingled, or at least he imagined it did, as he watched Ellen and her father walk around the corner. His spirits took wing on his own walk to his streetcar, already thinking about when he could next see Ellen.

◆　◆　◆

Next morning, a Sunday, Tom was due to report to barracks at noon, so after spending Saturday night with his family, he was in uniform when he arrived at Evans's office, ten minutes early. The outer door was locked, but when he knocked it was opened by John Evans himself. They shook hands, then the lawyer ushered Tom through a well-appointed reception area, down a hall lined with law tomes, and into a corner office. Tom couldn't help noting the contrast between the posh, dark oak panelling and Henry Zink's chaotic premises.

Evans waved Tom into a clients' chair and sat behind his broad desk. It was clear of paper and clutter but for a neat stack of files off to one side. Tom had a moment's regret at the thought that, but for the Kravenko jailbreak fiasco, he might now be practising law in an office with organized files and affluent clients. He placed his peaked cap on the desk in front of him and waited.

Evans spoke without preamble. "Bloody Jack has been apprehended. Your erstwhile principal, Henry Zink, has been formally charged with assisting his escape, as has his employee, Bernard Inkmann, and one of the jailers, who was apparently in on the conspiracy. The jailer has given the police a statement implicating them all. All four are in cells."

"I'm surprised Bloody Jack didn't make it out of the jurisdiction, even though the police were buzzing around like a bunch of angry hornets."

"I have been told he was badly injured in his fall from the police station. No doubt it will all be in the papers tomorrow." Evans gave Tom a sharp glance. "Which brings us back to you and me. We've both been tarred to some extent with the muck of the whole affair, and I wanted this opportunity to drive home to you how lucky you are to be well out of it. But Inkmann and Zink may yet try to paint you into the plot while attempting to exonerate themselves. And there's Inspector Boyle, who was embarrassed by Kravenko's escape and is looking for blood."

"For what it's worth, the truth is that I didn't have anything to do with Kravenko's escape."

"That, of course, is what I believe. If I thought otherwise I would totally forbid Ellen to see you."

Tom felt his face redden. He didn't want even a hint of disapproval from Ellen's father.

Evans continued. "Things have not been easy for me recently, Mr. Macrae. Ellen's mother was ill for years, and I spent large sums on treatment for her in the east and the United States. In spite of that, we lost her. Then there was the cost of Ellen's schooling in Toronto. I made some risky investments and lost what savings remained."

Tom nodded, wondering what was coming next.

"I tell you this so you will understand my involvement with Henry Zink. I could see you had questions. Well, no fool like an old fool. I borrowed heavily from Zink, and he demanded my help with the Kravenko file in return for not calling my note." Evans managed a rueful smile. "Desperate times all around, Mr. Macrae."

Tom didn't know how to react. He understood the older man's dilemma, but he resented Evans's apparent doubts about him. "May I ask, Mr. Evans, what concerns you have about me?"

Evans stood and paced behind his desk. Tom followed him with his eyes.

"To be perfectly frank, young man, it has more to do with your situation than with you personally. You are in the army, and I understand you'll be overseas soon. By all accounts this will be a bloody war. Mr. Macrae, I lost my wife not long ago. I have only two children, and one of them has now been rendered a . . . physically incapable. I do not want my daughter hitching her wagon, so to speak, to a soldier who may or may not return. I do not want her hurt any more than she has been."

Tom rose to his feet. He had been afraid that Evans's reservations about him had something to do with his standing in society and his humble Red River origins, and was only too happy to put that out of his mind. "Sir, I have every intention of returning home. In one piece."

"I don't doubt that, Mr. Macrae."

Evans came around his desk; the meeting was over. Tom picked up his cap. Evans was nervous, and he had every right to be. His unlikely association with Zink would be difficult to explain to his fellow lawyers and might even make him the subject of a police investigation. In the meantime, at the personal level, his son's condition was a drain emotionally and no doubt financially. He would not want Ellen involved with a soldier at risk.

"Best of luck over there."

Tom wasn't sure Evans meant it, but he looked sincere. Leaving the building, Tom was a bit shaken at the thought that Evans really doubted his survival. Maybe he should be more concerned himself. "Hell, no," he muttered to himself. "I'm going to be just fine."

♦ ♦ ♦

Small, puffy clouds formed a washboard pattern across the blue prairie sky. The thirty men and horses of the 1st Reinforcement Troop trotted westward on the right-hand shoulder of the arrow-straight gravel road. Fields of stubble with a skim of snow stretched to the horizon on both sides.

The horses were well warmed up and the troop had settled into a mile-eating trot. Tom's thighs and buttocks were over their initial saddle sores. He and Rusty had reached an understanding: Rusty would still try to embarrass him whenever he could, but once Tom got him through the first hour or so of their day, the horse just couldn't be bothered.

To Tom's surprise he was starting to enjoy army life. His days started at 4:30 in the morning, when he tended to the needs of his "long-nosed soldier" in the stable, and ended when Rusty was bedded down for the night. Between those times, they and their troopmates walked, shot, trotted, stabbed at dummies with swords, and galloped. Then they rode some more.

Quartermain had started the day off by having the men fall in on foot on the Fort Osborne Barracks parade square. He was a ruler-straight figure in his gleaming, calf-high riding boots, belt, and shoulder strap. He paced in front of them, his riding crop in its familiar position in his right hand with the other end tucked under his arm.

"You are a useless rabble. You want to be cavalrymen and the army wants you to be cavalrymen, but I have my doubts. A few of you can ride, but I still see bank tellers, teamsters, store clerks. Even a bloody lawyer if you can believe it."

Tom grinned as the troops guffawed.

"You have two weeks to prove to me you can do the job. If you can't ride to the army's standard by that time, you will be shipped off to England to join the God-forsaken, boot-stomping infantry. Any volunteers at this point?" He waited. "All right then, mount up. Let's see you look like a cavalry troop and not a bunch of farmers out for a Sunday ride."

Two by two the troop trotted west for an hour. When they reached a small stream, Quartermain led them off the road and ordered the dismount. Tom loosened Rusty's girth and took him down to the stream to drink.

Bruce Johanson, who had ridden at Tom's side all morning, stretched and farted. "Nothing like a good ride to make a guy regular." A broad grin, Johanson's usual expression, split his face. "Can't believe my good luck. The army pays me to ride a horse. They even provide the horse. Shoot—at a dollar a day I'll be able to afford one of those fancy Winnipeg whores in no time."

Quartermain waited until the horses had drunk their fill before ordering the troop back up to the road.

"Listen here," he shouted. He waited for the creak of saddle leather and the men's chatter to quieten. "Line up in single file along the side of the road and on my order, walk back toward town. I'll order the last man to trot to the head of the column and then walk. Then the next man, and so on. If it goes well, we'll move everybody along at a trot and do the final manoeuvre to the front at the gallop. Any questions? No? WALK—march."

Sounds easy, thought Tom. Johanson had contrived to be last man in the file in order to go first, as usual. Rusty and Tom were fourth from the rear. On Quartermain's order Johanson reined his horse to the left into the centre of the road and trotted to the head of the column. The next two men in their turn followed suit. Tom waited for the signal. Quartermain nodded at him.

Tom turned his horse to the left and touched him with his spurs. Rusty shot ahead, bolting up the road. Tom grabbed his saddle with one hand, sawing at the reins with the other. His mount bucked into the air, planted his forelegs hard and kicked up with his hindquarters. Tom nearly went over his head but somehow stayed in the saddle. The boys yelled and whooped as Rusty danced along the road. Tom transferred the reins to both hands and fought to hold him in.

Quartermain cantered up alongside. "Let him go!" he shouted. Tom eased the reins and they hurtled forward like a rock from a slingshot. The mounted riders, ditches, and fields blurred by. Tom was quaking, terrified that Rusty would pull his sidestepping trick and dump him face first onto the gravel.

After a hard half mile Rusty started to slow. Tom knew he had to assert control over his horse or his life would be miserable, and they'd both be at risk in battle. He spurred Rusty ahead into a ground-eating canter for a few minutes, then let him slow to a trot, finally turning him back toward the troop, which trotted toward them. He put the horse through his paces, turning him from side to side in the road, pulling him to a stop, walking again, then trotting back to join Quartermain and the rest of the advancing riders.

"Fall in at the rear," Quartermain ordered, and Tom reined Rusty into position.

"Nice ride, cowboy," Johanson drawled as he passed. Tom took it as a compliment, and gave Rusty a hard pat on the neck. The gelding shook his head and snorted.

♦ ♦ ♦

That afternoon Tom spent extra time brushing Rusty, who had settled down after their wild career of the morning, while Johanson, Gordon Ferguson, and a few of the other soldiers lounged outside the box stall. Ferguson, the former North West Mounted Policeman, was regaling the men with his adventures on the western frontier. Tom was amused by his Scottish accent, which put him in mind of some of the older Highlanders living in Winnipeg. Fergie, as everyone called him, would quote Robert Burns on any pretext. When Tom had mentioned his own Scottish roots, Fergie had grasped his hand and shouted, "Gie us yer hand, mon! Gie us yer twa hands!"

One of the sergeant instructors, Ronald Planck, walked briskly into the stable. He pointed at Ferguson and another man, Wayne Milroy. "I need two men—you and you—for a cleanup detail."

". . . So I said get inta the cell or I'll put ye in," Ferguson continued, then looked at Planck. "I did cleanup yesterday. Ye'll need someone else, Sergeant."

Even the horses seemed to stop swishing their tails and stamping their hoofs. Planck was English, a regular British army soldier who had been promoted rapidly after his infantry regiment had been decimated in the first months of the war. He was in Canada to teach bayonet drill and shooting, and was now wearing the badge of Lord Strathcona's Horse. Planck's working-class accent grated on Canadian ears; he was especially hard to understand when he was excited.

"I said you, Ferguson. On yer bloody feet and get over to the mess hall."

Ferguson, whose dislike of all things English was well known, stood and brushed straw off his breeches. "Go ta hell."

Planck and Ferguson stood toe to toe, Planck flexing and unflexing his fingers. He grimaced. "So it's like that, is it?" he said, and took off his tunic, calmly folding it and placing it, along with his cap, on a bale of straw. Fists raised in the classic Marquess of Queensberry stance, he advanced on Ferguson. "Come on, then, you Scottish refugee. I've not got my rank on now."

Stripped to the waist, Planck was thick-chested and muscular, and looked like he knew what he was doing. Ferguson is up against it this time, Tom thought.

Planck crouched, left arm extended, right fist cocked and ready. Ferguson put up his fists, shot out a left jab—then without warning lashed out with his left boot, catching Planck square in the crotch. The sergeant was lifted off the ground then collapsed, groaning, in a heap. Clutching himself, he curled into a fetal position.

The boys let out a collective gasp and melted away, apparently remembering duties elsewhere. Johanson clapped Ferguson on the back.

"Better get lost," Tom said to Ferguson, who left the stable.

Tom and Johanson helped the sergeant to a sitting position, then to his feet, handing him his tunic and cap, which he eventually managed to put back on. Planck was very pale, his lips pressed together into a determined line. He didn't thank either of them.

The next day was cloudy, bringing warmer fall temperatures to the men of the 1st Reinforcement Troop, and Sergeant Quartermain cut short the morning ride to allow Lieutenant Inkmann and Sergeant Planck to march a section of eight men off to the rifle range. Inkmann rode ahead.

Planck appeared to be functioning pretty well, considering he could barely stand upright the night before. Tom was surprised there was no hint of anything arising out of the incident. Planck was a solid man, burned brown by years of soldiering in far-flung corners of the Empire, and he kept up a running commentary on the shortcomings of the recruits. "Get in step, Ferguson. Didn't they teach you to march in the Mounted Police? Pick it up, Johanson. You're not behind the plow, boy."

The men marched grim-faced, trying to ignore the swarms of mosquitoes that still, this late in the year, attacked any exposed skin. Boots clumped a steady cadence on the gravel road, rifles over their left shoulders, right arms swinging high.

In a few minutes they reached the rifle range. Tom could see Inkmann on his horse, a hundred yards down range toward the targets.

Planck halted them and turned the section into line, so they were shoulder to shoulder. "Present—arms," he ordered. Tom slapped his right arm across his chest to the stock of his rifle, pushed it upright, dropped the rifle into the "present" vertically in front of him, left hand on the pistol grip, right on the forestock, and slammed his right foot at a forty-five degree angle back of the left one. The boots of the other men in the section hit the ground at various intervals. Even Tom knew it wasn't well done.

"Shoulder—arms."

"Order—arms." The rifles were lowered to the ground, right hands on the forestock, butts just clear of the right toes, left foot raised and stamped down into the attention position.

"That was a shambles." Planck shook his head. He took them through the drills again, until at last they got their timing down so they were acting in unison.

"Stand at—ease. Now—pay attention to musketry detail."

Musketry? Tom grinned. Where are the ramrods and powder horns?

"Find that amusing, Macrae?"

"No, Sergeant."

Inkmann had ridden up. Planck called the men to attention and saluted the lieutenant. "Squad ready for musketry practice, sir,"

"Carry on, Sergeant."

"Yes, sir." Planck saluted again, then turned back to the squad. "Johanson—give me your rifle. The rest of you fall out, and pay attention."

When they were gathered round, Planck ran over the basics of the Ross rifle. A bolt action, .303 calibre repeating rifle with a built-in magazine, it was standard issue in the Canadian army. The Ross was manufactured in Canada, and the Canadian government had had much to do with its development.

"Nobody other than Canadians uses it," Planck continued. "Extremely accurate. Winning rifle at Bisley in 1913. For those who don't know, that's a shooting competition that includes the whole Empire. Questions?"

Freddie Martens, a short, muscular, nineteen-year-old whom Tom was just getting to know, spoke up. "My cousin is back home in Calgary, injured in training," he said. "He says the Ross is a piece of crap. They always jam up. We should get some other rifle."

Sergeant Planck reddened under his tan. "That's not for you to decide, soldier. Anyway, you can thank your own Canadian government for the Ross."

Ferguson interjected, his brogue a contrast to Planck's English accent. "Why couldn't the army buy Winchesters? That's what I had out west. Perfect for mounted work."

Planck turned to his latest tormentor. "You're in the cavalry now, and your main weapon is your sword. If you don't like the Ross, I couldn't care less. You've still got to use it. I don't give a damn about what you did in the police or when you were cowboys or what you used to fight off the redskins." He glared at the men. "The British army has been fighting wars since Christ was a boy soldier. You're in the army now, and you'll do as the army says."

"We're not in the British army," Johanson observed.

"All right, enough," fumed Planck. "Retrieve your rifles. Fall in."

Tom picked up his rifle and lined up with the others, standing at attention.

"Rifles at the high port," bellowed Planck. The men let out a collective groan and raised their arms overhead, their rifles, weighing in at just under ten pounds, held horizontally.

"Right turn." The men turned into a single file. "Double—march."

They moved off at the double, an awkward, painful run over rough ground, the rifles heavier with every step. Tom had been in the army only a few short weeks, but he had seen quite enough of this form of punishment.

"Right wheel."

Tom was at the front of the file of doubling men. He turned right and the rest of the section followed him. Planck kept them running, wheeling every forty or fifty yards, in a square pattern, while he stood in the centre and watched them.

Tom's back ached from the unnatural posture. His arms shook, and just as he started to waver and stumble, there was a commotion behind him. He saw over his shoulder that Martens had collapsed. Johanson tripped over him and fell.

"Halt. Shoulder arms."

Tom and the rest of the section fought for breath while Planck growled at Martens and Johanson. "You two—on your feet. All you men will report for extra stable duty tonight."

Planck ignored the chorus of groans. "Now, back to the task at hand. Fall out. On the firing line, prone position. Open breeches. Check your bores are clear and magazines empty."

Guiding them through safety procedures on the rifle range, Planck paced behind the soldiers, correcting firing postures, adjusting grips, ensuring rifle butts were firmly tucked against right shoulders.

"Load magazines."

Tom took five .303 shells from his pouch and pushed them into the rifle's magazine.

"Ready."

Eight rifle bolts opened, caught shells pushed up from eight magazines, and closed, propelling shells into breeches. The rifle felt cool to Tom as he moved his right hand from the bolt to the pistol grip, index finger to the trigger. His left elbow was on the ground, hand clamped firmly on the forestock. The Ross was cocked, ready to fire.

"Aim."

Tom peered through the rear sight and lined up the foresight on his target, the second one from the right. It was only fifty yards away but suddenly looked a lot farther as he squinted down range.

"Fire."

A scattered volley of shots rang out. Tom flinched at the deafening reports on both sides of him, then bore down, sighted again, and fired. The Ross leapt, banging his shoulder.

"Open your bolts," Planck ordered.

Ears ringing, Tom slid his bolt back.

Planck pointed out what hopeless specimens they were; at only fifty yards there were just two bullseyes, Tom's and Ferguson's.

On Planck's order bolts were cycled, pushing fresh rounds into the breeches. The firing drill was repeated, each shot followed by Planck's comments.

"You bleeding hayseeds," he complained. "The British army is over in Belgium right now firing fifteen aimed shots a minute. So let's get it right, shall we?"

He was scathing and meticulous as he stalked from man to man. "It's not going to bite you, Martens. Press it into your shoulder. Grip firmly, like you would a dancing partner, if you had one. Ferguson! Nice shot."

Slowly, the ragged volleys became more synchronized. Magazines were reloaded and the men told to fire at will. When magazines were empty and bolts drawn back to demonstrate there were no rounds in the breeches, the privates rested their weapons on the ground. Planck led them down range, where they removed the now-shredded paper targets. They placed new ones, then lined up at a hundred yards, twice the previous distance.

Tom noticed that Lieutenant Inkmann had reappeared and ridden his horse to the back of the firing line. He dismounted, tied his reins to a post, and stood, hands clasped behind him, watching the action.

This time around Planck had to use binoculars to spot the bullet holes. The men shot two more magazines, and Planck ordered them once again to ground rifles.

Inkmann spoke up. "Macrae, you didn't do so well at this range."

"I thought I did, sir."

Planck led the men to the butts, mounds of earth banked up to absorb the rounds after they passed through the targets. Tom's target had three shots outside the bull; the rest had been in the black. The centre of the bullseye was shot away.

Inkmann mounted and joined them at the butts. "Couldn't see bullet holes from back there," he muttered. He yanked on his reins, forcing his horse to cramp its neck back and stamp nervously, and raised his voice to add, "You missed three, Macrae." His horse shook its head, and Inkmann turned it in a tight circle. "Carry on, Sergeant." He dug his heels into the horse's sides and trotted back toward barracks.

Ferguson nudged Tom in the ribs. "I don't think he likes ye much. What'd ye do t' him?"

"I knew his brother back when. It's a long story."

"Cut the cackle on the firing line," Planck interrupted. "Back you go, men. Prone position, stand by to reload."

Johanson spoke up. "Hell, Sergeant, why don't we fire standing up? See who can really shoot?"

"Standing? Let's see you cowboys show me you can shoot prone first. I haven't seen much yet."

An hour later, amid grumblings about tender shoulders, Planck decided they'd had enough. Tom's ears were still jangling from the gunfire, but his shooting was the best of the lot. Shooting had always seemed straightforward: line up the sights, deep breath, let half out, stay on the target, squeeze, and . . . fire.

Planck turned to Tom. "Where'd you learn how to shoot, Private?"

"When we were kids we had to get a rabbit with a .22 before we had any breakfast."

Johanson had walked up. "Don't give us that! I know you Red River types—you'd have oatmeal, not rabbit. Breakfast, lunch, and dinner."

Planck interrupted. "Right—enough chatter. Fall in."

The men shambled to attention and squared off.

"Right turn. Quick—march!"

Planck drove the men hard all the way to their barracks, at times halting them, turning them back, then marching them forward again. Whenever he was out of earshot, the privates kept up a running commentary about Limeys, sergeants, and other irritants.

Ferguson panted, "How come, for Christ's sake, we sign up to fight the Hun and we have t' fight the army first? And I thought the police force was hidebound!"

Tom laughed.

Planck stopped the section and stalked from one end of the line of men to the other, eyeing each of them. He stopped a foot from Tom. "So we're pretty tough, are we? Spoiling for a fight? Is that what you want?"

What Tom wanted was to get dismissed, now that they were back at barracks, and make use of a weekend pass. Mixing it up with a sergeant would not help with that. "No, Sergeant."

"Easy to talk, isn't it?" Planck snarled, once again pacing in front of the men. "What makes you think you can fight the Hun if you don't even have the guts to take me on?"

A voice piped up from down the line, "I'll fight, Sergeant!"

"Who said that?"

"I did, Sergeant," volunteered Martens, the nineteen-year-old.

"Well, good for you," said Planck. "I like a man who'll own up." He undid his jacket, folded it, and handed it, along with his cap, to Tom.

Here we go again, thought Tom. He watched as Planck snapped his suspenders and rolled up the sleeves of his undershirt. Martens threw off his jacket and cap, turning his back on Planck and winking broadly at his comrades.

The men in other sections were taking a break and sensed something was happening. A growing crowd of wisecracking Canadians gathered to watch as Planck prepared to take on yet another private.

Martens squared off with Planck, right hand close to his chin, left ready to jab, left foot forward. Planck moved cautiously, fists up. Tom could see what was going to happen. Martens was lined up to box, but he was keeping the weight off his back leg. He's heard about Ferguson kicking Planck, and he's going to do the same thing. Tom almost felt sorry for the sergeant.

The two men circled each other warily, Planck leading with his left, even more than he had done when fighting Ferguson. Martens held back, waiting for an opportunity to lash out.

Planck shot out a left jab, straight from his shoulder. Martens ducked it and turned to his left, giving Planck an opening. The sergeant swung his right foot hard, catching Martens in the crotch. He followed up with a sharp left hand to the jaw that put the kid down on the ground with an audible thump.

The silence that followed was broken only by groans from Martens.

Planck retrieved his cap and put it square on his head. Tom handed him his tunic. Planck draped it over his forearm.

"Carry on, men," he said, "and report to stables at 1900 hours for that extra time you earned with your horses."

♦ ♦ ♦

It was mid-November, and the ground was covered in early snow. Ellen was up before sunrise, dressed in woollen stockings and layers of warm clothing. With the part-time cook's assistance she packed a lunch of sandwiches and thermos bottles of hot soup.

Ellen knew Tom and her father had met on the day following her lunch with Tom, and John Evans had not been in a good mood afterward. A few days later, over breakfast, she had brought up the topic. "Is Tom finally clear of that jailbreak business?"

Her father had been very deliberate in his response. He put down his coffee. "My dear, Mr. Macrae is a client. We met at my office. I gave him some advice. But yes," he allowed, "I believe he will soon be clear of the Zink fiasco."

"I do enjoy his company, Daddy. He won't be in Canada for much longer."

Ellen's words, meant to allay her father's disapproval of Tom, were proving prophetic. The war news was grim. The Canadian Expeditionary Force was still in England but expected to see action soon. Everybody assumed more men would be on their way overseas within days.

Ellen knew that her father didn't like the attention Tom was paying her, but in spite of that, she had asked if she and Tom could take her high-spirited mare and cutter for a drive into the country. Evans was reluctant but eventually acceded, perhaps because he knew that Tom's days in Canada were numbered.

Now the day had come, and Ellen's thoughts were interrupted by the ringing of the front doorbell. She flew back up the stairs to finish dressing, and as she did so she heard her father greet Tom.

Their voices receded as she shut the door to her room and added a sweater to her layers of clothing. She pulled from a drawer a red-and-white scarf that had been her mother's and paused a moment to hold it to her face, breathing in the fading perfume. Oh, Mother, I wish you could be here now. Would you approve of my young man? She wrapped the scarf around her neck and glided sedately down the stairs and into the front parlour.

Tom stood as she entered the room. "You look like you're ready for the North Pole," he said, with a grin.

He, too, was bundled up for the cold. His hair was still cut extra short, for the army, she supposed, and she wondered what it would feel like to rub her hand through it. His grey eyes met hers, and her heart fluttered in her chest. She could feel herself colouring.

"I've frozen nearly to death in the past, and I didn't like it," she responded, smiling back at him. She pulled a heavy checked coat from the hall closet and Tom was immediately at her side, holding it as she slid her arms into the sleeves.

John Evans appeared in homburg and topcoat, and the three of them walked out to the front driveway where Ellen's mare stood, harnessed to a cutter. Ellen and Tom climbed into the sleigh and Ellen held the reins while Tom pulled a buffalo robe over their knees.

Evans stood by the mare's head until they were settled, then went back to the cutter, patting the horse's back and flank as he went. "Now, Ellen, I know you've driven Belle many times, but do be careful."

"Of course, Daddy. I won't do anything you wouldn't." Ellen's father raised his eyebrows. "I'll be careful," she reassured him with a smile, and called "Giddy-up" to Belle. They headed out the driveway and down the snow-packed road.

A short distance from home, Ellen eased Belle back to a walk, and handed the reins to Tom. "What a glorious day," she cried, and leaned back to take in the sweeping blue prairie sky and the white snowfields that stretched in all directions. The road, running straight west, met the horizon at the edge of the world. The bright winter sun was at its highest point, part way up the southern sky.

Tom put his free arm around Ellen and she snuggled against him, pulling the buffalo robe up to her chin as Belle's spirited walk kicked up a chilly breeze.

If only this ride could go on forever, Ellen thought. If only Tom didn't have to join the army. If only . . . but she was being silly. Tom was in the army and would soon be going overseas. What then? I'm getting ahead of myself—maybe he doesn't even care.

As if in response, Tom's free hand slid up around her shoulder. She turned toward him, closing her eyes as he kissed her, a lingering kiss that left her breathless. Ellen pulled away, and Tom turned forward, smiling, to cluck at Belle, who broke into a trot.

Tom wasn't the first young man to kiss her, but this was different.

To Ellen it seemed like something had been decided, pinning down her future.

Tom turned to her and grinned. "All this fresh air," he said. "Gives a guy ideas."

"I hope one of them includes being hungry. We've got enough food here to feed your army."

Two miles beyond the city limits, Tom turned Belle into a side road that ended on the north bank of the Assiniboine River. He tightened the reins to bring the cutter to a stop and climbed down to ease the bit from the horse's mouth so she could paw through the thin crust of snow and nibble at frozen grass. That was nice of him, Ellen thought; not everyone would do that. She unwrapped the sandwiches and poured hot soup into cups. "I'm so glad we could get away. Will you have more free time soon?"

"I certainly hope so. There are rumours, though."

"Rumours?"

"We may be shipping out soon."

Ellen flinched; she didn't want to face the fact that Tom's days in Winnipeg were numbered. She must have shown her distress, because Tom took her hand.

"I will tell you as soon as I know."

Ellen nibbled at her food, feeling distracted. Tom was attractive: tall and strongly built, with a square jaw and level grey eyes. Her father didn't approve, but she was prepared to deal with that if she had to. And what if he left sooner rather than later? The threat of his pending departure heightened a feeling of urgency. In the meantime, between the soup and the buffalo robe, and the pressure of Tom's thigh against hers, she was feeling unaccountably warm, and her hand undid the top buttons of her coat, seeming to have a mind of its own. She hardly realized she had done so when Tom turned toward her, pulling her into a close embrace. They kissed, awkwardly at first, then hungrily, Ellen feeling the heat spreading through her body. She had never felt such a strong physical need before, and her body responded to Tom's with a fierceness that at other times would have stopped her from sheer self-consciousness. She gave herself fully to him, matching every demand, abandoning all restraint.

Afterward, Ellen lay in Tom's arms, her mind's eye looking down from above, seeing them with only their heads visible above the robe, Belle stamping her hoofs and snorting into the icy air. Beyond them was the frozen river and unending snowy fields. She saw her breath and Tom's, mingling, rising straight up in the still air. This was a turning point, she knew. From here on, her life would not be the same.

The shadows were lengthening, and Ellen sat turned toward Tom as he guided Belle back toward town. She put her arms around his waist and he bent his head to rest his cheek on hers; the slight rasp of the stubble on his face struck her as very human, and she clung to him more tightly. "I want this trip to go on forever," she said. "Just as it is, so it's just the two of us. You know?"

"Me too. Be nice if it was possible."

"Well, I'm going to pretend it is, just for now." She gave a determined shake of her head. "I love you, Tom."

"I love you, too." He transferred the reins to his left hand and hugged her, hard, in his right arm, bending to exchange a kiss. "But I don't know where we go from here. Maybe I'll be back soon, and it'll all work out. Your father thinks . . ."

Ellen didn't want to hear what her father thought. She put her gloved hand over Tom's lips. "Shush. You'll be back, and you can leave my father to me."

He looked at her then, his face serious. "I'll be back."

The sky had clouded over and a gentle snowfall showered them, light flakes drifting downward, laying a fresh patina on the old snow. Belle smelled home, trotting with her head high, the bells on her harness jingling a counterpoint to her hoofbeats.

As they reached the city streets and passed a hedge, a jackrabbit darted across their path. Belle snorted and shied, rearing high into the air, only to thump down onto all four legs and bolt. The cutter skidded to one side, crashing into a utility pole and shattering its left shaft. Belle's hoofs thrashed frantically and she slipped and fell, the broken shaft jabbing her in the ribs. The frightened horse gave a piercing whinny and lurched upright as Tom tried to keep her under control with the reins. Ellen recoiled from the front of the cutter, terrified of Belle's hoofs flashing just inches from her face. The cutter rolled left, throwing Ellen onto Tom, then just as suddenly jerked the other way. Ellen flew through the air and slammed to a stop, face down in the snow. Everything went black.

Her first conscious thought was of sharp pain in her left wrist and arm.

"Are you all right?" A stranger's voice came from somewhere.

"I don't know yet." Tom's voice, from farther away. "Are you hurt, Ellen? Are you hurt?"

She heard him clambering toward her on the frozen ground and snow. He helped her roll to her side and then onto her back, taking off his coat to put it under her head.

"My arm. It hurts." She cradled her left hand and forearm in her right. Somehow her gloves had flown off and her hands felt numb with the cold.

Tom bent over her. She could see that his face was scraped and he was bleeding over one eye. He turned to a man who was close behind him. "Can you get help? We need a doctor."

"I have a car," the man said, and ran off. He was back in minutes, which seemed much longer, and he and Tom helped Ellen into the backseat.

Tom took a quick look for Belle and saw her standing quietly a few yards away, tethered by her harness and the wrecked cutter. She'd be fine for now.

"Take me home," Ellen said. "Please. I just want to go home."

"The hospital," said Tom firmly. He sat beside Ellen and put an arm around her. Ellen was embarrassed when she realized tears were streaming down her face. She gritted her teeth against the pain. That, and the thought of facing her father.

When they pulled up to the hospital on Sherbrook Street, the man jumped from behind the wheel and ran in for help, returning with an orderly who pushed a wheelchair to the door of the car. Tom and the orderly eased Ellen into the wheelchair, and she was whisked away into an examining room where nurses who recognized her as a volunteer at the hospital crowded around. A doctor appeared and shooed the extraneous help from the room.

Tom left to call John Evans. Ellen smiled when he returned to her side and put a reassuring hand on her shoulder. "Your father is on his way," he said, sounding grim.

The doctor took off her coat. "I'm just going to palpate your arm, and it may hurt. Please try to remain still."

Ellen kept her eyes on Tom, who had moved to the side of the room at the doctor's request. His steady gaze held hers as she winced under the doctor's hands.

The doctor straightened from his examination. "A fractured ulna," he announced. "Fortunately, not in the wrist itself—higher up. And not displaced, near as I can tell. We'll immobilize it." He turned to the orderly hovering by the door. "Take her to the cast room."

Ellen was wheeled down the hall, Tom walking alongside. The doctor reappeared to give her something for pain, then mixed plaster of Paris. Ellen felt drowsy, her eyelids heavy, and she watched, detached, as the doctor applied the cast. Forcing her eyes open, she glanced around for Tom and saw him standing by the door. He looks so worried, she thought. She tried to smile at him and she must have managed it because he smiled back.

Footsteps pounded down the hall; her father hurried into the room. He was bareheaded, his overcoat unbuttoned and flapping around him. "What the devil went on with you two? What happened?"

Ellen tried to talk but her tongue felt thick.

"Belle shied from a rabbit," Tom replied. "The cutter tipped over and we were both thrown out. I'm very sorry."

Ellen looked at her father, whose hands shook as he took off his coat and wrapped it around her shoulders. He glared at Tom.

"It wasn't Tom's fault," Ellen managed.

John Evans turned away from Tom. He bent and put an arm around his daughter. "Never mind, my dear. We can sort this out later."

The doctor smoothed a last wrap on Ellen's cast. It looks so white, she thought. Just like the snow outside. What happened to my beautiful day?

"Aren't you coming?" she asked Tom, as her father wheeled her down the hall toward the exit.

"Tom will collect Belle and see she is properly looked after," said her father in a decided voice. "And I will look after you."

Tom did collect Belle, who had been taken in hand by the helpful neighbour who had driven them to the hospital. Once Belle was led home, stabled, fed, and watered, John Evans invited him into the house.

"I will be taking Ellen to stay at my sister's, at Bird's Hill, in the morning," he told Tom as Ellen sat, wrapped in a comforter, on a couch. "Anne will be happy to look after her for a few days."

Tom and Ellen had a few minutes alone in the parlour. She was pale and tired-looking, her arm, with its heavy cast, in a sling. They were both conscious of her father, who hovered in the next room.

"How is Belle?" she asked.

"She's doing very well, none the worse for wear. But what about you?"

"I think I need sleep. When will I see you?"

"Just as soon as possible."

Ellen reached toward Tom and he took her hand, which warmed with his touch. "I'll be away for a few days," she said. "And then . . ."

"And then, we'll be together again. You look after yourself, and get better. Don't worry—I'll be here when you get back."

"You'd better be," she said, giving a toss of her head and doing her best to smile.

♦　♦　♦

The long-awaited figurative trumpet call sounded at Fort Osborne Barracks the next day at 0800 hours, when the commanding officer addressed the men of the 1st Reinforcement. "You have until 1600 hours to pack, at which time you will be granted leave until midnight tonight. Final kit inspection and parade take place at 0700 hours tomorrow, after which you will march to the CPR station for entrainment to Halifax and a ship to England to join your regiment. Good luck."

The rest of the day went by in a blur of packing and double-checking uniforms and equipment. Tom squeezed in a last ride on Rusty, who would be left behind to train the next recruit assigned to him, then rode the streetcar to his family home in East Kildonan.

He tried to reach Ellen on the telephone, but the operator could not connect with anyone named Evans in Bird's Hill, and there was no answer at the Evans residence. Thoughts of Ellen were uppermost in his mind, making it extra hard to say goodbye to his brothers, sister, and especially his mother, who was not doing well. He worried that he'd never see her again.

His father drove him back to the barracks gate where they stood a moment. Bill put out his hand for Tom to shake, then clasped him in a strong embrace. "Good luck, son. I know you'll make us proud."

A sudden upwelling of emotions hit Tom at the thought of not seeing his family or Ellen again, perhaps for years. If ever. But that was too hard a notion and he banished it from his mind. Bill, who had never been a man to show his feelings, held Tom a moment longer, and when they stepped apart he brushed his sleeve quickly across his eyes.

A lump in his throat meant Tom could only mumble, "I will, Dad." He reached out and touched his father on the shoulder for a moment, then turned and walked into the barracks, a sense of leaving part of himself behind crowding out fear of the unknown.

LIFE AT SEA

◆ ◆ ◆

It seemed to Tom as if one minute he was in Winnipeg and suddenly, the next, he was marching from the Halifax terminal to a dock where the men of the 1st Reinforcement boarded ship. Now that their vessel had butted its way into the teeth of an Atlantic gale, he couldn't believe there were men who actually enjoyed life at sea. He was on his hands and knees, scrubbing the deck in the officers' head. As the Royal Mail Ship *Cape Wrath* rolled, he clung to a water pipe so he wouldn't carom across the space and crash into a bulkhead. Water in the drains gurgled and growled with the ship's movements. He felt queasy and didn't know how long he could handle it—one instant he would be pressed into the deck and seconds later almost weightless, grabbing at whatever was handy to avoid flying through the air. Without warning his stomach rebelled. He bent over the nearest toilet and vomited the dry crackers he had forced down at breakfast.

Physical weakness and a previously unrevealed fear of the sea took hold of him. He staggered down the passageway and onto a ladder to the upper deck. He made it to the leeward rail and hung there, staring down at the grey, heaving seas and shivering in the biting, North Atlantic wind.

A diminutive sergeant named Flowerdew approached along the passageway and stopped, hands clasped behind him. He swayed in time with the gyrations of the deck.

"Keep your eyes on the horizon," he advised. "I learned that trick on my first crossing. It helps."

Tom wiped his mouth on his sleeve, waited for his stomach to settle. "Seems to help that my belly is empty now, too."

Flowerdew nodded and strolled off. He was typical of many who had volunteered as soon as war broke out. British originally, he had homesteaded in Saskatchewan and grown fruit in the interior of British Columbia. When hostilities commenced he had been a junior officer in a reserve cavalry unit, but in order to get into the regular army and go overseas immediately with the cavalry, he resigned his commission and volunteered as a private. Flowerdew made no secret of his ambition to distinguish himself in battle. Tom had heard other sergeants call him "Flowers," obviously not a reflection on his manhood.

As the fresh, cold air cleared his head, Tom followed Flowerdew's suggestion and concentrated on the horizon. They had been four days at sea, and for the first time he saw a sleek shape, low on the horizon. When a sailor passed behind him, he called out, "What's that?"

The sailor squinted. Tom envied him—he didn't have to hold on to the rail.

"Destroyer. They'll shepherd us, kind of like sheepdogs. In case of submarines. Of course, they'd be no help against a battleship." The sailor went on his way, oblivious to both the rolling of the ship and having planted the seed of something new for Tom to worry about.

Tom distracted himself as best he could by focussing on the destroyer as it moved on a parallel course, much faster than the *Cape Wrath*, a faint blue haze trailing from her funnels. Maybe the sailor was kidding about the battleship.

A pale Bruce Johanson joined Tom at the rail. "I couldn't stand being down there one more minute. That damn Planck had me shovelling out horse manure. Lance-Corporal Hicks is still down there—he's worried about horses going down in this weather and not getting back up. I told him I was sick. Sick of being on this tub, more like."

"Can't be any worse than scrubbing the deck of a stinking head on your hands and knees."

"They figure another ten days of this till we get to England." Johanson's young face perked up. "Maybe there'll be some fillies who've never met any real cowboys. We can give them a good gallop."

Spray shot over them as the ship rolled heavily. Tom looked down to see the grey sea foam high against the black hull, and tightened his grip on the rail. "Maybe. Personally, I just want to get on dry land. Fighting the Germans can't be any tougher than this."

Johanson went below again to help with the horses. Tom took a last look around but could no longer see the destroyer. He left for his cleaning station, where the drains still gurgled and his stomach still churned.

Next day the weather was worse than ever. Rain and strong winds lashed the sea and huge swells bore down on the *Cape Wrath*'s starboard bow, adding a sickening pitch to her wild rolls. Aft, where the reinforcements were quartered, the deck corkscrewed under Tom's feet.

He forced down some dry bread and coffee, then went back to the upper deck to clear his head. A group of miserable soldiers huddled at the base of the ship's smokestack: the "funnel watch," sailors called it, where seasick men gathered at the ship's most stable location.

A corporal joined them and took charge, allocating the men to various housekeeping tasks: cleaning washplaces and heads, helping the cooks with meal preparations, tending to the horses below. Tom got lucky—the corporal ordered him to report to the cook, to "peel spuds." At least the galley would be warm and dry. He could wedge himself into a corner with a paring knife and a sack of potatoes.

"One moment, Corporal." Lieutenant Inkmann had appeared, looking freshly shaved.

"Sir?"

"The officers' mounts need extra attention in this weather. Macrae needs the experience." Inkmann turned and walked away, swaying with the roll of the deck.

The corporal had a quizzical expression on his face as he turned toward Tom. "You heard the lieutenant."

"Bloody hell. Since when does an officer say who does what?" Tom spluttered. It was unusual for an officer to interfere with a noncom's work, and he didn't trust Inkmann.

"Since right now. I don't know what he's got against you, but get at it. Hicks is already down there. Go give him a hand."

Tom took a deep breath of the clean air. The cold, wet, upper deck he left behind looked good as he climbed down the series of ladders to the lower hold where the officers' horses were stabled. On each deck the smell was worse than on the one above it, reeking of hot engine oil and dank air. As he reached the bottom, he felt as though he had descended into a seaborne hell.

He looked around for Eddie Hicks, a gangly young man from Dauphin, Manitoba. He had been an early recruit who just missed the departure of the regiment for Europe, a keen but inexperienced soldier. Down here, the smell of urine and horse manure mingled with the fetid odour of the bilges. Tom steadied himself, clinging to the ladder with one foot on the deck.

The horses were haltered and tied in narrow stalls that had been thrown together in Halifax. One horse lay jammed down on the deck, its head jutting out into the passageway that ran the length of the compartment, its eyes rolling in terror.

Lance-Corporal Hicks yelled, "Get over here, Macrae. Hold his head so I can check him out."

Tom lurched along the passage, grabbing at posts as he went so the violent heaving of the ship wouldn't catapult him into the far bulkhead. He hunkered down on his knees by the pitiful animal's head, one forearm across the long nose, his other hand tightly around the horse's ear.

"Hold him steady," said Hicks. "I'll have a look." He peered into the dark stall. "Can't see a thing." He clambered past Tom to get in closer. The horse twisted its hindquarters off the deck and lashed out with a hoof, catching Hicks on the leg. He dropped with a curse.

Tom hung on until the animal quieted, then shifted to put his knees on either side of its head. He took hold of a groaning Hicks by the shirt with both hands and pulled him out of the stall.

"Feels like my fucking leg is broke," said Hicks through gritted teeth.

Tom looked around, hoping someone else would appear to lend assistance. "Listen, I've got to get help. You'll have to control this horse."

"How?" Hicks moaned. "The son of a bitch has already kicked me."

Tom pointed. "Bite his ear."

"What?"

"Bite his ear. He won't move."

Tom eased part way off the horse's head and Hicks, with a doubtful glance at Tom, bent to clamp his teeth over its ear, lips drawn back in a fierce grimace. The horse froze in position, no longer struggling.

Tom backed away, steadied himself against a nasty roll of the deck, and scuttled to the ladder. Within minutes he returned with Bruce Johanson and two other privates. Hicks was only too happy to let go of the ear. He spat repeatedly. "Damn horse hair."

Cowboy Bruce wasted no time rigging up a sling with canvas, ropes, and pulleys, and together they hoisted the horse to its feet. One of the men left to fetch a farrier—there were no veterinarians on board—who checked the horse over and pronounced him none the worse for wear after his ordeal. Not so Hicks: he was half dragged and half carried up the ladders to the sick bay.

Tom finished Hicks's watch with the horses, then went to see how he was doing. The lance-corporal looked pale but chipper, sitting up on a narrow bed that was bolted to the deck, his injured leg supported on cushions. His knee looked twice normal size and already displayed various hues of yellow and purple.

"Nothing busted, if you can believe this excuse for a medic," Hicks reported. "Sure as hell hurts, though."

Tom smelled brandy; the orderly had broken out the medicinal supply. Hicks offered Tom a swallow from his cup. "I couldn't believe it when you said to bite his ear. Where did you learn that trick?"

"Well, I've never actually done it, but I heard it works."

"I guess I have something to write my mother about now. I'll tell you, though, I was pretty worried. I figured he'd fling his head up and knock out my teeth for good measure." He reached for the brandy.

The medical orderly turned from where he'd been stowing his equipment. He wasn't much more than a kid, who'd either lied about his age or whose parents had signed for him. "Hey, Hicks—maybe you can use that technique when you're in one of those fancy English dancing establishments."

"Don't get smart, buddy. You ain't old enough. Why don't you make yourself useful and go get my cigarettes from the mess."

The orderly laughed as he left the compartment.

Tom figured he'd wash up before reporting to the galley. Strange— he hadn't felt sick since he'd first seen the horse flailing in fear down on the lower deck, and he was grateful for the respite. Not to mention the brandy.

◆　◆　◆

When they were still three days from England, the Atlantic decided the *Cape Wrath* and her passengers had been through enough. The winds died and the seas calmed, leaving only a long, slow swell that overtook the ship from the starboard quarter. A million tiny, breeze-swept wavelets sparkled like jewels in the early morning sun.

Quartermain assembled the troop on the upper deck and outlined the morning's program. "Something different today, men. Sergeant Planck tells me some of you fancy yourselves as pugilists. Let's see what you're made of." There would be two teams, odd-numbered eight-man sections against evens.

The ship's crew had rigged a rough boxing ring with a single strand of rope outlining the space. Boxing gloves were produced and the men squared off two at a time for two rounds, then the next pair put on the gloves.

The sergeants were in their glory, taking charge of the affair. Quartermain was in one corner and Planck the other. They yelled instructions to their respective fighters, who went at each other with great enthusiasm and, for the most part, not much skill. The men crowded around, cheering on their friends and shouting insults at their opponents.

Tom had sparred before, in school, so he at least knew enough to keep his hands up and not expose his chin more than necessary. His first bout was with a shorter opponent who couldn't match him for reach, and Tom was happy to stay out of his way. The sergeants decreed it a draw.

When his name came up a second time it was against a Metis soldier named René Carbonnier. Carbonnier was the only man in the troop who could ride as well as Cowboy Johanson. A professional soldier, he was years older than Tom. He had been ill when the Straths were first sent overseas and was attached to the reinforcements to get him back to the regiment.

Tom didn't figure on having much trouble putting him away. What would a half-breed know about boxing?

Carbonnier wasn't a boxer, but he was canny and Tom had trouble pinning him down. He was tall and angular, and didn't hit hard, but his wiry physique helped him avoid Tom's punches. With seconds left in the final round Tom saw an opening and went for it, slashing a hard right over his opponent's guard. He was sure he had won, but just as his shot hit home he was rocked by a roundhouse blow that he had not seen coming. The bell rang. Again it was a draw, but this time both men were roundly applauded for their efforts.

Tom held his hands out so Johanson could take the gloves off. "Never knew a Metis who could box," said Tom.

"I reckon Carbonnier's been in the army long enough to pick it up. I know lots of Metis from out west, and maybe they can't box, but they can sure as hell ride and shoot. Hell, he's probably a better trooper than I'll ever be, and likely you, too."

Tom thought it over. A lot of his contemporaries back in Winnipeg looked down their noses at Indians and people of mixed blood, but the descendants of Red River settlers included many with Indian ancestry as well as Scots. And Manitoba's history was intertwined with that of the Metis, people of French Canadian-Indian descent. His mother had hinted that her parents had aided Gabriel Dumont to leave the country after Canadian troops had put down the Northwest Rebellion. Ironically, Tom knew of several Strathcona troopers who were, like René, of part or full Indian ancestry and had found a home in the army.

After two bouts Tom's arms felt like lead and he was happy to stand at the back of the crowd and cheer on the boys. Absorbed in the action, he jumped when Lieutenant Inkmann came up behind him and spoke. "Just wondering, Macrae. Did you hear before we sailed that my brother Bernard has been sentenced to jail?"

"I did. My mother wrote me about it."

"I am convinced they got the wrong man. You were Zink's student, and you were with him in the jail when he visited Bloody Jack Kravenko before his escape. Surely you know Bernard had nothing to do with Kravenko's jailbreak? You could have helped him in court."

"Your brother and Zink were like that," and Tom held up two fingers twisted together. "I couldn't do anything to help him. I just about went to jail myself."

Inkmann's face turned rigid and his hands shook. "I want the truth, Macrae. I'll not stop until I get it." He turned and stalked away.

Tom looked back toward the boxing ring. Quartermain was standing on a hatch cover making an announcement. ". . . and those who did well will have a chance to show us how good they are. We'll post a list of this afternoon's matches. Three rounds, if you last that long." He jumped down.

Tom followed his friends to line up for the noon meal, but not before he saw Inkmann take aside a corporal named Alton, a street brawler with a mean streak who had fought earlier. He was obviously at home in the ring but had held back during a bout with Bruce Johanson, who was a popular soldier, well liked by all.

The afternoon bouts attracted off-duty seamen as well as the troop's officers. There was great excitement while the various matches played out to the cheers of teammates and jeers of the opposition. Tom watched as Cowboy Johanson pursued a lanky private who took advantage of his long reach to stay out of range of Bruce's flailing fists.

Sergeant Planck, who was in Bruce's corner, yelled at him as he mopped off his face between rounds. "What do you think you are, a bloody windmill? Keep your right up and jab with your left."

A seaman rang the bell and Johanson leapt at his opponent, swinging his fists like a navvy with a sledgehammer. His opponent grinned and backpedalled, then slipped a wild punch and caught Johanson with a hard right. Johanson sat down with a thump. Planck and Quartermain charged in and pushed the other fighter away. Tom jumped forward and helped Planck get Johanson to his feet; blood leaked from one nostril. The victorious soldier skipped around the ring, arms in the air, as the crowd clapped and whistled.

Gordon Ferguson and Tom sat Johanson on a nearby crate. "Nice try, mister," said Ferguson, "but I think ye'd do better to stick to bronco busting. Just hope ye show more against the Germans."

Johanson grinned through a split lip. There was blood on his teeth. "I don't figure to box with Fritz. I'll club him with my bloody Ross rifle if it comes to that."

A buzz went up from the crowd behind them as another bout came to a close with no clear winner and no casualties.

"Macrae. Alton. Get the gloves on," Sergeant Planck yelled.

Tom swallowed hard. Alton was a tough guy, comfortable with the gloves on, and Tom had no desire to be in the ring with him for three rounds.

Ferguson pushed him forward and Planck tied the gloves on. "Ye can do it, Tom," Ferguson yelled.

He found himself standing in the jury-rigged ring, suddenly remembering that Inkmann had taken Alton aside after he had words with Tom. That could only mean trouble, and here it was.

Planck whispered hoarsely into his ear. "You're going to have to protect yourself. Be patient and wait your chance—he's too good a boxer. Keep your hands up and your feet moving." He nodded at a sailor and the bell rang.

Alton danced, shuffled to his left around the ring, and advanced. Tom swung to his left as well, hands tucked close to his face. They circled warily, trading jabs for the first minute or so. Tom moved forward, peered over his gloves, threw a harder left. Alton easily evaded the punch and snapped a left of his own off Tom's forehead. Tom shook his head and stepped into Alton. They clinched, and as Quartermain pushed them apart a sudden searing pain shot from Tom's lower back up his torso. You son of a bitch, he thought. A cheap shot in the kidney.

Tom bent forward, clutching his left arm to his side. His knees felt as though they were made of rubber. Alton landed two businesslike punches on his face and Tom sagged. Before Alton could hit him again Planck was into the ring and holding Tom around the shoulders. He pushed him into his corner and sat him down on an overturned bucket. Ferguson crowded in. He wiped Tom's face with a wet cloth and it came away bloody.

Tom had trouble focussing but he could make out Alton in the opposite corner, relaxed and waving his gloved hands to the cheers of his teammates. Beyond him, Lieutenant Inkmann stood with his peaked cap pushed back, a satisfied expression on his face.

Planck knelt in front of Tom. "That's enough for you, laddie," he said. "I'm throwing in the towel."

"The hell you are." Tom forced himself to his feet. "Ring the bell."

"I'll grant you your nerve, but not much in the way of brains." Sergeant Planck shook his head, and looked over his shoulder at the opposite corner. "Corporal Alton is a back-alley fighter," he said. "Just keep out of his way for two minutes—hands up. Remember to keep those feet dancing. Watch him in the clinches—he's bound to try something else."

The bell rang, and Tom strode directly to the centre of the ring. Alton looked at him and shook his head, grinning at the crowd. Tom crouched, hands raised to guard his chin, elbows low to protect his body.

Alton stepped forward and they exchanged punches. Tom stumbled back, breathing hard, while Alton closed in. They clinched; Tom jammed his arms under Alton's and thrust his elbows out to protect himself against another kidney shot. Quartermain came in to wave them apart and as they separated Tom threw himself at Alton. His left hand went behind the taller man's neck so he couldn't pull away, and his right fist smashed into Alton's nose. Blood sprayed onto Tom's face and shoulders as he stepped back. Alton went down like a sack of coal falling off a wagon.

Pandemonium broke out as the bell was rung again and again by the excited sailor.

"Attaboy, Tom!" yelled Ferguson.

Tom heard a muffled voice. "Macrae. Macrae."

He looked around. It was Alton, a wet towel held to his face. "One more round," he yelled. "One more round."

The crowd went quiet.

Above the din Tom heard Quartermain say to Planck, "We gave your guy a second chance. Fair's fair."

Planck looked at Tom while the crowd yelled encouragement.

"What the hell," Tom shrugged.

The bell rang, and Tom again took the centre of the ring. This time Alton was cautious and kept his distance, jabbing from long range. I've got him, Tom exulted, and closed in, taking a punch to the cheek. Alton feinted high, slashed a low blow to Tom's crotch, doubling him over, and hit him in the face with an uppercut. Tom saw a brilliant flash of light as he fell to the deck, men's voices yelling furiously in the background.

He struggled to his hands and knees, his head too heavy to lift, and toppled onto his side. The shouts of his troopmates faded into the background, like a wave dwindling on a beach. It's a rough sea tonight, he thought, as he turned his head to the side and puked.

Ferguson and Johanson supported him to his bunk, where he drew his knees up to his chest and passed out.

GROUNDWORK

◆ ◆ ◆

The morning after they landed at Portsmouth, Tom woke from a fitful sleep to the juddering of the ancient railway carriage as it slowed to a crawl, almost stopped, then speeded up again. The train rattled and creaked, continuing northward across a low, rolling landscape. A grey sky hung close over farms and cottages. Tom looked around the railway car in the half-light of dawn. Men in khaki sat or leaned, propped against each other, as the wet, green English countryside slid by outside the window. Every inch of the carriage was taken up by semi-reclining soldiers who were draped on, around, and sometimes under heaps of packs and duffel bags. There was a steady drone of snores, coughs, and muttered phrases, the air thick with the smell of damp clothing and the sweat of thirty men in the confined space.

Johanson's head flopped onto Tom's shoulder. His friend's breath was enough to gag a rat, and Tom elbowed him; Johanson grumbled and slumped the other way onto Ferguson. Tom's body still ached from the punches he had taken on board ship four days before.

The train slowed again. Tom dozed, his head against the rain-spotted glass. His mind wandered, the partly glimpsed landscape taking him back to train trips across the prairies. Trips on the Canadian Pacific main line west of Winnipeg when he was a young boy, where grass stretched to the horizon; trips when he would gaze out the window of the train and daydream about the buffalo herds which, short years before, had stretched to the horizons, Indian and Metis hunters in pursuit; daydreams interrupted by the shriek of a steam locomotive . . .

The English train's whistle brought him upright as they slowed and stopped at a platform in a rustic village, whitewashed cottages and ancient oaks, bleak under the lowering sky. Carriage doors banged open. A tall corporal stuck his head in and shouted, "Move it, you lot. Boots and saddles. Grab your gear and fall in on the platform."

Tom didn't recognize the corporal. Their own noncoms had been hived off to a different train, for some unfathomable army reason.

A mass groan arose from the reinforcements.

"Just when I was getting comfortable," someone muttered.

"Are we at holiday camp yet?" asked another anonymous voice.

"Corporals piss me off."

The corporal shouted, "At the double," and stomped out.

The men dragged their gear off the train and fell in. The corporal and a lance-corporal did a head count.

The corporal turned to the lance. "Carry on, Heskitt," and the lance-corporal stepped forward. Heskitt was a small man sporting a thick mustache. He didn't wear Canada badges, the brass identifiers on the shoulders of the Dominion's soldiers. Tom figured him for a particular type, an Englishman who had found a home in the small, permanent British army, regulation all the way. He reminded Tom of Sergeant Planck, although Planck had grown in Tom's estimation as he learned to deal less formally with the Canadians.

Heskitt spoke up. "Listen here. Transport is waiting outside the station. You," he said, and pointed at Tom, who happened to be at the front of the end file. "Get these men aboard. I want a head count once they're in the bus. Report back to me. Carry on."

Mentally vowing never to be end man in the front rank again, Tom grabbed his pack and turned to the soldiers lined up on the platform. "Let's go, boys. You heard the man." He led the way around the end of the station to where a decrepit, double-decker, London omnibus waited, belching smoke. The vehicle's red paint was faded, its height accentuating a list to one side.

As the men struggled up the narrow steps with their loads, the ones in first tried to wedge themselves and their packs into the cramped front benches.

"Hold on," Tom said. "You men in front—take your packs to the back of the bus. The rest of you, form a line. Pass the rest of the packs along and stack them in the back. Jam them in. Once all the packs are on, everybody take a pew."

In short order, all thirty packs and bags were stowed in the rear of the bus; the men piled into the remaining seats on the bottom level and the upper deck. Tom did a head count and went in search of the lance-corporal. He looked for the single chevron on the uniform and saw him with the corporal.

"All aboard and accounted for, Lance-Corporal."

Heskitt ignored him for a minute as he continued to talk to the corporal. Then he said, "Who the hell told you to separate the men and their packs?"

"The bus seats are too small for both."

The lance tucked his chin in, arms rigidly at his sides. "See this?" he shouted, and pointed at the chevron on his sleeve. "That says you do what I tell you, and nothing else." Tom couldn't place his accent, but it sounded as though he said "nuffink else." "What are you smiling at, you colonial sod? I'll teach you to follow orders. Get those men off the bus, unload the packs, and get them back on with their packs. Do it now," he screamed, spittle flying off his lower lip.

"Hold on," interjected the corporal. "We haven't got time for this. Leave things where they are." He looked at Tom. "You'd better hope everybody finds their own gear when we get to camp, or you'll be walking back for it. Now climb aboard, and next time listen to instructions."

Tom turned away to head for the bus. As he did so Heskitt moved quickly to his side. "I'll teach you to laugh at me," he hissed.

Tom climbed into the front seat on the overloaded bus and it lurched off, the driver laboriously working his way up through the gears. Tom glanced out the window and spotted Heskitt climbing into the driver's seat of a small truck. Goddamn Limeys, he thought. Goddamn army.

The bus clattered through the village, its rusted-out muffler rendering it noisy at any speed. The irregular roar of its engine echoed off white-painted churches and neat cottages. Passing scattered farms, the overloaded vehicle swayed ominously in rain-filled ruts. A weak sun that slid into view between banks of clouds cheered Tom up a little. His stomach growled.

As if on cue, someone shouted from the back. "Hey, Tom, since you're in charge here—did your pals tell you when we'd get fed?"

"Lance-Corporal Heskitt promised boiled mutton. Sound good?"

Laughter rippled through the bus; the sun broke through between dark banks of cloud. Someone stomped on the overhead deck and yelled, "Looks like we're here."

The bus squealed to a stop, and the men piled off. The last ones out passed the packs down the line, and owners claimed their gear. Tom took a moment to look around. Pond Farm Camp was in Wiltshire, on Salisbury Plain. Long lines of soggy tents sagged against their guy ropes and though here and there bits of turf remained, for the most part men's boots and horses' hoofs had churned the ground to mud. The smell of cook stoves, saddle soap, and fresh country air was a welcome change from the fug of the *Cape Wrath*'s hold. In the distance men were drilling on horseback. The reinforcements grinned at each other in anticipation.

The tall corporal fell them in once again, then reported to a smartly turned out sergeant-major, who stepped forward and looked up and down the line of newcomers.

"At ease. Welcome to Salisbury Plain, gentlemen. I see you've brought a little bit of Canada with you. This is our first sunshine in two weeks, so we're doubly glad to see you." A few of the men chuckled.

"I'm RSM Ballard." Regimental sergeant-major, next only to God, Tom knew, the senior noncommissioned officer in our army world. At least he's Canadian. Ballard went on to explain that the Strathconas were assigned to the Canadian Mounted Brigade. Other regiments in the brigade were the Royal Canadian Dragoons and two batteries of the Royal Canadian Horse Artillery, along with a British regiment, the 2nd King Edward's Horse.

"Lord Strathcona's Horse is now up to full strength. You'll be assigned your billets later today. In the meantime, you'll be shown where you can stow your gear and the corporal will take you to the mess tents. At 1400 hours the colonel will inspect. That gives you an hour to get cleared away. That is all." He turned to the corporal and nodded.

"Atten-SHUN," bellowed the corporal. "Dis-miss!"

The men fell out and trooped after the corporal through the glue-like mud of the camp.

So far, so good. Tom and his compatriots had worked hard to qualify and train for this day; now they had finally joined their regiment. Fresh mounts would be assigned soon. The common feeling among the high-spirited Canadians was a hope that the war wouldn't be over before they got into it. Tom kept his reservations to himself. Part of him wanted to have at it, and the sooner the better. Get it over with, get home. But he also had a gut-wrenching fear: a fear of death, to be sure, but in particular a fear of losing limbs, abetted by his own vivid imagination and the memory of Sergeant Grey, the man with no arms.

Tom was now a member of C Squadron's 1st Troop. The squadron had four troops, each composed of approximately thirty-five men and horses. The troops were further broken down into sections of eight, led by a corporal or lance-corporal. A troop had a sergeant as well as a junior officer in command, usually a lieutenant. The 1st Troop of C Squadron was commanded by Lieutenant Tilley.

Tom looked for Inkmann's name on Daily Orders, the typewritten schedule posted outside the orderly room. It wasn't there. He had apparently been posted elsewhere, swallowed up in the growing monster of the British and Empire war effort. Good luck to him, and good riddance.

♦ ♦ ♦

The good weather lasted all of four hours. By nightfall heavy clouds had scudded in from the west and a misty rain drifted over the Strathcona camp.

Tom had been allocated half of a two-man tent. After stumbling through mud that was inches deep he managed to locate it, one of many in two long rows. He stuck his head in and introduced himself to its occupant, who sat on his bedding cleaning a rifle. Charlie Fricker was a wiry soldier with a gaunt face and black hair.

"Okay, Macrae. Here's the deal," said Fricker, talking fast out of the corner of his mouth. "You keep on your side of the tent and I'll stay on mine. Right? Don't touch the inside of the tent. Water collects on the outside of the canvas and if you touch it, it'll leak. I hope you don't snore. This place is the shits. Most of the officers are okay. Stay out of Heskitt's way—he hates Canadians, along with the rest of the world. Oh yes—put lots of Dubbin on your boots or they'll rot away within a week. Don't—"

Tom thought he should interrupt or Fricker would bust a gasket for want of taking a breath. "What do you hear about the regiment getting to France?"

"Nothing's going to happen in a hurry. The colonel said the generals don't see any use for cavalry when both sides are bogged down in trenches. Hell, the way I hear it, the Allies and the Germans are mostly within a mile of each other. No room for cavalry." Fricker sniffed. "Bloomin' English generals don't have any bloomin' imagination."

It was ironic, listening to Fricker go on about the English, Tom thought, because, like most of the volunteers in the Canadian army, Charlie had a British background. Even those born in Canada could usually trace their roots to the British Isles. Fricker had an English accent but didn't leave any doubt about how he identified himself. He told Tom he had been in Lord Strathcona's Horse since its early days, when the predecessor regiment was raised in the Canadian west for service in South Africa. Tom reappraised the diminutive veteran.

The Canadians in the cavalry considered themselves the elite among their army brethren: "going to war on horseback, like a gentleman," as Bill Reagan had said way back at the Evans garden party. They were often the butt of derisive comments by other soldiers, who thought them anachronistic.

"What about horses?" Tom asked Fricker. "Do we all have horses? Only the officers brought theirs over on the ship."

"No problem there," said Fricker. "We have enough to go round, though the countryside is being raided for more all the time. There are thousands with the British army units in France."

Tom knew the fighting was hard on horses. The huge armies on both sides of the trenches used horses and mules as their main method of moving supplies of all kinds around. Trains and motor vehicles worked behind the lines, but only four legs could support the men in the vicinity of the actual fighting, where the earth itself was flayed by constant shelling.

"The RSM said the brigade gets paraded tomorrow. What's going on?" Tom asked.

"Don't know. Could be anything. Or nothing. You never know with the army. Hurry up and wait, what? I hear the infantry is getting all shot up. Come on, I'll show you around."

If the infantry was getting shot up, what hope was there for men on horseback? Or for that matter, for the horses? Tom and Fricker sloshed off in the muck to inspect the horse lines, tents, camp kitchens, headquarters, latrines, storage areas, and magazines, all of which were surrounded by mud and water; there was no dry ground anywhere. Tom's breeches and tunic were wet, right through his waterproof poncho.

Everybody they talked to grumbled about the weather, but to a man they were cheerful in spite of it. Even Tom was glad to be with the regiment, a fighting unit, no longer just part of a training squadron.

But the training went on. Tom was in with a new section, with a new horse. He named him Johnny, after a favourite uncle.

The familiar voice of Sergeant Quartermain greeted the mounted troop. "Pay attention, men. Check your swords, and follow me."

Tom glanced down to where his Pattern 1908 cavalry sword hung from his saddle, just behind his left thigh. The deadly weapon had a straight, tapered, thirty-five-inch blade and was designed to stab, not slash. To draw it, he would reach across his body with his right hand, grasp the handle, pull it out of its scabbard, and bring it back across to his right side.

Quartermain led them to higher ground, where spring-loaded dummies had been set up. "We will walk through the drill. Watch me." He walked his horse toward one of the dummies, and drew his sword while continuing to talk. "Draw sword. Point at your man. Lean forward, buttocks off the saddle. Grip firmly—knees and thighs. Reins in left hand, sword extended straight ahead in the right." The sergeant leaned over his horse's neck, sword as far forward as he could reach, well past his steed's head.

"Sword horizontal. Arm straight. Carry right through your target." Quartermain's sword was thrust into the dummy, which swayed as his horse moved past it. "Don't let me see you swinging your sword at your target. The sword is a stabbing weapon. As you pass your man, let your right arm swing back. Hold on, or you will lose your weapon. Pull it out, swing it overhead so you don't skewer your mate on your right, and line up your next target."

Quartermain had the men walk through the drill several times, then do it at the trot. Tom's horse, Johnny, tried to shy away from the dummy.

"Take charge of that animal," Quartermain growled.

Just like old times. Tom felt a stab of nostalgia for Rusty.

◆　◆　◆

"Time, gentlemen, time," sang the pub-owner's wife. She was a middle-aged blonde who flirted with the soldiers on an equal basis, while making sure they knew she was married to the guv. She was as cheerful to the privates in the public bar as she was to the officers in the adjoining saloon.

The raucous crowd of Canadian soldiery thinned out, with late-filled pints gulped down. Tom and Bruce Johanson were among the stragglers, and as they left, they were joined by George Windell, a private who had worked in a Calgary bank.

Tom breathed deeply of the still air, glad to be out of the pub with its nicotine-coated timbers and thick blue smoke. The cobbled streets were slick with rain, although none was falling at the moment. They had another two hours before curfew.

The three men wandered through the quiet village to the square, where an ancient king gazed down on them from his stone pedestal. A worn bench faced the statue. Tom took off his cap and sat, his arms folded and legs stretched out in front of him. A gentle easterly breeze, scented by miles of gorse and bramble, ruffled through his short hair. "I'll be glad when we're out of this English weather," he said.

Windell peered at the horizon, as if he could see through Kent and across the Channel. "What makes you think it will be any better in France? I expect it rains over there, too."

Bruce struck a match. He cupped his hands around its flare and dragged deeply on a cigarette. "Guess I won't be doing this in the open air where we're going," he said with a grin. "I hear the Germans have some pretty good snipers."

"I reckon we have some of our own, eh, Tom?" Windell had been yanked out of training with the rest of his troop and employed with the regimental staff because of his typing ability. He had access to various reports, one of which listed Tom as a top marksman with the Ross rifle.

"That'll probably change now that we have the Lee Enfield. I haven't had a chance to practise with it. Anyway, I'm no more interested in being a sniper than I am in being a general."

Tom was thinking about Ellen's latest letters, a bundle of which had arrived as the army's postal service had finally caught up with the Strathconas. They covered a six-week period, and he read them in order. Ellen's tone seemed to change as time went by. More distant, more newsy, and less personal. She had been going to social functions, where she'd been mingling with her own friends—people he didn't know. And here he was, in England, where he might as well be on the moon for all the prospects of seeing her any time soon. He hoped he wasn't reading too much into it.

"Personally, I'm having the time of my life," Bruce interjected. He took another puff on his army-issue cigarette. "I'd be happy to stay here and plant more wild Canadian seed in English soil. And that reminds me—I've got an appointment. See you later, boys," and he set off through the village. Tom envied him his nonchalant attitude. Bruce didn't spend his time brooding about a girl back home.

"I'll be glad when we get to France. Maybe I'll get back with the troop," said Windell as he sat on the bench beside Tom. "If I'd wanted to be a clerk, I could have stayed in Calgary. I didn't enlist in the cavalry so I could type out requisitions for bully beef and plum jam."

"You might want to rethink that. Regimental headquarters might be out of artillery range. A hell of a lot safer than the front lines."

"Maybe so." Windell paused. "I hear from my family that the Yeomen got hit hard. Almost wiped out. There'll be widows and orphans in Gloucester." Windell was originally an Englishman and had a slew of aunts, uncles, and cousins in the Old Country. They kept him up to date with his native village's war news.

Tom found it hard to imagine his troop facing decimation as had so many Allied units. Ypres, the Marne: sickening rumours of casualties in the hundreds of thousands. How would his mother carry on if he were killed? At least he had siblings; many families had seen their only children march off to war. And what of Ellen? She'd probably move on fast enough, he thought unhappily.

He gazed unseeing to the south and east toward the Channel and France, where he would soon find himself. Thoughts that he couldn't articulate hovered at the very edge of his consciousness, like the vague, low sound of a distant thunderstorm on a humid prairie night.

"Do you hear that?" asked Windell.

"No. What?"

The two of them sat, totally still. There it came again—low, growling, barely audible.

"Guns," said Tom.

"Artillery," Windell corrected. Being a clerk in headquarters, he always had to have the last word. "Big guns, howitzers. Night-firing practice. Sounds nasty. Maybe I'll keep on typing, at least until we see how the ground lies."

That night Tom's sleep was interrupted by a dream about Ellen. She was looking for him, but couldn't see him. And he couldn't call out to her, no matter how he tried. She slowly faded from view, but toward him came something evil and unknown, creeping from a distant, bleak horizon.

◆　◆　◆

Ellen gazed into the mirror, reached without conscious thought for her hairbrush, and ran it slowly through her hair. Her father was being so tedious. Not that she minded acting the chatelaine at his endless dinner parties and social events; she knew her role and played it well, and also more frequently, now that she was twenty years old and there was no other woman in her father's life. No, what was bothersome was his insistence on matching her up with eligible men—"The Eligibles," as she thought of them. I wonder who The Eligible will be tonight. Not that it mattered, her thoughts turning to Tom. She was desperate for the war to end so he could come home and they could be together, her father's concerns dealt with.

Later, she mingled with the female guests who sat with tiny glasses of sherry. Through the door to the study she could see the men, dark-suited and assured, speaking in quiet tones with her father. The men drank Scotch whisky, straight or with water, brought to them by the butler, her father's last remaining extravagance; he kept the man on out of a sense of duty, in spite of his failing economic circumstances.

Ellen listened with little attention to comments by Mrs. Ellison, wife of the manager of the Hudson's Bay department store. "My Jeffrey is of course overseas, waiting in England for a chance to get into action. He says they . . ." Not an Eligible in sight, Ellen thought with some relief. Although having one around would at least lend a little interest to the party, let her flirt or ignore him at her whim.

Just then the doorbell rang, and Ellen joined her father in the foyer to greet the late arrivals. John Evans opened the door and a tall young man in a cashmere overcoat and white silk scarf thrust his hand out. "How do you do, sir. I believe my parents are here already. Harry Hepwell."

Well, well. Tonight's entry in the marry-Ellen-off sweepstakes. Let's see how he makes out.

Her father took Harry's hand. "Welcome, Mr. Hepwell. Indeed they are." He turned to Ellen to say, as he had so many times before, "This is my daughter, Ellen. She runs my life."

Ellen smiled. "Don't pay any attention to him, Mr. Hepwell."

"Let me have your coat," Evans continued, then, taking it, passed it off to the butler who had appeared at his side. "Whisky, young man? Ellen, why don't you entertain Harry while I get him a drink."

"How is it we haven't met before, Mr. Hepwell?"

"Please call me Harry." Hepwell paused as if waiting for a response, which Ellen did not give him.

When she thought the awkward silence had gone on long enough, she said, "And you must call me Ellen. How is it we have not met before . . . Harry?"

"I've been at university in Toronto. My parents moved here two years ago. If I had been here, we most assuredly would have met."

Forward, thought Ellen. Confident. And he certainly is good-looking. They exchanged small talk, and Ellen sized him up when his gaze was elsewhere. He looked physically fit but on the slim side, and there was something about him that made him seem somehow frail. Why wasn't he in the army?

As if reading her mind, Harry blinked and responded. "I spent eighteen months in a sanatorium with TB. All over it now, but not up to fighting standards, the recruiters tell me."

Ellen was flustered. Good heavens—she must have spoken her thoughts aloud. "Oh dear. I'm so glad you recovered." She glanced toward the dining room, where she saw her father beckon. "I see dinner is about to be served," she said, with some relief.

Harry laughed, and presented his arm with a flourish. "May I, Miss Evans?"

Ellen, still embarrassed, took his arm and they led the other guests to the candle-lit dining room. Amid the scraping of chairs and rustle of the women's clothing as they sat, Ellen glanced at her father, who looked awfully pleased with himself.

Later, after the last guest had gone and the butler was cleaning up in the dining room, John turned to Ellen. "A pleasant evening, my dear?"

"Better than average, perhaps," Ellen replied, knowing her father was asking about more than the social niceties that had been observed.

◆ ◆ ◆

"Okay, Gordon, what's the latest poop?" Tom asked.

Gordon Ferguson, since his friend George Windell was on regimental staff, was always good for whatever hot rumours were flying around. Tom, Gordon, Bruce Johanson, and a few others were seated at a table in one of the mess tents. The duty personnel had cleared the tables, and the men were taking advantage of a respite from the tedium of training. It was late April 1915, and a wet winter had blended seamlessly with a soggy spring. Rain pattered steadily on the canvas roof and the wall dripped water into the already saturated earth.

"Windell doesn't know what's really going on. Besides, he's not supposed to talk about what he knows."

"Come on, Gordon," Johanson teased. "You just like to be coaxed. What does Windell say? Is the war gonna be over before we get into it?"

Some of the men chuckled. Gordon grinned and shook his head. The Strathconas had been in England for months, and from what they could see, the war wasn't going to wrap up any time soon. The Canadian infantry, artillery, and supporting units of the Canadian Expeditionary Force had crossed the English Channel in February. They had seen heavy action and suffered many casualties. Meanwhile, the cavalry still languished in England.

"The British and French generals have their heads stuck in the mud, along with their armies," said Eddie Hicks, still wearing the single chevron of a lance-corporal. "All they can think to do is to push more troops into the trenches and chew 'em up. It's a bloody meat grinder over there."

"At least the boys over there have Canadian commanders," Johanson contributed. "Speaking of which, how is our new, very own British general doing?"

"Seely's a good man, apparently," Ferguson said. "Did you lads hear about him outlawing Number One punishment?"

"Why would a general do that?" asked Hicks. "Number One is pretty useful. Nothing like being lashed to a stationary wagon wheel for two hours to cure a man of being absent without leave, or drunk. At least until the next time."

"The story is when old Seely heard what it was, he had himself lashed to a wagon wheel. After five minutes his back seized up. So he made them turn him loose and announced, 'No man under my command will undergo this torture.'"

"Well," commented Hicks, "I hear he ain't that old—and by the way, did you know he was in the British war cabinet, then quit to join the army? Who knows, maybe he'll be okay. Even if he *was* a bloody politician."

"I reckon having Canadian cavalry to command will bring out the best in him," said Johanson. "Anyway, Fergie," and he turned to Gordon, "you haven't told us. What's the latest from headquarters?"

"Don't know. But I hear we're getting paraded tomorrow morning for Seely's inspection. I'm guessing something's on."

The group broke up soon afterward and Tom went back to his tent, where he sat on his bunk, intending to write some letters. Without thinking about it he picked up his Lee Enfield, took out the magazine, checked the bolt action, cycled the safety. He pinched the bolt between his thumb and forefinger and pulled the trigger, letting the pin down gently.

Tom had never seen himself soldiering, laying his life on the line. Zink and his machinations had changed all that, so here he was, on Salisbury Plain, training ground for British armies for God knew how long. Across the Channel a generation of the Empire's young men was being tested. And getting wounded. And dying, a lot of them. Tom had every intention of making it through this madness however he could, returning to Ellen, maybe dealing with the people who had fed him into the war's gaping maw.

The men around him were keen to get at the Germans. They saw themselves as Canadians and only secondarily as citizens of the British Empire. They were proud of being here to fight, proud to represent their country. But greater minds than theirs had decreed there was no place for the cavalry in modern warfare, so the Strathconas and their brothers in the Canadian Mounted Brigade fretted, drank too much, and raised hell away from camp, testing the patience of both their officers and their English hosts.

Tom was too keyed up to write a reassuring letter home. His rifle was oiled and spotless. Veterans in the regiment were fatalistic about their futures and sometimes commented that if a bullet had your name on it, there wasn't much you could do about it. Tom fleetingly pictured a German, cleaning his rifle, thinking about home. He put his muddy boots back on and tramped around the camp until he was tired enough to sleep.

◆ ◆ ◆

"Atten-SHUN," bawled Regimental Sergeant-Major Ballard, and the Strathconas came to rigid attention. The regiment was fallen in and a merciful God had allowed a break in the rain. The RSM turned and saluted Lieutenant-Colonel Macdonell. "Regiment ready for inspection, sir."

Tom glanced at the sky. Shafts of watery sunlight broke through in a couple of places, illuminating far-off, translucent columns of rain. In the distance he could hear the other regiments of the Mounted Brigade falling in, to be inspected in their turn.

The colonel returned the salute and said, in a voice that carried to the last man in the ranks, "There will be no inspection today. General Seely will address the regiment." The colonel turned and saluted the brigadier-general. Tom saw a slim, upright figure with an air of command about him.

Seely stepped forward and started to speak in a rather dandified English accent, his voice resonant. "Strathconas, I don't have to tell you about your proud history, your origins on the Canadian prairie, your predecessors' gallantry in South Africa—where, incidentally, I also served."

There was an approving rumble from the men.

"As you know, to date there hasn't been much call for cavalry in these hostilities. Perhaps one day our friends in the infantry and artillery will blast a hole in the Hun's lines that will allow us to gallop through and put the enemy to the sword. But that day has not yet arrived."

And maybe never will, Tom thought, as the general paused.

"In fact, our Canadian comrades-in-arms, the rest of the Canadian Expeditionary Force, have been in a heated battle since their deployment in Belgium. Most recently, when attacked with poison gas, they stood steadfast and beat back the enemy. The Canadians are establishing a reputation as superb fighting men. But they are in the fight of their lives, and they need help."

Where is he going with this? Tom didn't like the sound of it. Soggy breakfast eggs twisted in his gut.

"Mounted men are not currently required. Help in the trenches is. Strathconas, I believe we have a job to do. Your brothers and cousins are in the thick of it." He turned to the colonel.

"We are calling for volunteers," said Macdonell. "We will have to leave our horses behind for now. I want us to go immediately to the continent to join our Canadian brothers in the trenches." In the sudden silence, Tom heard the gentle soughing of the wind. "All those who volunteer take two paces forward."

Tom's mind raced. He knew of men who had gone overseas into battle, men who had come back wounded, shattered . . . or who never would come back. He had no intention of joining that ghostly cadre. But in that instant the world slowed. He saw clearly the faces of the men around him—Johanson, Ferguson, Hicks, Windell, and all the rest—and he knew what they would do.

The mass of men surged ahead, Tom with them, as a great roar rose from the ranks. The colonel, not able to totally conceal a smile, called them to attention.

The hubbub died down, and General Seely stood like a rapier before them. "I told the commander-in-chief that would be your response." He nodded. "Carry on, colonel."

"Three cheers for General Seely," shouted the colonel.

Cheers rang out, defiant in the face of a cold wind that had begun to blow; rain closed in once again when the men were dismissed. As Ferguson and Tom sloshed through the mud, Johanson ran up behind and jumped between them, whacking them across the shoulders.

"Here we go, boys, here we go! No horses, but that'll come. We'll get a crack at Fritz after all."

Lord save us, thought Tom. We're in for it now.

FRANCE

♦ ♦ ♦

It was May 22, 1915, only days since the Canadian Mounted Brigade had volunteered to go into the mud of Flanders. A flash of lightning behind a cloud to the northeast lit the night sky and for an instant, Tom saw the long, sinuous line of poncho-covered, hump-backed men ahead of him, burdened with haversacks, bedrolls, and rifles. It snaked toward the front to disappear into a communication trench. Then the image was gone and he was left with the murky shadow of the man in front of him. Tom could too easily imagine Germans peering over machine gun sights—sights that were aligned on him.

The 1st Troop leader, Lieutenant Tilley, had addressed his thirty-two men before they set out to replace troops in the trenches, but Tom couldn't bring the lieutenant's words to mind, try as he might. He knew they were full of admonitions to do their duty, to stand firm. But what everybody knew, and nobody talked about, was that this night, or the next, or the next, some of them would be dead. It stood to reason. The front, with its trenches now hundreds of miles long, was where battles were fought in this modern war, and that was where men died. The Strathconas were going into the trenches and some of them would die. Maybe all. Maybe Tom.

Slimy mud caked his boots, making every laborious step a challenge. He became aware of a panting sound and realized it was his own breathing. He hitched up his shoulders to settle his pack and without warning bumped up against the man in front of him. He could just make out a clump of men huddled together in the darkness and the rain.

"What's going on?" he whispered.

"Don't know," someone replied.

Everyone had stopped. Tom couldn't see anything beyond the length of his arm. Then the rustle of wet ponchos from ahead signalled that those in front were on the move again, and one by one the men in the little knot resumed their march.

For some reason Tom thought of a time when he had drifted in a canoe over white sandy shallows on the eastern shore of Lake Winnipeg. An inkblot of black had appeared, several feet across, then expanded so he could see it was a mass of tiny minnows. At some unknowable signal they coalesced once more into a dark mass. From one side a two-foot-long pike suddenly appeared and shot through the ball of fish, leaving an empty streak that quickly closed. The pike struck again, and again, then drifted off. Tom had watched the reformed, amorphous school of minnows until they disappeared into deeper water. Maybe he'd be one of the lucky ones. He gripped his rifle tighter and vowed for the hundredth time to do whatever it took to survive.

More lightning flashed, and there was a rumble of thunder in response. Tom was concentrating on his footing when a screaming arc of sound slashed across the sky. The high-pitched shriek of the shell faded as it passed overhead and terminated in a flash of light and an ear-shattering blast behind them.

Tom sensed rather than saw the men ahead of him flinch, and they increased their speed as more shells landed. Now a new sound met them—a brutal chatter they recognized as machine gun fire. They had heard machine guns before—the regiment had Hotchkisses of their own, and many of the men were trained to fire them—but this was new. This was the enemy: Germans armed with Maxims that spat five hundred steel-jacketed slugs a minute. Stray bullets whined and ricocheted around them.

At last Tom made it into the communication trench. He followed the man in front of him, keeping in contact with an outstretched hand as the landscape was blotted out by the six-foot-high sides of the zig-zagging ditch. Not deep enough, he muttered, wishing, for the first time in his life that he were shorter. If he craned his neck to look up he could see the bitter sky with its low clouds and competing lightning and shell bursts.

The men reached the reserve trench, which ran parallel to the front. An officer directed them a short distance to the east into another communication trench, which deposited them into the front line, the forward trench. To Tom's searching eyes this glorified ditch seemed deeper, perhaps eight feet. There was a foot of mud and water in the bottom; the sides were alternately slick with slime or gritty with sandbags. His stomach clenched at the stench of animal and human excrement and rot, and the smell of death, his feet already wet and cold.

Sergeant Planck posted Tom's section of eight to a short, straight section of the fighting trench. It was already populated by ghostly infantrymen of the 1st Canadian Division, dirty-faced and stinking. The newcomers instinctively pressed themselves up against the front of the trench, hoping the earth would protect them.

"Got a smoke?" asked a dark figure. His eyeballs reflected flickering light from the flashes of exploding shells.

Tom produced a package of Players and the two of them bent low to shield the flame of the man's match. "Where you from?" asked Tom.

"Toronto."

"How long have you been in here?"

"Two weeks. Glad to see you horse soldiers. We need a break."

Tom was glad the infantry were getting a break. He was only sorry he had to be part of giving it to them.

The soldier's name was Clark, and he told Tom he had enlisted as soon as war was declared. Now he just hoped to survive to see his new wife again.

Tom hesitated, then asked, "Have you been attacked while you were here?"

"Twice in the last week."

Tom's heart sank.

An infantry sergeant came through, giving his troops a warning.

The foot soldiers would be withdrawing immediately.

"Not bad compared to what came before. But it's the boredom that gets you," Clark continued.

Tom knew these men had seen brutal action at Ypres in Belgium. "Wipers," they called it. They had taken huge losses, in spite of being trained infantrymen, not cavalry troopers who had undergone instant transformation.

Behind his cupped hand, Clark took a last drag on his cigarette and ground the butt into the side of the trench.

Tom was nervous. What good would all those months of training on horseback do him now? The Straths had been trained to attack with horses, swords, and the Ross rifle. Now they had been handed Lee Enfield rifles and bayonets, and were up to their knees in mud and shit in the trenches, with no horses in sight.

An infantry officer passed behind Tom on his way to the communication trench with a string of indistinct other ranks trailing him, sloshing and stumbling in his wake. They moved like sleepwalkers, dark figures in deep shadows.

Clark moved off to join them. He turned to Tom. "Good luck, soldier of the horse. See you in Berlin."

Tom waved in salute as the infantrymen rounded a corner in the trench and the sound of their passing faded. He shivered, and a shell buzzed overhead. He was a long way from Winnipeg.

◆ ◆ ◆

Sergeant Planck detailed Tom as a sentry for the first two hours. He stood on a low platform so his head was just below the top of the trench, peering through a slot between two sandbags. He felt exposed, but tried to convince himself that the enemy couldn't see any better than he could.

Planck appeared and explained that an attack would be carried out before dawn, but not by the Strathconas. They were to lie low and be prepared for an expected German counterattack.

At the end of his watch Tom shook Gordon Ferguson, who took over on the lookout platform. Tom wrapped himself in his bedding and poncho and squeezed into a shallow cave carved in the forward wall of the trench. There was just room for him to scrunch into a semi-sitting position, his left side to the enemy and his right exposed to the men passing by in the trench. He tried to relax but his eyes wouldn't close. He had been concentrating for too long, trying to see where there was nothing to be seen, and his eyelids refused to stay shut.

The German shelling increased. Most of the explosions were well behind the trench, and Tom hoped he was safe so long as he kept his head down.

An hour later a series of explosions echoed from the direction of the German lines. Shouts and screams drifted back to the men in the trench, overlain by a sudden, nearly continuous stutter of machine guns. Everybody was up on their feet, and some of the men climbed to the lip to peer into the night. Artillery fire increased to an ear-splitting crescendo that seemed to go on for hours, much of it now coming from behind the Canadian lines. As the anxious men strained to hear through the roar of shelling, Tom pictured grey-clad Germans, firing wildly, pouring into the trench, a death trap for its occupants.

Ferguson, up on the parapet, yelled, "Who goes there?"

The men in the trench froze.

"Hold your fire," came a shout. "We're Canadian. We're coming in."

"Keep your hands where I can see them," Ferguson yelled back. They had been warned that the Germans sometimes impersonated Allied soldiers.

Tom leapt to the platform to stand beside Ferguson. Gordon had his rifle levelled at what Tom now saw was a private supporting an officer who stumbled, barely able to keep moving. Tom reached out, grabbed the officer's jacket at the shoulders, and helped him over the parapet. Other Strathconas eased the wounded man to the bottom of the trench, holding his head and shoulders above the water and mud. The private slid down the side of the trench and collapsed in a heap, breathing hard. His face was blackened, his uniform caked in mud.

Sergeant Planck sent for medical help and he and Tom knelt over the officer, a lieutenant, who was wounded in the shoulder. They cut away his tunic, exposing an entry wound in front and a larger exit hole in the back. A shaded lantern showed what had looked black in the darkness to be dark red blood, oozing from the officer's wounds. Planck applied iodine and a field dressing while they waited for stretcher-bearers. The wounded man's face was still blackened to facilitate night operations, but deathly pale under the burnt cork, and he mumbled incoherently.

Tom saw the insignia of an Ontario infantry regiment. "What happened out there?" he asked the private.

"We were on a raid. We got across No-Man's-Land okay, but there's a row of barbed wire in front of the German trench. So far, so good. The lieutenant found a way through the wire and waved the rest of the raiding party through, but the machine guns caught us before we could get into the trench. We got cut up pretty bad." Then he added, "I got all turned around on the way back. I didn't know who was in this trench but I'm damn glad it wasn't Germans."

Tom shivered at the thought of crawling across No-Man's-Land, waiting for the machine guns to open up.

Stretcher-bearers appeared and carried off the lieutenant, making hard work of it along the dark, cramped trench. The private splashed after them.

Ferguson was replaced at the parapet by Freddie Martens, the youngster who had been kicked in the balls by Sergeant Planck back at Fort Osborne Barracks.

By now Tom figured there wouldn't be much sleep for him, but he hunkered down in a corner, his Lee Enfield propped beside him, and forced his eyes to close. Luckily, the German gunners were concentrating their fire farther back in the Allied position, and he dozed, in spite of the enemy artillery.

He awoke with a start, his neck sore from the way his head dangled, weighed down by his sopping wet cap. Something was wrong. There was total silence outside the trench. He stood, stiff with cold but fully awake. The members of his section were still huddled in cramped postures, jammed into corners and shallow dugouts in the side of the trench. Martens remained at his post, standing on the platform, but as Tom watched, his head bobbed forward then snapped back up. Christ, Tom thought, he's asleep.

"Martens," he hissed, not wanting to wake everybody up. At that instant a rifle cracked and Martens was flung backward, cap falling across his face. Ungodly screams filled the air, and a grenade bounced into the trench, landing at Tom's feet. He snatched it up and flung it back over the parapet. Instantly, a sharp explosion buffeted his ears and fragments slapped into the sandbags above his head. He looked up to see a dark figure looming over the parapet, rifle in hand, shooting down into the men below.

Tom swung his rifle up and fired without aiming. The German doubled over and tumbled into the trench. Tom's ears were ringing as he ejected a shell and cycled another round. Shaking, he kept his eyes on the lip of the trench. He was aware of Johanson, now on his feet beside him, as shots rang out from inside and outside their lair. The German on the ground was trying to get up, reaching for his fallen rifle. Johanson shot him in the back of the head. There was a spray of blood and the man fell across Martens. This time he didn't move.

Ferguson was up on the platform, firing as fast as he could work the bolt on his rifle. Sergeant Planck appeared from around a corner and flung a ladder up against the side of the trench. "Up you go, lads," he shouted. "Give them what for!" He pushed Tom toward the ladder.

Before he knew what he was doing, Tom was over the top and had thrown himself prone on the ground, his rifle at his shoulder, Planck at his side. In the vague light of a murky dawn he saw grey figures scrambling away. He fired and kept firing, not knowing if he was hitting anything. He emptied his magazine and reloaded, firing again and again until Planck tapped him on the shoulder.

"Hold your fire, Macrae. They're gone. Don't worry, you'll get another crack at them."

A high-velocity shell hit the parapet a hundred yards away, exploding with a loud crack.

"Come get your head down, son." Planck slithered into the trench as a renewed barrage opened up from the German side. The British guns to the rear responded and shells whistled overhead. Tom crawled backward until he could get his feet on the upper rungs of the ladder and clambered down into shelter.

An ugly dawn revealed three Canadian casualties: Martens dead, and two wounded. The dead German remained face down, blond hair crusted with dried blood. He still lay across Martens, their bodies entwined. Two young men on opposite sides, Tom mused, neither of whom had wanted to die. Both of them would have families, loved ones at home. Planck ordered up medical assistance, and the military machine went about its business. Wounded were helped away, bodies carried out.

Cooks came up the line lugging steel pots of food and gallons of hot tea. Tom was ravenous and wolfed a bowl of porridge and half a loaf of bread, washed down by the tea. He clutched his hands around his tin cup and let the warmth from the hot, sweet liquid spread into his body. Planck conjured up a flask of rum, and gave each man a shot in his tea.

Poor Martens. No, too late for him. Poor Martens's family. And because Martens had dozed off, it was damn near poor a whole lot of other people, too. They could all have been killed like rats trapped in a barrel.

One skirmish, survived. Thank God for Planck, who had been under fire many times. Tom had never liked the man, but now he saw him in a different light. Maybe the Canadians did have a few things to learn. As he finished his tea a light drizzle added to their misery. Tom draped his poncho over his head and shoulders and sat on an ammunition box.

In 1914 everybody at home had feared that the war would be over before Christmas, and the Canadians wouldn't get a chance to fight. God, thought Tom. One night so far. One night at the front, with two wounded and one dead, that he knew about. Three men gone. Now, in the spring of 1915, Tom no longer worried about the war ending too soon; he worried about it going on too long. He dozed, his elbows on his knees and his tin cup dangling in one hand. The cup dropped from his fingers. He twitched but let it lie, as rain pattered on the mud.

◆ ◆ ◆

Lieutenant Tilley led the way out, followed by the twenty-three surviving men of the 1st Troop. They were due for two weeks of relief and training, the pressure of battle off for the time being. Tom hitched his pack higher, and glanced back at the men who followed. His section was last in line, and Sergeant Planck was pushing them along from the rear. They were dirty and they stank, just like the infantry they had replaced two weeks before, their gear and clothing soaked through and caked with mud. Losses had mounted—four killed and eight out of action with wounds. But the noncoms had kept morale high during these first weeks of life in the trenches, and the regiment had given as good as it received.

The plan called for a three-mile march to transport that would take them to their quarters. All Tom could think about was the promise of hot food and dry bedding. Packs and rifles seemed lighter with every step away from the front line, in spite of an ongoing drizzle.

Tom felt rather than heard a high-pitched whine. "Down," yelled Planck from behind. At that instant there was a tremendous explosion and something banged off Tom's head. Clumps of earth pelted him as he crashed down. He lay as small as he could on the ground, a ringing in his ears the only sound in the otherwise sudden, aching stillness. He raised his head and saw the men behind him all face-down, partly covered with earth.

Ferguson looked up, his mouth moving, but Tom heard nothing. He felt as if he were buried under a layer of blankets, his movements slow and difficult. He got up on his elbows, then his knees. Now he could hear men's voices, muffled but real.

Ferguson came closer. "Are ye hit?"

"No—don't think so. You okay?"

Fergie nodded.

Tom retrieved his cap from where it lay, feet away. He clapped it back on, and turned to look for Planck, who lay on his back beside a raw shell hole, wisps of smoke rising from the ground around him. Tom stumbled over to the sergeant, his feet slipping and catching in the mushy clods of dirt. Planck's cap was missing and his uniform was black and charred. He was conscious, and his eyes fastened on Tom. He struggled to raise his head, enough to look down to where his left flank and hip should be. They were gone, and a great mass of blood and guts flowed from his side.

The sergeant's eyes rolled back in his head, then refocussed. He looked up at the sky, as if there were something there to see. "I'm going, boys," he said, as his eyes glazed over. He never moved again.

Tom collected the sergeant's cap. Planck, you son of a bitch, how could this happen to you? You, as tough as they come, a survivor of the Boer War, for God's sake. We couldn't stand you back in Winnipeg, but you brought us through. Who will watch over us now?

Johanson and Ferguson marked the spot by jamming the shattered limb from a nearby tree into the muck, and Tom wedged Planck's cap into a split in the branch. Lieutenant Tilley crossed himself, and the troop marched on. They'd send a party back for the body.

Tom held back as the rest of his troop slogged past him. Their route was through a blasted landscape recently torn up by enemy artillery. Two of the youngest members of the troop trailed behind. They were in bad shape, having suffered more than most with the short rations and lack of sleep during the nightly bombardments. Sergeant Quartermain had taken Planck's place and urged them on like a collie herding sheep. Quartermain was carrying one man's rifle for him, and

Tom took Liam Fogarty's. In spite of that Fogarty bogged down in the mud; Tom shouldered his pack and helped him along. Anything to avoid thinking about Planck. This war could get any of them, at any time. There was no way out.

◆ ◆ ◆

"I need a rest," Ellen gasped, and Harry led her toward their table. An evening of square dancing and Scottish reels was pleasantly tiring. Ellen's normal physical exertions involved walking to work at the hospital in good weather and climbing up and down stairs when necessary, so she was relieved to sit and fan herself with the printed dance program.

Three times over the past few weeks she had gone out with Harry and his friends, and this was the most active evening of all. Harry sat close beside her. She leaned back in her chair while she caught her breath. Swirling dancers swooped by, the men in everything from dress trousers and shirts to kilts and jackets. The women wore long, colourful, loose dresses and skirts, with practical, low-heeled shoes.

"Back in a minute. I'll get you something to drink." Harry picked up their glasses and made his way around the dancers toward the bar.

Ellen watched him go, a lithe figure, assured and confident as he greeted acquaintances. He had been in Winnipeg only a few months but already was an accepted part of the social set. Come to think of it, a part of *her* social set.

The war dragged on, and Tom's letters were still coming, as regular as the weeks that rolled by. They were unfailingly cheerful, in a superficial way. He hoped to go on leave to Paris but would not be allowed to cross the Atlantic. She understood that the men's correspondence was censored by the officers, but couldn't he say something to help keep the home fires burning? Yes, he loved her, she knew that, or least so she told herself. Time was intruding, though, on her precious memories of Tom, of their trip in the cutter with Belle, of the heat of their bodies under the buffalo robe.

She wrote back, at least twice a week, but she found she had less and less to tell him. The work at the hospital was depressing. She certainly couldn't tell him any details; it would be too mournful. He had enough on his mind dodging bullets and God knew what. She couldn't write about her social life: no need to upset him. Not that they meant anything, these outings with Harry.

Harry returned with freshened drinks, and they were soon joined at their table by the Bergers and Hugh and Sandra Jenkins. Hugh worked with Harry at the Hudson's Bay store. John Berger was in the grain business.

Ellen enjoyed the company of the other young women, who were only two or three years older than she was. She laughed at Sandra's story about her children's latest escapades, although what was funny about changing diapers and sweeping up food spilled on the floor she didn't know. I think I'd better slow down with the punch, she cautioned herself.

"Well, I've just about danced myself out," said Harry, looking from John to Hugh.

"I think the time has come," John responded. "Come on, ladies. Let's collect our coats."

"John Berger," said his wife, Cecile. "It's far too early to go home. What are you up to?"

"You'll just have to wait and see," and Harry took Ellen by the hand toward the cloakroom, where they recovered their coats. John Berger directed them to a waiting taxi, and they all squeezed in.

The vehicle moved south along Sherbrook to Cornish Avenue, then turned down Assiniboine to pass between immaculate homes to the very end of the street. Harry steadied Ellen as she alighted from the taxi and it glided away.

"This way, everybody." Berger spoke quietly in deference to the sleeping neighbourhood. He and his wife walked toward the Assiniboine River, where the water lapped at a float tied to the bank. The men gallantly aided the women down the ramp to a motor launch, its engine purring. A man stepped off the boat onto the float and saluted Berger.

"Over to you, captain," he said cheerfully.

Berger got in behind the wheel, Cecile beside him. Hugh helped Sandra and Ellen on board while Harry loosened the ropes that secured the boat to the float.

"Let go the lines, mate," ordered Berger.

"Aye, aye, sir." Harry threw the ropes aboard and jumped after them.

The little vessel chugged downstream toward the Red River, the low banks sliding by in the moonlight. Harry produced chilled wine from a locker and poured generous glasses for each of them.

"To further adventures," John said, turning in his seat. They clinked glasses all round.

Ellen and Harry sat side by side, watching the silent ripples on the dark river. Occasional lights in houses along the bank winked from behind a screen of willows and elms. Ellen wasn't really listening to the casual conversation around her as she gazed out at the water. Harry draped his arm over the back of the seat, his hand on her shoulder. She turned and glanced up at his face, hidden in the shadow cast by the boat's canvas canopy. He pulled her toward him and kissed her full on the lips.

Ellen's heart raced as she broke off the kiss. What was she to do now? She had promised herself to Tom, but Tom wasn't here, and Harry was very desirable.

♦ ♦ ♦

It had not been a dream, then. Tom had woken to the trumpet, clear and sharp in the chilly air. He stumbled from his tent, snapped his suspenders up over his shirt, and was greeted by a blue sky, scudding white clouds, and the neighing of horses looking for their morning feed. The rain had stopped, the regiment was out of the trenches, and they had their horses. Life was good.

Tom, up on Ranger, his new ride, went off on a morning exercise with the other members of his section under the relaxed leadership of Lance-Corporal Hicks. The eight horses and riders meandered down the road toward the nearest French village, a couple of miles away. After a fifteen-minute warm-up they broke into a trot.

It was March 1916, and change was in the air. Not only had the brigade finally become mounted, they now wore British army helmets for the first time, replacing their cloth caps. Artillery shells exploding overhead had caused a high percentage of wounds among the Allies, even more than bullets. The helmets took some getting used to, but Tom felt safer with the extra protection.

Their formation was now known as the Canadian Cavalry Brigade, made up of three Canadian regiments: the Strathconas, the Dragoons, and the Fort Garry Horse, which had replaced the 2nd King Edward's Horse. They were more "Canadian" than ever, but ironically, the brigade was now part of the British army command structure, serving separately from the rest of the Canadian Expeditionary Force.

They were well back from the immediate area of the front, and Tom, as always, was astounded at the peaceful countryside that showed no sign of the carnage a few short miles away. Rolling hills with scattered woods and fields, golden brown with last year's stubble or lying fallow, stretched one after another to the distant horizons. Hedges with new, bright green foliage snaked along shallow waterways. Villages were tucked into folds in the landscape, seeming none the worse for wear considering the total devastation just over the horizon. He was amazed to see no fences—it was countryside suited to horsemen, or an invading army. There were no natural obstacles; they could have galloped for miles without hindrance but for occasional streams and gullies. Just like the prairies, Tom thought.

The blue sky and clear air, combined with the thrill and exercise of a morning ride, lifted the men's spirits. Tossed aside were the memories of the brutal times in the trenches. They were young and healthy, and they were alive. They had survived the hell and uncertainty of two-week rotations in the front lines for most of a year.

"Beat you to the bridge," shouted Bruce Johanson, and kicked his horse into a gallop.

Hicks didn't hesitate a moment. "Like hell," he said, and spurred after him.

Tom and the others gave chase. The mass of men and horses thundered the half mile to a small bridge, clattered across, then slowed their mounts to a walk on the far side to cool them off.

Tom rode beside René Carbonnier, the wiry, half-breed veteran and career soldier who had boxed him to a draw on the *Cape Wrath*. Tom had heard that René had twice made it to the dizzy height of corporal, but brushes with authority and regulations, usually related to excessive consumption of alcohol, had propelled him back to the ranks as a private.

"What do you think, René? Are we going to hang on to our horses?" asked Tom, as the men followed a circular route back to their camp.

"You never know what the damn army's going to do next." René thought a while. "Those trenches are no place for a cavalryman. Let the infantry and the artillery blast a hole in the lines, then we'll gallop through and put the sword to the bastards."

It wasn't the first time Tom had heard that sentiment. "If our last months are anything to go by, blasting a hole in the lines is going to be the tough part."

"I figure we'll get our chance. Sooner or later we'll have a crack at them in the open, then watch out. The cavalry has always been special. We do the cleanup."

"Those poor guys in the infantry look pretty beaten up."

"Yeah—and they were trained for the trenches. We weren't. Doesn't matter. The cavalry is the cream on the top of the milk jar. We can fight in the trenches if we have to, or we can fight on our horses."

Since he found himself in the army anyway, Tom had happily accepted the fact that he was on horseback, at least part of the time, not constantly marching and slogging around in the mud. He was impressed by his fellow Strathconas; they were tough, elite horsemen—professionals.

From the commanding officer to the lowest-ranking shoveller of horse manure, they saw themselves as heirs of a glorious tradition of mounted warriors. The exploits of the regiment in the Boer War and the élan of their brigade's leader, the aristocratic Brigadier-General Jack Seely, only added to the mystique.

Some of the villages they encountered were in valleys along rambling streams; some were on hilltops or ridges, where they commanded views all around. Tom was reminded of fairy-tale picture books that he had read as a child. The villages typically were made up of houses and shops built right to the edge of the streets. The buildings abutted one another, presenting a solid front to passersby. Many streets were cobbled; others simply earth and stone packed by centuries of use.

Few inhabitants were to be seen when the mounted men passed through the villages. Occasional housewives or shopkeepers would appear in a doorway, shielding their eyes from the sun, watching the riders, as if they had seen it all before.

Back in England, an officer had given the men a lecture. He explained that in 1914, most Frenchmen had been only too happy to be at war with Germany once more, but the stalemate on the front and heavy losses had cooled their ardour considerably. The French wanted to reverse the results of the War of 1870, when Germany had wrested Alsace-Lorraine from France. And that was just the most recent war. For centuries, invaders had swept across the low hills of Picardy, plundering and killing, only to be beaten back until the next time. Like their ancestors before them, these villagers and farmers waited stoically for the outcome of the present conflict so their lives could be restored to normal.

◆　◆　◆

Sometimes Tom didn't know which was worse—living in a trench with half the regiment for two weeks or slogging it out in reserve, looking after the horses for the whole regiment. After a week away from the trenches, spending eighteen hours a day training, exercising, feeding, watering, and otherwise caring for horses, the front lines could look pretty good. At least in those spells when nothing was going on.

Life in a cavalry regiment, like any other part of the army, often meant waiting for something to happen. As the order said so many times, "Stand to your horses," and the men, fully kitted and spurred, would stand by their saddled mounts, ready for action. For most of the war so far, the cavalry had waited in vain for the infantry and artillery to crack open a fissure in the German lines so they could charge through. Now, in the fall of 1916, the inactivity, combined with the constant, routine attention to their horses, was too much for many of them. Some of Tom's friends requested duty elsewhere.

Just a week before, George Windell brought news that Eddie Hicks— recently promoted to sergeant—had been reassigned to a Highland infantry regiment in the 1st Division.

"Guess Hicks never did get over having to bite that horse's ear on the way over," Bruce Johanson laughed. Tom wondered if Clark, the infantry soldier he had met his first night in the trenches, was still alive.

Tom was confident in the saddle and comfortable with the regiment. His first loyalty was to his section, the small group of men with whom he fought, trained, bivouacked, and drank. They were his new family, his closest friends. If a sergeant was wounded or departed for promotion or training, a corporal could take over and perhaps be promoted into his new role. Tom had now been in the same section for two years and had been promoted, as gaps in leadership opened up, from private to lance-corporal.

♦ ♦ ♦

Tom's section was in a forward trench when Lieutenant Flowerdew located them. Flowerdew, who had risen rapidly in rank and been granted a commission, was now the lieutenant in command of C Squadron. He took Tom aside. "The Brits in the listening post out front are due for relief. Draw enough ammunition from stores for an extended stay, plus extra rations and a radio. You and your men will take over from them tonight."

Tom was well aware of the listening post. It had once been a German dugout, a deep, elaborate underground shelter in a former trench, both of which were now abandoned and all but obliterated by shellfire. A communication trench—just a ditch, really—so shallow that it would allow German snipers on their high ground to fire on any occupants during daylight, had been dug to the post by the Straths under cover of darkness the previous night.

Tom duly drew the stores and equipment, then after midnight he and his men crawled forward on their bellies from their own front lines via the communication trench and slid into the sandbagged post. Happy to withdraw for their two weeks in reserve, the Brits did a turnover and headed back the way the Canadians had arrived. Tom's section was on its own, eight men two hundred yards in front of the rest of the Canadian troops. Eight hundred yards away across No-Man's-Land were the Germans.

The dugout, originally twenty feet deep, now measured only ten. It had been filled in partly by earth flung up by exploding shells, partly by heavy rains that had pelted down over the previous weeks. Firing steps, platforms set into the side walls, were five feet from the top. There Tom crouched and peered into the shadows, senses stretched like banjo strings. Below, in the total darkness, were the other seven men of his section. Private Walter Reynolds, a newly arrived replacement, manned a telephone connected to regimental headquarters.

Tom climbed as quietly as he could down to the floor. He still wasn't used to the steel helmet that was now standard issue, and he banged it against a wooden post set in the wall. "Simpson," he whispered.

Private Reg Simpson was squatting right at Tom's feet. "Here, Lance."

Tom touched Simpson on the shoulder and bent close. "Up you go, Simps. Keep your head down and your eyes open. We're expecting a German patrol. If they see you first, we're all dead."

Tom laced the fingers of both hands together to give Simpson a leg up, and the nineteen-year-old scrambled up the dirt wall. He was new to the regiment, having been assigned to Tom's section only three days before. He had impressed Tom with his keenness and even more, his intelligence. They had all been briefed on the situation, but Tom figured it didn't hurt to remind Simpson this was not an exercise. It was real.

◆ ◆ ◆

A boot scraped the side of Tom's helmet, and he looked up from his perch on a splintered table they had found in the dugout. Against the barely lighter sky he saw Simpson beckon him. Tom climbed up, rifle in hand.

"Heard something," Simpson whispered.

Tom listened and heard only distant shelling. A light breeze from the direction of the German lines carried the faint scents of torn earth and cordite. A half moon was covered by a gauzy layer of cloud, leaving the slightly rising land in front of them dappled with impenetrable shadows.

He stayed with Simpson for ten minutes, then sent him down for a break, and Bruce Johanson climbed up beside Tom. "Simpson thought he heard something a few minutes ago. Make bloody sure you stay awake."

"Okay, Tom. Heck—new guy, Simpson. Probably hearing things."

Tom wasn't so sure. Something didn't feel right.

Flowerdew had briefed Tom's section personally and told them the Brits they relieved had conducted a trench raid against the Germans. If the Hun was true to form, he'd counter with an aggressive patrol of his own.

Johanson leaned close. "Hope the bastards do come. I want to get one for Lindman." Lance-Corporal Lindman, a popular noncom, had been shot through the neck two weeks before. He had moaned without letup for three hours before they could get him out of their trench; it had taken him another two days to die.

The section was heavily armed with rifles, bayonets, and Mills bombs, the British hand grenades. In addition Tom had a Webley .455 revolver.

If they detected the enemy, it was their job to phone headquarters and keep their heads down. A large enemy patrol could wipe them out.

Johanson covered the left front, while Tom scanned the front and to the right.

◆ ◆ ◆

Tom felt Johanson stiffen. He nudged Tom in the ribs and pointed right. Tom held his breath and turned that way. Maybe Bruce *had* heard something; he knew his own hearing wasn't as good as it had been before he encountered the brutal, explosive sounds of war. He slowly swung his head left to right and back, thinking his peripheral vision might pick up something otherwise missed. He looked back to his right, and thinking he saw a shadow move, he unfastened the flap on his holster, drawing the Webley.

A scraping noise made Johanson bring his rifle to his shoulder. Tom swung the Webley, cocked it. A figure loomed over him, and he started to squeeze when, against the grey sky, he saw the outline of a British helmet.

"Who goes there?" he hissed, and reached up to grab at the front of the figure's jacket. He pulled, rammed the muzzle of the Webley at where the face would be and connected with flesh and bone.

"I'm Canadian, damn it."

Tom thought he recognized the voice of Lieutenant Tilley, one of the regiment's junior officers. "Who goes there, goddamnit?"

"Rocky Mountain House," came the whispered and, mercifully, correct response.

Tom lowered his revolver, while, beside him, Johanson kept his rifle at the ready. Tom could now make out that it was, indeed, Lieutenant Tilley. He uncocked the Webley, hand shaking and heart pounding. He and the lieutenant slid down into the dugout. The men all had weapons in their hands.

"I came out to see how you were coping," said the lieutenant. "Quite efficiently, I see." He pulled out a handkerchief to wipe away the blood that trickled down his forehead, black in the low light.

"We weren't expecting you, sir."

"No, I dare say you weren't. The major felt we shouldn't ring you on the phone—too noisy. Nothing going on, I take it?"

"No, sir. But you came from the wrong direction, off to the side."

"Got lost. Not much of a trench to get here in, is there? But I'm going to leave you to it. And Macrae—glad you gave me the benefit of the doubt."

The lieutenant crept off toward the Canadian lines. Tom was shaken. If he hadn't recognized the voice, he might well have shot the man. Two fresh men went up to the platform, and Johanson came down. Tom was restless, but he stayed below for a few minutes to let his nerves settle down before climbing back up with the sentries.

♦ ♦ ♦

It was two hours before dawn, the darkest part of the night, and all was quiet. Even the distant artillery had packed it in. The moon was playing peek-a-boo behind scattered clouds brought in by a chilly breeze, and Ferguson and Simpson had just taken over as lookouts. Tom had them change around every thirty minutes, to reduce the fatigue and boredom of staring at the dark landscape. There was no room to pace in the crowded dugout, but he stood and stretched. He checked for the hundredth time that his Webley was not cocked but ready, his rifle at hand. Just as he crouched to flex his knees, he heard a distinct metallic clank.

Tom looked up and saw Ferguson, his right arm extended horizontally and palm down, clear against the murky sky. He already had his rifle in front of him and lowered his head to press his cheek against the stock as if aiming. As Ferguson's right hand went to the pistol grip and trigger, Tom put one foot on the rickety table, now propped against a side wall, and started up.

There was a flash and a bang as Ferguson fired. Tom sprang to the firing step, Webley in hand.

"To the east," Ferguson yelled, as he worked the bolt on his rifle. He fired again.

Tom jammed the Webley into his holster, jerked a Very flare pistol out of a bag at his waist, cocked it, and fired. In the flash of brilliant light he saw the ground swarming with enemy soldiers who leapt to their feet and ran, screaming, toward the Canadian line. Only forty feet away, some of them looked in his direction and swerved toward the dugout. The fading light of the flare flickered off bayonets.

"Everybody up," Tom shouted, and threw himself forward, prone on the ground outside the dugout, to make room for the men hurrying up from below.

They fired as fast as they could work their bolts, pointing their rifles at the closing Germans with no time to aim. Tom pushed himself up to one knee, threw down the flare pistol, and grabbed his Webley. A screaming figure charged toward him, only feet away, and fell as one of the men climbing from the dugout shot him. The German got up again, and charged at Tom, who shot him at pointblank range. As the man collapsed, his bayonet pierced Tom's left shoulder. He sagged, gagging with pain, but hung on to his revolver.

Thirty feet out another German dropped to one knee and aimed. Tom, shoulder searing, swung the Webley with both hands and fired, but saw no reaction. The man's rifle flashed, and the bullet zipped past Tom's head. The German dropped to the ground and frantically worked the bolt on his rifle. Tom fired at him and missed, fired again and the soldier collapsed, face down in the dirt.

Somewhere behind the Canadian lines a howitzer banged, and a moment later a starshell burst over the scene, its brilliant light revealing a long line of Germans, momentarily frozen by the light, in a shallow depression east of the dugout. The phosphorous flare floated slowly downward. A fusillade of rifle and machine gun fire roared from the length of the Canadian trench, and the Germans rushed forward into it, bypassing the men at the listening post.

A second starshell burst into life before the first one hit the ground, and the attackers staggered to a halt just short of the trenches. The leading men went down, cut to pieces by a hail of bullets. The second wave threw grenades and were shot down in their turn. Some turned and ran, and a few might have tried to surrender, but the Canadian blood was up, and the slaughter continued until the light faded.

Tom saw a straggler or two crawling back toward the German lines, weapons abandoned, despairing. "Cease firing," he ordered. His voice sounded as though it came from far away. "Simpson, Johanson, take lookout. Everybody else below."

The men clambered down and fell silent, gathering around a dark form on the floor of the dugout. It was Reynolds. He groaned, still alive. Two of the men checked him quickly, finding blood on the front of his tunic. Ferguson cut away the uniform and located a bullet hole in the junction of his neck and shoulder. Tom helped Ferguson with first aid, applying iodine and dressings.

Reynolds was conscious. "Hurts, Lance. Can't move my arm."

"Doesn't look bad, Reynolds. We've stopped the bleeding. Just have to get you back and the docs will take care of you, boy. Get on the blower," Tom said to Ferguson. "We don't have to worry about being quiet now. Tell them we need stretcher-bearers."

While Ferguson cranked the phone Tom took stock. The light had improved with the approaching dawn. "Anybody else hit?"

Nobody spoke up. Tom counted heads, needing to know if anybody was lying up top, unable to move. All accounted for. "Okay," he said. "Somebody look at this for me." He eased off his jacket and pulled his sweater and shirt back from his neck to expose the wound from the German bayonet.

"Not deep. Looks clean," said Simpson, and sloshed iodine on the gash, making Tom wince.

Ferguson spoke up. "Got the lieutenant on the line. He wants you. Says he can't get body snatchers out here until dark."

Simpson pressed a dressing to Tom's neck as he bent his head to the earpiece and took the microphone from Ferguson. The line crackled. Tom thought he heard someone talking but wasn't sure. "Say again," he yelled into the box, and waved for silence in the dugout.

The static eased, and the voice of Lieutenant Flowerdew came through. "Well done, Lance-Corporal. The brigade commander says . well done."

"Thank you, sir. I'll pass that on."

"You'll be relieved by Section Two after sunset tonight. They'll bring a stretcher for your casualty so you can bring him in."

"I'd like to get him in now, sir."

"No can do, Lance-Corporal. Not in daylight. He'll just have to wait."

Tom replaced the receiver on the wooden phone box. He straightened and looked around the cramped quarters at his men. "General Seely says well done, and I second that. Good work, boys."

"Bastards will be licking their wounds after that little effort," said Ferguson in his soft burr. The others nodded agreement.

Tom knelt by the recumbent form of Private Reynolds and put a hand on his good shoulder. "Hold on there, trooper. We'll get you out of here as soon as the sun goes down."

Reynolds nodded. "Pain is worse, Lance." His teeth were chattering.

Tom turned to Ferguson. "Break out the morphine. Use as much as he needs." While Ferguson looked after Reynolds, Tom gathered bedrolls and greatcoats to bundle up the wounded man.

The only sign of activity during the day was the mutter of far-away artillery. The men brewed tea and heated bully beef in tin mess kits. Tom kept two men on watch at all times but did not anticipate problems before nightfall and their scheduled relief. He fingered his bandaged neck. Not enough to get me out of here, he mused. Not like poor Reynolds.

By blind chance, the German attackers had all been to the east of the dugout, just abreast of it, when the careless sound that Ferguson heard gave them away. It had been like shooting fish in a barrel for the alerted Strathconas in the main trenches, Tom's listening post having done its job. In the aftermath, Tom shuddered at the thought of what might have happened had the enemy attackers been a hundred yards farther west, centred on the dugout.

Tom took his regular turn at lookout, up on the firing step. German bodies were scattered where they had fallen. They looked small, shrunken, as though they had never lived. Except for the man who had bayoneted Tom. His body was splayed with arms outstretched, its opaque, lifeless eyes only two yards from the lip of the dugout.

Bodies were plentiful in the country of the trenches, a country that snaked across Belgium and northern France, only hundreds of yards wide. In the eighteen months the Canadians had spent in and out of that blasted territory Tom had seen plenty of bodies: lifelike bodies; shriveled and putrified bodies; cold, clammy bodies. They were dragged back for burial when they were your comrades and it was possible to do so. But hundreds—no, thousands—were out there: torn and ripped, half or fully buried, apt to be stepped on or crawled over in the dark, slowly becoming part of the blood-soaked earth.

Tom could see pale eyelashes and stubble on this particular body, that of a very young man, probably under twenty. He was reminded of his own younger brothers. Somebody, somewhere, would hear of this boy's death and would grieve.

It didn't seem right, leaving the body exposed to its enemies, even in death. Tom looked carefully around and warned Johanson, who was beside him. He slipped out of the dugout and, squirming flat to the ground, dragged the German body twenty feet farther away, toward the German line. He pressed its eyelids shut and crawled back to where his section waited and watched for the enemy.

RAIDING PARTY

◆ ◆ ◆

In the fall of 1917 the regiment moved to their winter quarters. They had settled into a relatively pleasant existence, considering they were living in tents in miserable weather far from home. For the time being, at least, they were out of the firing line and back in reserve. The brigade still hoped in its collective heart that a hole would be blasted in the German lines and the cavalry would come into its own, but it looked unlikely, given the terrible losses and total stalemate that were the legacy of the Battle of the Somme. Twinned, parallel lines of nearly static trenches still zigzagged from the Swiss border to the English Channel.

Tom had managed a shave and wash in a rudimentary bathhouse set up in an abandoned factory and was on his way back to his tent when he saw Bruce Johanson approaching.

"Hey there, Corporal Tom," Bruce said with a grin. "Are you still associating with the hoi polloi? Or is it just other noncoms you hang around with now?"

Tom knew his recent promotion had a lot to do with casualties and promotions in the ranks above. The troops were being thinned out. Only a few of his original troop of reinforcements were still in one piece and in the regiment.

Bruce didn't expect an answer and didn't wait for one. "I've got good news, which I'll even share with a corporal. Our leave has come through. Paris, here we come!" He did a little jig, incongruous in muddy boots and puttees.

Tom clutched his friend and the two of them sashayed in a circle, yelling and laughing. They stopped to catch their breath.

"How soon? When do we go?"

"This coming Saturday. What I'm thinking is, there are going to be lots of those little French mademoiselles skipping around, with nary a French soldier to be found. We probably won't even have to parley-voo the French to have one on each arm."

Ferguson appeared and hurried along the line of tents to where Tom and Bruce stood, grinning. He was waving a letter. "I see you've both heard the news. Anyway, here's some mail. Nothing for you, my boy," he said, clapping Bruce on the back, "but one for His Majesty's newest corporal," and he bowed, sweeping his hand with the letter in it to Tom. "Let's you and me, Bruce, go and see if the cooks have dinner ready yet in the dining lounge and leave lover boy to his mail."

Tom watched the two of them wander off, then sat on the remains of an abandoned garden wall. Ellen's familiar handwriting on the envelope made his heart leap as he ripped open the envelope.

Dear Tom,

I haven't heard from you for two weeks, but there are always delays. Perhaps I'll get another bundle all at once, just like last time. This will be the shortest letter yet. I don't know where to start.

Tom, I have met someone else. It's not your fault, it's mine. I don't know what to do. You have been gone so long. Why couldn't the army have sent you home like they have some others? What if something happens to you? I don't know what to do. I am going to mail this, no matter what.

I'm sorry, Tom, but you have been away so long. I feel I've waited half my life. Whatever happens, I will always care.

Ellen

Tom doubled over in agony, feeling as if he had been kicked by a mule. The pain was worse than when Alton had caught him with that low blow, way back on the trip to England. He sat frozen, the letter crumpled in his hand. He didn't believe this was happening to him. To other men, maybe. Their wives or sweethearts were unfaithful or simply fell out of love due to the passage of time and the ongoing temptations of life at home. But not Ellen; not him.

How could she do this to him? A sudden rage flared. He ripped the letter, shredded it again and again until it was like confetti. Confetti, he thought in a detached portion of his mind: that's a good one. He squeezed the scraps of paper in one fist, and threw them into the air. The wind swallowed the fragments, whipping them away as if they were dandelion seeds on a blustery day.

In a daze, he stumbled to his tent and sat on his cot, his elbows on his knees and his head in his hands. He rubbed his face, sitting still as someone walked by outside the tent, then got to his feet, threw on his tunic, and went out.

Blind to where he was going, he walked. At times he staggered like a drunk, at other times he charged up grassy brown hills and down the other side, oblivious to the dark groves of beeches and shrub-choked gullies that surrounded him. Why wouldn't the earth open up and swallow him? Anger fading, he wallowed in self-pity, even while another part of his mind commented that it was a good thing the regiment wasn't on the front line or he'd have been felled by a sniper by now. He found himself on a dirt road and walked for miles into the countryside.

He eventually made his way back to camp, the searing pain easing. So she thinks she's found someone better, does she? He shook his head. He would not accept that; he could not. When he got home he'd sort this out in short order, by God. In the meantime—what? What could he do? He suddenly regretted tearing up Ellen's letter. What would he hold on to now? Did it matter whether he lived or died?

He shook off the thought and walked to the horse lines. Stopping by Ranger, he picked up a curry comb. Ranger nickered and swished his tail, twitching his skin in anticipation. Tom brushed his horse from nose to tail, the rhythm soothing his mind, while he concentrated on nothing but the task at hand. When he finished, he went in search of Bruce and Fergie. Paris it would be.

◆　◆　◆

The main rail line from Amiens south to Paris ran, straight as an arrow, down the spine of France. Four of the dozen Canadians in the passenger compartment played poker, hoping to increase the cash saved up out of their pay before they hit the fabled city. Tom and the others watched the countryside glide by, interrupted from time to time when they were shunted to a siding to allow northbound trains to pass. Tom looked out at a series of railcars loaded with glum-looking French Zouaves, colonial troops, headed toward the charnel house of the front.

The mood of his comrades presented a fine contrast. The card players shouted in triumph or cursed, depending on the throw of the cards; Tom, Gordon, and Bruce sporadically joined the game. The three of them had a bottle of brandy between them, with cheap glasses bought in the station. Before they were thirty minutes out of Amiens most of the liquor was gone.

The men were not shy about their requirements: food, liquor, and female company topped their list of priorities. Of Tom's section, one was away on a course to learn the latest in radio communications, one was confined to camp for his misdeeds, and one was hospitalized. The latter, like many of his Canadian comrades, had been a little too uninhibited in his youthful and energetic pursuit of female company, having chosen the objects of his affection while his mind was clouded by strong drink. To compound his error, he had not heeded the sergeant-major's exhortation to always use a condom, and the resulting syphilis ensured he would not be available for the firing lines either in Paris or on the front for some time.

They arrived at the Gare du Nord late in the day. Tom had the address of a hotel that catered to servicemen on leave, so they commandeered taxis and, after protracted negotiations with the drivers, piled in and were taken to the Normandie, a four-storey building a few blocks from the Paris Opera.

Tom threw his bag on the bed and started a bath running. It had been months since he had been afforded such a luxury, and after stripping to his underwear he laid out his shaving gear and breathed deeply of the warm, steamy air. Shaving with hot water and a mirror that was more than a piece of tin balanced on an upturned ammunition box was an unimagined indulgence. He soaked for an hour in the tub, adding hot water from time to time, resolutely thinking about everything except the war. Afterward, he dressed in his only clean uniform and went down to the lobby.

Gordon was there, smoking a French cigarette, and the two of them went in search of food. At the end of the block was a small restaurant named for its proprietor, Jacques, who, they assumed, was the Frenchman who waited on them; Mrs. Jacques was no doubt the aproned lady in the kitchen. There was no menu as such, just a blackboard with a couple of items scrawled on it. M. Jacques sadly admitted that due to the exigencies of war he could not supply the restaurant's advertised veal or chicken specialties, but, much to Tom's amusement, he did have a highly recommended stewed rabbit. In the meantime, would the gentlemen care for a litre of the house wine?

"*S'il vous plaît*," Gordon responded. "Make it *deux* litres, if you please."

Their friend Jacques was happy to comply and to keep the wine coming. The rabbit stew was indeed delicious: "Much superior to snowshoe hare," said Gordon. Tom was dismayed to find he could eat only a fraction of the food on his plate; his stomach had shrunk from the months of short rations.

The long day in the railcar, the alcohol they had consumed there, and now the rich food combined with an excess of wine took its toll.

"Me for bed," Gordon said. He looked a little dazed.

"I feel like I haven't slept in a month. Let's go."

They paid their bill and returned to the Normandie, where they had to wake the concierge to get in. It wasn't even midnight, their first day of leave, and all Tom wanted to do was sleep. As he and Gordon parted company in the lobby, Tom commented, "I bet when you signed up in Winnipeg you never thought you'd fight your way to Paris, and end up eating a snowshoe rabbit."

"That was no snowshoe rabbit, my boy. That was a French *lapin*, very highly prized in the salons of the rich."

Laughing, Tom climbed the stairs to his room, threw off his clothes, and collapsed into bed.

◆ ◆ ◆

Tom slept until noon, then went for a late breakfast at a sidewalk café. He strolled in a shopping area and bought postcards he planned to mail home later. The day was blustery, with a weak sun breaking through the clouds. He hiked the Champs Élysées as far as the Arc de Triomphe and crossed the broad Seine, a stiff breeze propelling him from the Eiffel Tower up the Left Bank. The grandeur of the city astounded him.

He felt clear headed and calm, and was even mildly amused by the efforts of Gypsies to sell him a "guaranteed gold ring, monsieur," which they pretended to have just found on the street. Groups of French, British, and colonial soldiers on the streets were reminders that there was a war going on, but they, like him, were on leave and wide eyed at the sights of Paris. There were no young and few middle-aged civilian men to be seen.

Every new vista made him wish Ellen could be there to see it with him. He couldn't resist a return to the hotel in the late afternoon for another bath, then wrote a long letter to her. He refused to accept her decision that it was over between them. He would be back, and he loved her.

When Tom emerged from his room his comrades were nowhere to be seen, so he ate a solitary meal with a half bottle of red wine in the hotel dining room. Growing tired of his own company, he prowled the lobby and was given a note from Ferguson. It had an address, which he handed to a taxi driver.

The Café de Paree catered to Allied servicemen. When Tom opened the door he was assaulted by a roar of sound, and it took him a moment to discern Canadian voices singing—if it could be called that—"Mademoiselle from Armentieres." The atmosphere was thick with blue smoke from pungent French cigarettes and Players pipe tobacco. Shutting the door behind him, he stepped into a long, narrow room. The back section, farthest from the street, was two levels, with half flights of stairs going up and down from the floor he was on. The bar was to his left, running the length of the main floor. A sweating Frenchman in a stained apron was wiping it with a rag.

Tom walked toward the rear and saw Canadian shoulder flashes on a uniformed figure on the lower level. He looked down the stairs and was greeted by a shout from Bruce Johanson.

"Hey, Tommy. Made it at last—come on down here. Got lots of room." He slid sideways on a bench at a table, propelling the girl next to him farther in, then lurched to his feet. "The rest of the boys are here already," he shouted. He pushed Tom onto the bench and squeezed in behind him. "Meet Yvonne. She likes Canadians."

Yvonne was a petite brunette with lots of makeup. Her hair was cut fashionably short, and she wore a white, low-cut blouse and a dark red skirt.

"Ferguson, look who's here," Johanson continued. He waved at a passing waiter. "More wine, *garçon*."

Tom looked around. Lots of Strathconas were there, scattered among tables, sharing them with women who ranged from late teens to middle age. At the very back of the room was a tiny dance floor, with an accordion player jammed into the corner. Two couples bounced off each other and the surrounding tables to the merriment of the onlookers.

The waiter brought him a glass, and Yvonne poured it full.

"*Merci*," he said in his best French accent.

She smiled.

Tom danced with Yvonne, and she held him close. Her breath was hot on his throat; her right hand caressed the back of his neck. The music slowed, and she moved even closer, her body clinging to his.

The accordion player took a break, and Tom went in search of the washroom, a tiny space with a fly-specked mirror. For the first time since he had been on leave, he looked, really looked, at himself. In the harsh overhead light he was shocked to see a thin, haggard face peering back. God, he thought. That's not the same man who was raised on the banks of the Red River, the man who loved and won Ellen.

Well, Tom, he said to himself, you're a free man now, and you're having the time of your life. Good joke. He went in search of his cap and left the café to walk the lonely streets of wartime Paris.

◆ ◆ ◆

Tom had been back with the regiment for a week, and it felt as though he had never been away. It was December 1, 1917, and Lord Strathcona's Horse was in action in No-Man's-Land near a place labelled Chapel Crossing on their British maps. A seventy-seven-millimetre shell exploded on the other side of the cutbank beside the sunken road where Tom, already face down, was making himself as small as possible.

"Goddamn whizz bangs," said Bruce, on his left. The men hated the high-velocity, mobile German 77s. The bang of the gun firing could not be heard until the shell had shrieked past, thus giving almost no warning, unlike the low-velocity howitzers that lobbed huge shells, often from miles away, but with the sound of the gun forewarning any potential target.

Tom and the rest of C Squadron were in reserve. A and B Squadrons were lending assistance to the Royal Canadian Dragoons and other Empire forces in an attack at Chapel Crossing. C Squadron's 1st Troop sergeant had been sent ahead to get further instructions from Colonel Docherty, who was up with the lead squadrons.

The steady racket of rifle, machine gun, and artillery fire from the forward positions attested to a hot action under way. Below the rim of his helmet Tom could see René Carbonnier crouched up against the cutbank on the other side of Johanson. Carbonnier looked up, past Tom, who turned and saw the troop sergeant running toward them.

"Holy shit," the sergeant yelled, and threw himself face down beside Tom. "The old man has been killed."

All the men within earshot crawled closer. It was as if the battle had stopped.

Johanson was the first to speak. "What happened?"

"He was talking to me—he wanted us to bring up the Hotchkiss machine gun and give some covering fire—when he got shot in the head. Sniper. The major has taken over."

Tom felt cold. How could the commanding officer of the regiment, the "old man," be killed? Lieutenant-Colonel Docherty was figured to be indestructible. He had been in the army longer than Tom had lived, had held every rank up to regimental sergeant-major before taking a commission. Although Docherty, in his mid-forties, had only recently assumed his command, he had long been a familiar father figure. Tom knew that every man in the regiment would feel more vulnerable and alone than he had the day before.

The men around Tom looked stunned. Somebody clambered over the backs of his outstretched legs. He turned and saw René Carbonnier who continued crawling until he was face to face with the sergeant.

"Where's the colonel?" Carbonnier asked.

"Right where he was shot. But they were loading him on a stretcher to take him back."

"Where did the shot come from?"

"Not sure, but probably a grove of trees to the right front of us." The troop sergeant raised his voice. "We're still in reserve. Sit tight and keep your heads down." He moved off cautiously from cover to cover, talking to knots of men as he went.

Darkness fell and a half moon rose, the noise of battle easing to sporadic firing. The troop sergeant came back and ordered the men to slip to the rear. They would not see action that day.

A few moments later Tom looked around and realized that only he, Johanson, and Carbonnier were still up against the bank in the sunken road. Johanson and Carbonnier were talking quietly. Tom couldn't make out what they were saying. "What are you two waiting for? Let's get out of here," he said. He turned and started to crawl away from the front.

"Hold it." Bruce grabbed Tom's ankle.

"What's going on?"

"René wants to get into the action."

"Don't be crazy. Our troop has been ordered to the rear."

"They won't be going anywhere for a while."

Tom stared at Bruce. Why the hell would he want to go into harm's way if he didn't have to?

René said, in a flat voice, "I've been in this regiment a long time. It's my family. Someone got the colonel."

The sniper, for God's sake, Tom realized. He's after the sniper. He glanced at Bruce, who ducked his head and shrugged. "Someone's gotta cover his back."

"You're both nuts."

René and Bruce had been watching each other's backs ever since they had both excelled as riders back at Fort Osborne Barracks, but this was too much.

"You want to miss the fun?" Bruce slithered after René who was inching to his right, down the sunken road.

Carbonnier was sometimes a hard man to talk to; if he had made up his mind, there wasn't much Tom could do about it. Giving him a direct order would have no effect. But Bruce was Tom's closest friend so, his heart in his mouth, he went after them.

Tom couldn't tell precisely where the front was, but he could make out a party of dragoons, partially dug in behind a low ridge. From miles away in the direction of the enemy lines came the thunder and growl of howitzers. Shells whistled overhead, some buzzing, some screaming, low and high velocity. The dragoons answered with occasional rifle and machine gun fire.

The moon went behind a cloud, and they took advantage of it to run, doubled over, along a shallow depression that angled in an easterly direction toward the Germans and past the ridge occupied by the dragoons. They hugged their rifles to their chests, making as little noise as possible. After covering several hundred yards they could make out a small wood. Skeletons of beeches were stark against the sky, but lower down was a tangle of branches, undergrowth, and the splintered trunks of shell-shattered trees.

Again they hugged the earth, rifles cradled in forearms, with elbows, knees, and feet pushing them, snakelike, over the churned-up ground. Tom's straining ears detected scrapes and clinks as René led the way to within a hundred yards of the wood. Still sheltered by the dissipating cloud, they came to a halt in a shell hole.

"You reckon the sniper's still there?" asked Tom in a whisper.

"Guess we'll find out," said René. "You boys stay here. I'm going to circle to the right and try to get behind him. If you wave a helmet around he'll fire. Maybe. Then we'll see."

Soundlessly, René was gone into the night. Tom was glad Bruce was still in the shell hole with him. What the hell was he doing here? They were between the lines, and their own troops could fire at them by mistake. Somewhere ahead a German sharpshooter with a hair trigger was waiting and watching, as seconds, minutes, half an hour dragged by.

"Long enough," said Bruce.

It was a whisper, but Tom jumped. He watched, mesmerized, in the breathless way an audience will watch a circus tightrope walker climb onto his partner's shoulders, as Bruce eased his helmet off and raised it six inches over the lip of the shell hole on his rifle barrel.

Nothing happened.

Bruce lowered his helmet and fumbled in his tunic pocket, producing a match and thumbing it with his nail. Tom squeezed his eyes shut to preserve his night vision as the light from the match flared and died. Bruce again put his helmet on the end of his rifle. He looked at Tom and shrugged, then slowly waved the helmet once again. Silence, and Tom breathed more easily.

Suddenly a rifle cracked, and there was an instantaneous, resounding bang as sparks flew from the helmet, which spun to the ground. Bruce dropped his rifle and fell to the bottom of the hole, covering his face.

Tom had a death-grip on his Lee Enfield, his eyes and ears straining. He reached for his friend but kept his eyes in the direction of the trees. Seeing nothing, he crouched down beside Bruce. In the moonlight he could see black liquid oozing between Bruce's fingers.

There was a thrashing sound and a muffled moan from the direction of the wood, followed by the rattle of a distant machine gun. Bullets sprayed the earth at the top of the shell hole, then moved away. Blind fire from the direction of the German front.

Tom listened but heard nothing more. He put his rifle down to help his friend into a sitting position. Pulling a dressing out of his pocket and easing Bruce's hands away from his face, he applied the fabric over a wound above his left eye. Bruce's other eye blinked in the faint light.

"How bad is it? My head is killing me," said Bruce. "What the hell happened, anyway?"

"Shut up," hissed Tom. "Hold this in place."

While Bruce put his hand on the dressing, Tom got out a bandage and wrapped it around his head. Risking a quick visual sweep from the lip of their shelter, he could make out nothing significant. Feeling around, he located Bruce's helmet and rifle. The helmet had taken a round right on the rim, which was bent downward as if it had been pounded with a blacksmith's hammer.

"A chunk of the bullet must have ricocheted and hit you, you bloody fool."

For once Bruce had nothing to say. He lay back with a groan.

Tom didn't know what to do. René might have taken out the sniper—or vice versa. How long should they wait? He would eventually have to lead Bruce back, hoping to get out of No-Man's-Land before daylight. He heard a low whistle from the direction Carbonnier had gone and peered cautiously, rifle at the ready. René crawled into view and slid over the lip into the hole. He looked battered. His tunic was stained with blood, and he was protecting one arm, holding it across his body.

"You wounded? Did you get him?"

"Got slammed with a rifle butt, I think," said the Metis. "Two of the bastards. When the sniper shot at you boys, I jumped on him and slit his throat. But he had a spotter, and he clubbed me on the arm and shoulder before I could get clear of the first guy. He should have shot me. I'd dropped my bayonet but I snatched it back up and got him, too."

No wonder he was drenched in blood. René had killed two men, in near-total darkness, hand to hand. Tom didn't want to think about it. "You okay to travel?" he asked.

"I'm okay. Bruce hit?"

"Ricochet."

"You boys sure attracted their attention. Have to hand it to you."

"Glad to help," Bruce muttered, his hand still pressed against the dressing.

Bruce's helmet wouldn't fit on his head with the bandage there, so Tom slung it on his own haversack. He shouldered Bruce's Lee Enfield, carried his own in one hand, and with the other supported his friend, who was wobbly on his feet. René was able to manage by himself. They crawled and walked, bent low, for what seemed like hours before they reached the sunken road where they had been when they heard about the colonel's death. They rested, then moved again. The sky was lightening when they were challenged as they rejoined their troop.

Bruce was still groggy and complained of a severe headache, so the troop sergeant sent him away to an aid station. René took off his bloody tunic, sweat-stained shirt, and underwear, despite the cold winter air. His left arm was swollen above the elbow, already showing vivid shades of black, blue, and yellow. He had full movement but his face was pinched with pain.

Tom sat in the wet trench, forearms on his raised knees, helmet pushed back. He was so tired he could have slept for a week. The troop sergeant came and glared down at him.

"I don't know what you sons of bitches got up to, but I'm giving you the benefit of the doubt. I reckon the Germans came out of this little escapade worse than you did. But I'm warning you, Macrae. I covered for you this time, but the next time you take your pals on an unauthorized absence, I'll make you wish you had never been born. And you can pass that on. Do I make myself clear?"

"Perfectly clear, Sergeant."

The sergeant stomped away. Tom saw René hunkered down, sitting on an ammunition box, carefully easing his shirt back on. Tom thought he smiled, but maybe it was only a grimace.

◆ ◆ ◆

Three months later, in the spring of 1918, part of the regiment was away with the horses, taking a break from the action, while Tom's squadron did their regular rotation in the trenches. Tom's troop sergeant took him aside and told him to be at regimental headquarters at 1000 hours. Now what, Tom wondered. For days, rumours had swirled that there was to be a major raid on the German trenches.

He'd know soon. The triple chevrons of a sergeant on Tom's arms had only been there for a week. They spoke of the constant loss of non-commissioned officers to promotion, death, and wounds, and to Tom's assumption of an understated leadership style. He wouldn't have any more control over his own life, but he would perhaps be privy to more of what was going on than he had been as a private or corporal.

The troops were nearing the end of another miserable winter, the

Strathconas' third year of fighting. For once it was not raining. Tom made sure his section was accounted for and usefully employed under the watchful eye of Lance-Corporal Gus Dunnett. Dunnett was a methodical, dependable man from a farm outside Regina, and he was putting three men who had recently joined the regiment through their paces with rifle and bayonet drill, while making sure they became familiar with their section of the trenches.

Tom knocked out his pipe, ground the ash with his heel, and headed toward regimental headquarters. He joined a group of junior officers and sergeants as Lieutenant-Colonel Macdonald, who now commanded the regiment, emerged from the headquarters hut.

"We've been ordered to conduct a large-scale raid, along with the Dragoons. Those of you who were with the regiment a year ago will remember our last successful show in the same area."

Tom remembered that night: a night of sheer terror, when the Straths had overpowered a company of Germans. As a private, he had no idea of the big picture, and had considered himself lucky to be assigned to a rear group that covered the withdrawal of the raiders. This time he would be leading his section, but the chevrons on his arm didn't make him feel any less vulnerable. He glanced at the clearing sky, wondering pensively if he'd be back here, looking at the sky, after the raid.

The colonel was still speaking. "The officers have been briefed on the latest intelligence. It is our job to make sure all of you have a clear idea of the objectives and the terrain, and what to do when or if things go wrong. You are to brief your men this afternoon. No one is to leave camp from now until the raid has been completed. Start time is 2200 hours."

Twelve hours from now, Tom thought. So that's why reveille was late this morning: resting up the troops.

"British intelligence has done a mock-up for our purposes. Follow me." The colonel turned and led the way to a second hut, in front of which was a table with maps spread across it. A tall captain in a British uniform stood behind the display.

Tom glanced at the captain. It was Cedric Inkmann.

"Right, men." Inkmann paused and looked at the assembled officers and noncoms. Tom saw no flicker of recognition, but the man's eyes were red-rimmed, his face thinner than Tom remembered it.

Inkmann pointed at a map with his swagger stick. "Here, we have our trenches. And here, the German front line. Distance between is almost two thousand yards. Your task will be to go in under quiet conditions, get as close as possible, then isolate and neutralize this area," outlining a length of German front line and reserve trenches, "and capture as many of the enemy as you can. We especially want officers. Now, come this way, and we'll look at the mock-up." He directed the men over to a thirty-yard-square area of soil and sand that had been raked and formed to recreate in miniature the Canadian and German trenches with No-Man's-Land in between.

Inkmann described the probable formation of the enemy troops they would encounter, the location of machine guns, listening posts, and artillery, and the topographical features. The attackers were to overrun the German fighting trench, the first one they'd encounter, then swarm past it to take prisoners in the reserve trench behind it. It all sounded very impressive to Tom. When Inkmann finished, Tom's squadron leader, Lieutenant Gordon Flowerdew, asked a couple of questions about challenges and passwords.

The colonel spoke again. "Artillery. When the signal goes up, our artillery will set up a protective curtain of fire to cut off German reinforcements. The curtain will be only one hundred yards beyond the first German reserve trench. We should have an overpowering number of troops against the Germans, who have been isolated by the artillery, but we have to rely on stealth to get close to their lines before the signal flare goes up. The barrage will last ten minutes, then it will retreat toward us so as to do as much damage to the Boche front-line trenches as possible, as well as protect your rear as you make your way back." He added dryly, "You won't want to still be in the enemy trenches when that happens. Questions?"

There were none.

"One more thing before we move on. Each man is to load only two rounds. This raid relies on stealth, followed by an overwhelming attack from in close. Our primary aim is to obtain German prisoners, especially officers, as Captain Inkmann said. Bayonets will intimidate and deal with any resistance. Firearms to be used only as a last resort."

The next stop was a full-size layout of the German trenches. White tapes staked to the ground represented the dimensions of the trench system to be attacked, while miscellaneous chunks of iron pipe indicated the likely location of heavy machine guns and artillery pieces.

"Questions at this point?" asked the colonel.

Tom waved his hand. He felt all eyes turn toward the most junior sergeant in the regiment. "How accurate is all this, sir?"

"Allow me, sir." Inkmann glanced at Tom, then addressed the men. "We have reports gleaned from prisoners over the last few weeks. In addition we are able to use the latest in photography from balloons and aircraft. The enemy emplacements can be seen quite clearly."

"Don't they try to hide things, same as we do?" Tom and his comrades had spent many hours cutting tree branches and rigging poles, canvas, and netting to obscure horses and equipment from enemy aircraft and ground spotters.

"Of course they do, Sergeant," said the colonel. "No doubt the captain has taken that into consideration. It's our job to drive home the attack, no matter what."

"Even in the face of possible inaccuracies," added Inkmann. He smiled an indulgent smile, and some of the officers chuckled. Tom felt his face burn.

The colonel laid down the timing and precisely which sections of the regiment were to go where and what each was to do. Challenges and responses—passwords—were reviewed: nobody wanted to be shot by their comrades when they were dashing around No-Man's-Land.

The men were dismissed. Tom turned to go.

"Sergeant Macrae."

It was Inkmann. "A word with you, Sergeant."

Tom walked back. The colonel had disappeared, and the other officers and sergeants had dispersed. "Sir?"

"We have unfinished business."

Tom had heard from his family that Cedric Inkmann's brother, Bernie, and Henry Zink were still in jail, but despite the passage of years, legal proceedings still weren't finished. He looked carefully at Inkmann, who appeared to have lost weight. His swagger stick betrayed a mild tremor.

"You look fit and healthy, Sergeant. I have followed your progress. I am happy you haven't been injured or killed. I want you to survive. You are no use to me dead. I intend to somehow get the truth out of you and clear my brother's name."

"I told you before I can't help you."

"We shall see, Sergeant. In the meantime, stay well. We do have a common enemy, after all. Over there," Inkmann said, and jerked his head in the direction of the German lines.

Inkmann dismissed him, and Tom hurried back toward his men. Cedric Inkmann's behaviour was stranger than ever.

◆ ◆ ◆

The hands on Tom's pocket watch seemed to have slowed almost to a stop. Two minutes to go. He could see Lance-Corporal Gus Dunnett going from man to man; if he's as nervous as I am, he's hiding it well, Tom thought. Dunnett had a word for each of them, ensuring their bayonets were properly fixed, safeties on, and they had no metal gear that would clank or rattle in the coming raid.

His second hand showed five ticks to go. "Ready, Gus?"

"Ready, Sergeant."

There was a half moon in the sky with a skim of cloud that all but obscured it. As Tom climbed out of the trench on the dot of 2200 hours and crawled forward, he could see nothing of the enemy lines a mile away. The horizon showed clearly against the lighter sky, but only the general shape of the intervening land was discernible. Strangely absent was any growl or roar of artillery, but behind him came the muffled sounds of the men of his section as they too crept forward. Dunnett would bring up the rear and ensure nobody got left behind or lost.

Tom's immediate task was to link up with other sections in the proper order. Flowerdew and many of the officers were out front, farther into No-Man's-Land, coordinating the multipronged attack. Tom caught glimpses of a group of soldiers advancing on his left. Their orders were to attack the front-line German trench; Tom's section would be part of the attack on the reserve trench behind it.

Once they were well away from the lip of their own trench, Tom waited for his men to gather around him. "So far so good, boys," he whispered. "Now, up on your feet. Watch where you step. Stay in close touch."

The ground here was lower than both front lines, which meant they could get off their bellies and move faster. The enemy would have artillery and machine guns zeroed in on the Canadian front-line trench, ready to hammer men who might pour out during an attack. Their current position was already past that killing zone, and it was a common belief that at night, machine gun fire tended to be high.

But the Canadians also knew there would be other German guns sighted in on the area just in front of their own trench system, ready to rake attackers in a vicious crossfire. A silent approach and a shocking, overpowering attack from close in were keys to a successful raid.

Tom's section formed part of a large group that went to ground where the land started to rise. They had reached their first objective, and Tom forced himself to slow his breathing. He looked to the right where a large wood dominated the dark skyline. The plan included an advance group that had infiltrated the wood the day before and with luck were still there, protecting the attackers' flank.

Tom waited, every stifled sound reverberating in his mind; surely the Germans must be forewarned. Staying still was torture.

A party of nine men led by a lieutenant crawled forward, past him, pushing along in front of them a three-inch metal pipe crammed with explosive. Known as a Bangalore torpedo, the device would be thrust under the twenty feet of tangled barbed wire that was strung parallel to the German trenches to stop attackers from rushing the trench. After the torpedo was properly placed and detonated, the Canadians would charge through the resulting gap in the wire and throw themselves on the Germans.

Tom's grip on his Lee Enfield tightened. Surely something would happen soon. He forced himself to ease his hands, and at that moment there was a deafening roar as the torpedo exploded. Flares shot up from his right, a signal sent into the sky from one of the officers to the waiting Canadian artillery. Almost instantly came the crashing reports of the howitzers and the whistle of shells headed for the German lines.

The roar of artillery was drowned out by the shouts and screams of the Canadians as they surged toward the opening in the wire. Tom swung to the left behind an officer who led the way. Flares now shot up from behind the German lines, and enemy howitzers joined the crescendo of shells that hurtled overhead. Near-constant flashes from exploding munitions lit up the sky in a staccato imitation of daylight.

"Stop!" yelled the lieutenant Tom was following, wheeling toward the men behind him and flinging himself to the ground. "Get down! Send for another torpedo!"

A runner dashed back. Tom, now face down, peered ahead and saw why—there was another row of wire. That hadn't been in Inkmann's briefing, damn him. We're done, now. All hell was breaking loose and the Canadians were pinned to the ground by enemy machine gun fire. He hugged the ground, trying desperately to stay below the deadly fusillade. Men cursed with frustration as they held their fire, saving their two rounds until they had firm targets.

A group of men charged up past Tom's section, carrying another torpedo, two of them cut down by German fire before they got to the wire. The lieutenant grasped the front of the torpedo, guided it under the wire, then hurled himself back and down to the ground. Again the crack of an exploding Bangalore rang out. The lieutenant stood and ran forward, limping, to throw himself on the loose strands of wire that waved in the air like severed blackberry tendrils in a windstorm.

"Let's go, boys," Tom bellowed and leapt to his feet, rushing past the lieutenant where he lay on the barbed wire, clearing their path. Dunnett was right beside him, yelling like a banshee as the two of them charged, their section right on their heels. Tom heard rifle and machine gun rounds zinging around him, and a man next to him went down. Canadian ordinance added to the din, as long-range artillery pounded the area behind the German line.

Suddenly a dark slot in the earth opened up in front. A forty-yard section of the enemy trench was filled with frantic, indistinct figures spewing fire at the Canadians. "Bombs, bombs," someone yelled, and hand grenades arced over Tom's head into the trench. One came sailing right back out, to land somewhere behind. The trench was filled with rapid explosions, and grenade fragments whistled around Tom's head. He was flung back, knocked off his feet by the concussive force. He struggled to his hands and knees as a wave of Canadians jumped into the trench, stabbing and clubbing, screaming at the Germans to surrender. He was helped up by Private Reg Simpson, the trooper who had done good work in the listening post.

Tom shook off the private and took stock. The Germans still standing in the trench were flinging down their weapons, hands raised in the air. Six of his section were still with him, and he waved them on to jump into the trench and climb out the other side. Their target was the reserve trench, fifty yards farther on. Another section had already started in that direction. From the corner of his eye Tom thought he saw Inkmann, down in the captured trench, rooting through German packs and boxes.

Lieutenant Black, one of the regimental officers, was in charge of the attack on the reserve trench where they hoped to bag more prisoners.

Tom saw him a few yards ahead, revolver in hand, as they ran. There was a flash from the lip of the trench; Tom fired at it from the hip and immediately worked his bolt. One round left. Black had fallen, still pointing his revolver.

Dunnett shouted "Bombs away!" and hurled a grenade into the trench as they ran toward it. There was a muffled explosion and a wall of Germans went swarming out of the far side of the trench and ran. A machine gun to the right of the trench was abruptly silenced as a Canadian lobbed a grenade into its bunker and ducked back out of the way.

Tom got as far as the front parapet of the trench. A knot of Germans stood in it, hands raised. One of them stepped forward, a revolver in his hand. A shot rang out and he fell, stumbling backward. The Germans were yelling something that Tom couldn't make out.

"Hold your fire, hold your fire." Lieutenant Black, grimacing with pain, had rejoined the attack, his shout barely audible above the racket of the heavy calibre Canadian shells landing only yards past their position.

Tom slid feet first into the trench and aimed his rifle at the Germans. He waved it, pointing in the direction of the Canadian lines. "Out, out!" The prisoners started up a ladder toward the waiting members of Tom's section, who had their rifles levelled, fixed bayonets glittering in the brightening moonlight.

As he watched the Germans climbing out, Tom checked his watch by the flickering light of artillery blasts. Only five minutes to get clear of the German trenches. Then the artillery curtain would start to march backward toward the Canadian lines, and a German counterattack would be right behind it. Not to mention the German artillery, which would be hitting their own trenches as soon as they realized they had been overrun. Already the roar of exploding heavy shells seemed closer.

All but a few of the prisoners were clear of the trench, so Tom stepped up onto a ledge to clamber out. Private Simpson held his hand out to help him up, then suddenly jerked it back, aimed his rifle at Tom, and fired.

UNDER ATTACK

◆ ◆ ◆

Tom momentarily wondered if he was dead or alive. He lay on his right side, aware of a droning noise that grew louder and louder. He pulled his knees up, lifted his head an inch, then fell back as pain ricocheted through his skull. Blinking, he managed to focus on a bed two feet away, where a man was lying on his back, breathing deeply, apparently asleep.

Hell, he thought. A hospital. He rolled his eyes so he could see more. Canvas walls and canvas ceiling. An aid station, then.

The droning noise reached a rattling roar and he realized it was an aircraft. It sounded as though it were on top of him until the engine noise was suddenly obliterated by a loud explosion. The walls and roof buckled and billowed. The drone died away, and a minute later white-clothed figures he recognized as nursing sisters moved along the aisle between beds.

One of them approached and took his wrist. "Awake, are we? Did Fritz wake you up, Sergeant?" She glanced down at a watch pinned to her breast.

Tom had trouble talking. His mouth was dry. "Awake already," he croaked. "Where are we? What day is it?"

"Casualty Clearing Station Forty-seven," said the nurse. "You arrived last night. And this is the twentieth of the month. Can you tell me the month and year?"

"March, of course. Nineteen eighteen. Did I pass?"

"Just checking. Now, let's have a look."

She helped Tom roll onto his stomach, making the room spin around him, and touched the back of his head. A wound just below the occiput, she explained. A concussion, but no infection by the looks of it.

"Do you often get bombed? I thought hospitals and casualty stations were out of bounds."

"The Germans are pulling out all stops, we hear. When they come over, Matron makes the staff get into a shelter. Afterward, we come out to see if any of our patients have been hit. She's thinking of taking down the red cross so they can't target us."

The nurse gave Tom painkillers and water to wash them down, and she was followed by an orderly who provided lukewarm soup. Tom wolfed it down, then dozed most of the day.

Just at dusk Bruce Johanson came to see him. "Some guys will do anything to get attention."

Tom sat up. The room tilted, although the pounding in his head had eased somewhat since morning. "What the hell happened, anyway? Last thing I remember is Simpson shooting at me."

"He wasn't shooting at you, Tommy. One of the prisoners still in the trench pulled the pin on a grenade. Simpson shot him over your shoulder and the German fell across the grenade before it exploded. Lucky for you. Guess you caught a fragment though."

"Glad you told me—I was going to go looking for young Private Simpson." Tom managed a grin, or tried to. "Guess I'll have to anyway. Look for him, that is. To thank him."

"Funny thing though, Tom. You went down in a heap and Captain Inkmann was into the trench in a flash. I never saw anyone move so fast. Slapped a hand over your wound and organized a stretcher real quick. The barrage was moving in our direction so we headed back as fast as we could. What's the story with him? I thought he hated your guts."

"He does. All I know for sure is he acts stranger every time I see him."

Bruce left to return to the regiment, and Tom thought things over. Inkmann was a constant worry: he never changed his insistence that Tom somehow help out his brother, one minute badgering him and the next rescuing him. In the meantime, Tom hoped for a few days of recuperation. He didn't have a serious enough injury to warrant a trip to England for hospitalization, but maybe time off would help get rid of the vertigo and the pain in his head.

Next morning the usual artillery heralded dawn, but it slowly intensified during the day instead of fading away as it normally did. In mid-afternoon Tom stood to walk up and down the narrow aisle between the beds for a few minutes. For the first time in thirty-six hours, his head felt clear, but he was still having dizzy spells. He sat on the edge of his bed and waited for the walls to stop swaying.

There was a burst of activity at the far end of the tent as nurses hurried in, followed by orderlies and uniformed soldiers with stretchers. They began transferring patients to the stretchers and carting them out.

"What's happening? What's going on?" shouted the man in the next bed.

"We've been ordered to move back. The Germans have broken through," said a nurse. "We'll get to everyone as quickly as we can."

Tom heard the rumble of a familiar voice. Quartermain. The broad-shouldered sergeant marched into view. "How is Sergeant Macrae?" he asked a nurse who ran along behind him.

"He needs bed rest, Doctor says."

Quartermain stopped at the foot of Tom's bed and peered down at him, hands on hips. "You can sit up, I see. Can you sit a horse?"

"I expect so."

"Then get your boots on, Sergeant. There's work to do. Johanson is waiting outside with your new horse." He turned and left the way he had come.

New horse? Tom wondered. Why do I need a new horse?

The nurse was still there. "Cancel one stretcher," she said. "Your uniform is in the locker under your bed."

Tom scrambled to climb into his uniform, do up his boots, and quickly wrap on his puttees. His helmet was there too, and he clapped it on, momentarily staggering with a mild vertigo, then hurrying from the aid station to see Bruce Johanson sitting calmly on his bay gelding, smoking. All round him was a confusion of ambulances coming and going, stretcher-bearers sweating, and red-faced, harried nurses trying to bring order to the chaos. Bruce was holding a second horse, big and raw-boned, a dun with a white star on his forehead and a white, off-side fetlock. He had an independent air about him, and he carried Ranger's tack.

Bruce handed Tom the dun's reins. "This guy's name is Toby."

Tom held Toby's bridle and scratched him behind his ears. "Ranger?"

Johanson wheeled his horse to face Tom. "I was back with the horses during the raid, and we were shelled right after it. Took a terrible pounding. Lost three horses and two men. Ranger was killed. Direct hit."

"Ah, the hell you say."

"I knew you'd be upset." Johanson paused and looked at his friend. "We tried to find you a good replacement. Seems kind of poetic. Toby's soldier, a corporal in the 2nd Troop, was wounded in the same shelling. Figured he's a good match for you."

Tom still stood by Toby's head. He numbly checked the saddle, his sword in its scabbard, his rifle in its bucket, and mounted to ride beside Johanson, who brought him up to date. "Wouldn't you know it, after our big trench raid, by some ugly coincidence, the whole German army attacked all along the line. The colonel said it was the biggest artillery shelling of the whole war. Bloody Huns are breaking through everywhere."

When they reached the regiment's bivouac, Tom quickly located his section, whose members were already standing to their horses, ready to march. All around, men with their horses were doing their best to prepare for whatever was to come, stoically awaiting direction, with a sort of overarching, organized confusion in the background, orders countermanding orders in quick succession.

◆ ◆ ◆

Tom was dead tired and could have dozed in the saddle if he had dared. If he let his attention wander, the rolling hills of Picardy might have been, in the early dawn, a frozen seascape in pinks and greys. A white mist, like the foam at the edge of a wave broken on a beach, swirled and ebbed with the rising sun. He reined Toby to a stop and raised his right hand as René Carbonnier and Reg Simpson brought their horses up on either side.

The three mounted men stayed in the shadows of a grove of trees, where they'd be hard to spot. Tom pulled his binoculars from his saddle-bag and scanned the edge of a forest a mile ahead. Between them and the woods was a rough pasture, with no cover except a clump of undergrowth with a couple of tall beech trees part way across.

Nobody knew how far the Germans had advanced. There were rumours of scattered actions to the east, in the French section of the front—the former front, which had all but disappeared beneath the German juggernaut during the previous week. Tom's scouting mission was a classic use of cavalry. Probing and reaching for the enemy and, with any luck, reporting back to the colonel.

"Okay," he said to Carbonnier and Simpson. "Let's go. I don't see anything."

They started forward at a walk, the horses' breath streaming out in white gusts that were scattered by the breeze. For the first time in weeks there was a sunrise, the yellow globe visible through the fast-fading mist. Tom pulled his helmet down to shade his eyes, but even so he had a hard time seeing the forest ahead clearly. They came up to the grove with its two tall beeches and reined in.

Toby was skittish for some reason, tossing his head and prancing sideways, and Tom had to keep him firmly under control. "Steady, boy," he said, and patted his horse on the neck. Toby snorted.

Tom still missed Ranger, his big bay. He and Ranger had had lots of good times, riding the French countryside, training together. Tom had looked after Ranger for hours every day, and Ranger had looked after him. Thank God he went quickly, a direct hit.

"How far we going, anyway?" Simpson asked.

"Until we bump into Fritz," Tom replied. "Nobody knows how far he's penetrated."

The regiment had been on the move for days, fighting a rear-guard action on foot one day and dashing forward on horseback the next, looking for weaknesses in the German lines. The enemy had advanced across a broad front, the Allies forced to fall back by the sheer weight of the offensive. Men and horses ran on nerves and instinct, short of sleep, snatching food and shelter where they could. Allied High Command was desperate, and their desperation had passed down the line to division, to brigade, to regiment.

The Canadian officer corps had long since realized that every man in the army had to know what the immediate objectives were, what was at stake. Tom understood how bad things were, and so did his men. They were in muck up to their chins.

He glanced left and right at Carbonnier and Simpson, nodded, and nudged Toby with his spurs. The three of them moved forward at a walk. Tom kept his eyes fixed on the forest; the open country made him nervous. "Better speed it up," and he urged a reluctant Toby into a slow trot. The others followed suit.

Two hundred yards from the trees, Tom glanced right and saw something move. A dark, indistinct figure against the line of trees, then another.

"Shit!" he yelled. "Germans. Get out of here." He yanked Toby around to the left and spurred hard, bending low over his horse's neck and giving him his head. He glanced around and saw both privates, eyes wide, kicking their horses into a mad gallop. A bullet zipped somewhere close, then he heard the sound of rifle fire from the woods behind them. Another few seconds and they'd put the grove of trees between them and the enemy. Tom heard a cry and looked to his left.

René Carbonnier's horse was hit, its gait slowing. Without warning it collapsed and René was thrown headlong, face first into the turf. The Germans gave a shout of triumph and let go with a renewed fusillade. Tom pulled on his reins, but Toby had his head and was not to be stopped.

Tom yanked harder, got his excited mount under control, and swivelled in his saddle. René was on his feet, taking a slow step back toward his fallen steed when he spun around and fell to the ground, bullets kicking up dirt around him. Tom brought Toby to a halt and Simpson pulled up beside him. They were now well out of accurate rifle range, although bullets still zinged through the air. Tom looked back to see René struggle to his feet and begin a halting run toward them.

"Let's go," Tom shouted, and he and Simpson spurred back toward René. Tom swung Toby wide to the left and when he had thundered up even with the limping trooper, hauled his horse around to the right to come up beside René, who was running awkwardly, holding his hand over a bloody spot on his right leg. Simpson galloped up on René's other side, and pulled his right boot out of his stirrup, which René immediately grabbed with his free hand. Tom freed up his left foot, and René let go of his leg and seized Tom's stirrup with his right hand. The two excited horses had hardly slowed and were now running flat out, René being dragged between them. The enemy's bullets whistled around them for another hundred yards before dying away.

They didn't slow their horses until they were once again in the trees where they had started their reconnaissance, and Tom called a halt. René let go his desperate grip on their stirrups and slumped to the ground, chest heaving, grimacing.

Tom jumped down off Toby, handing his reins to Simpson, who was still mounted. Their horses pranced around, energized by their gallop and the excitement of the riders, who were jubilant after their bare escape and the improvised rescue of their comrade. Tom cut René's trouser leg away around a wound in his lower thigh, to reveal an entry hole in back and a slightly larger exit wound in front.

"Thanks, boys," René gasped. "I figured I was done for."

Tom was still bent over, looking at René's wound. "Lucky man. They won't have to dig out a slug, or set a bone. Good thing for you Fritz wasn't using a dum-dum." Rumour had it that the Germans would illegally doctor their rifle bullets so they'd spread open on impact and rip a ghastly wound in the flesh of man or beast; the rules of war required steel-jacketed bullets that should pass cleanly through, as if that wouldn't be bad enough. Tom got a gauze bandage and iodine from his kit and put an emergency dressing on René's wound.

"Might even qualify as a Blighty," said Simpson. "You *are* a lucky man."

René was a man of few words. He reached up and Tom hauled him to his feet. René tried a few steps; he was limping but able to put weight on his leg.

"Get ready to ride, Simps," Tom ordered. "Next order of business is to get back to the regiment and report to the colonel. René—get up behind him. You can change round halfway and ride behind me." The reality was that a horse could carry double for a time but would not be able to keep up over the ten miles back to the regiment's camp.

"Glad you came back for me, boys. But I'm not going," said René. He looked at Tom. "Give me your rifle."

"What the hell do you mean, you're not going?"

"Gabriel—my horse—he's not dead. I'm not going to leave him."

René was a superior horseman, as befitted a Metis. His forefathers had roamed the prairies, living wild and free. It was a source of some amusement among the Strathconas that he always named his horse Gabriel. A tribute to Gabriel Dumont, war leader of the Metis in the rebellion of 1885, Tom assumed.

"Your horse is dead."

"No, he's not—he's gut shot. He can't get up. I'm not leaving him like that."

Tom hesitated. René was a free spirit, often in trouble with army discipline. He could be led but not pushed. The most crucial thing now was to get word of the enemy's location back to the colonel as soon as possible, but Tom had also learned never to give an order that would not be obeyed. He turned to Simpson.

"Get back to the regiment as quick as you can. Tell the colonel we saw a large German patrol ten miles northeast of the camp, just east of the Avre River." There would be consternation in his troop when he and René didn't appear, so he added, "And tell Flowerdew that Carbonnier and I will be a couple of hours behind you, riding double."

Simpson trotted off, and Tom tied Toby to a tree. He took his Lee Enfield from its boot and his water bottle from his bag. He and René both drank, then he handed the rifle to René, who acknowledged it with a nod and started off across the field toward the clump of trees, favouring his right leg as he went. Tom hurried after him, drawing his Webley, hoping not to need it, thinking that if a German patrol was close enough for him to hit them with a revolver they might as well just slit their own throats.

René got down on hands and knees when he was nearing the beech grove, and Tom did likewise, staying close. He could hear René's heavy breathing, interspersed with the occasional moan. Tom felt like moaning himself. He could feel the hair standing up on the back of his neck as they reached the undergrowth at the base of the trees and crawled carefully forward. For all they knew the Germans could have advanced across the open field and be right on them.

René again took the lead, now down on his belly, Tom's rifle alongside him. As Tom watched, he reached out and with great care bent a clump of grass in front of him. There was no sign of the enemy. Gabriel was a hundred yards out on the field, legs pulled under his body, nose resting on the ground. As they watched he raised his head, struggling to get his forelegs under him, and heaved his front quarters off the ground. His back legs scrabbled at the ground but could not find purchase and he collapsed again. He screamed, a long, horrifying scream. Again and again he shrieked, as if he knew they were near and was crying for help.

"Oh, Jesus, Jesus, Jesus," Tom cursed. He had lived with men now dead and gone. Shattered, blown apart, dying of wounds and infection. Men had some control over their own actions, some sense of what they were fighting for, but horses did not. He could not bear the suffering of the horses, creatures that only did the bidding of men. Innocent, somehow. He had seen horses gutted, legs blown off, blinded, shot, even gassed, and he knew he would live with their screams for the rest of his life.

René brought the rifle to his shoulder, steadied the forestock with his left hand, elbow on the ground. He thumbed the safety off. Tom saw Gabriel toss his head, lower it. The Lee Enfield cracked.

Tom grabbed René's leg and pulled him back as a hail of bullets whistled through the underbrush, slapping the tree trunks behind them. The two soldiers scrambled back the way they had come, keeping low, René limping worse than ever.

When they reached the woods where Toby was tethered they were gasping for breath. Tom picked up the reins, mounted, and took his left foot out of the stirrup so René could use it to climb up.

René stood and looked at him for a moment, flexing his wounded leg, then handed Tom the rifle.

"Get up, René. We've been here too long."

René mounted behind Tom, who dropped the rifle into its boot and started Toby back toward camp.

"That was a good horse," René said. "I couldn't leave him."

"Okay," said Tom.

"I reckon you're in trouble for staying."

"Well—I guess I couldn't leave you."

"I'll get another horse. Another Gabriel." René fiddled with the edge of his bandage, which was oozing blood. "And this ain't no Blighty."

They rode double for a couple of miles, then Toby started to stumble. Tom climbed down and led him, with René now in the saddle. They stopped at a creek so Toby could drink, and Tom unbuckled the feed bag to give Toby the last of his oats. They pushed on, anxious to rejoin the regiment, Tom insisting René ride, even though Toby was all in. He sure as hell wasn't skittish anymore.

"One more hill to climb, old boy," Tom said, and gave Toby a scratch behind his ears. They kept going, and at times Toby rested his long head on Tom's shoulder as they walked.

The sun was low on the western horizon when they stumbled by the first sentries. Tom reported to Flowerdew, relieved to find that Simpson had made it back safely, then delivered René to a first aid man. He was near collapse when he was finally able to unsaddle Toby, wipe him down, and feed him. Ferguson had seen Tom at the horse lines and rustled up a tin of cold bully beef stew which Tom wolfed down before falling onto his bedroll, fully booted and spurred, his poncho for shelter against a drizzling rain.

In the instant before he slept, an image of Toby came to mind. His horse had been nervous and unsettled in the morning, just before Tom had spotted the enemy. If they had been a hundred yards closer to the Germans before seeing them, he, Simpson, and René would be bloating corpses, bled out on the Picardy grass. Next time he'd pay more attention to what Toby had to say.

The following morning, while the 1st Troop was standing to their horses and awaiting the day's orders, Sergeant Quartermain called them together. "As you know, Lieutenant Tilley has been appointed to head-quarters squadron. Lieutenant Harrower will be our new troop leader, but he's still on course. He'll catch up with us in a couple of days. I'll be acting troop leader, and Sergeant Macrae will be troop sergeant until Lieutenant Harrower gets back." He nodded at Tom. "Designate horse-handlers. We'll be reporting to Flowerdew up close to the lines, and fighting a rear-guard action. As soon as we're there, the handlers are to form up a half mile back. We'll need them in a hurry."

An hour later, the 1st Troop of the Strathconas was moving forward at a ground-eating trot, Troop Sergeant Quartermain at its head and Tom, as second sergeant, bringing up the rear. The horses and riders followed in pairs, nose to tail, strung out like a hundred-yard-long serpent that wended its way over the French countryside. The men were grim and silent. Tom checked his sword, rifle, and ammunition bandolier for the hundredth time. Word had it that the German advance was rolling on, and the French and British were retreating across a thirty-mile front. Valiant rear-guard actions were being fought, with some units overrun and wiped out, luckier ones escaping to fight again.

The troop had to stay off the roads, which were clogged with retreating soldiers, artillery, supply wagons, trucks. Civilians too were on the move with wheelbarrows and carts—anything that could be collected at short notice. Children and domestic animals added to the confusion.

Tom could see they were approaching the battle zone; there was no longer a stationary front. Sporadic German shells burst randomly across the landscape. Hoarse noncoms and junior officers bawled commands as thousands of men with whatever equipment they could carry retreated, heading in the direction opposite to the cavalry. They looked beaten, shoulders slumped, faces pale with exhaustion.

"Close up, dammit," Tom grumbled at the men ahead of him, who had allowed a gap to open up between them and the riders ahead.

Toby mounted a slight rise and Tom had a view of the troop, thirty-three mounted men with Quartermain in the lead, in a ragged line ahead of him. Other troops were off to the left and right, sometimes in plain sight on the rolling French landscape, sometimes obscured by groves of trees or hillocks. A quarter mile ahead he could see a group of dismounted men, and as he got closer he recognized Lieutenant Gordon Flowerdew, who was waving them on. The riders reached the advance party, where Quartermain and Flowerdew had a hurried conversation while the troop dismounted, rifles in hand.

"Good luck, boys," yelled Johanson as he wheeled away on his charger, lead ropes from Toby and four other mounts in hand, away from the front lines. He and six others had drawn short straws and would serve as horse-handlers. Flowerdew ordered Quartermain to move to the left to direct the men on that side, and kept Tom close to await developments.

At Flowerdew's direction the troopers spread out a hundred yards on either side of him and Tom, dropping to the ground behind a low wrinkle that ran across the field. Tom edged up beside the lieutenant, who was sprawled belly down across a heap of soil between two old shell craters, scanning the near horizon with his field glasses.

Within minutes they heard the heavy rattle of machine gun fire and the roar of trench mortars. Two dozen khaki figures burst from a scraggly grove a quarter mile in front of them, running hard, straight at them. Tom could see they were British Tommies, some without helmets, eyes wide in their white faces. They stumbled past the line of Canadians and collapsed.

"How bad is it?" asked Flowerdew.

A sergeant gave a hasty salute and gasped for air. "Bloody awful, sir. This looks like the real thing. Thousands of the buggers coming straight for us. Heavy machine guns raking our position. Trench mortars, field guns. The captain said to get out, stayed behind with ten volunteers to man our Vickers. I hope to hell he makes it." He looked around. "I lost six men on my way out."

"Get your men to the rear, Sergeant. We'll fight a delaying action from here—then we'll be dropping back too." Flowerdew turned back to his glasses.

Hell, thought Tom. This could be bad.

The brigade had been responding to often-contradictory orders as the French and British forces tried to slow the enemy. The cavalry was stretched thin. They would be up before dawn, saddled and ready to go, standing to their horses; with luck they'd be under their ponchos, horses tended to, by midnight, after a long day in the saddle.

Most days brought a brush with the enemy. Numerous firefights had broken out where German patrols or columns had broken through British or French lines. Sometimes the response would be a quick mounted skirmish, and sometimes, like today, the Straths would dismount and act as infantry.

Tom watched the line of trees as the rattle of small arms increased, then died down. The men peered forward. Tom saw Flowerdew's glasses steady.

"There they are," said the lieutenant.

Now Tom and the rest of the troop could see them too, a scant half mile away, grey-clad men swarming out of the woods. Flowerdew had deployed a Hotchkiss machine gun fifty yards to the right. Lowering his glasses, he turned to Tom. "Sergeant, get over there to the gunners. For Christ's sake stay down. Tell them to hold their fire until they hear my Webley." He undid the flap on his holster, pulled out his revolver, and rested it across his left forearm.

Tom backed away, then squirmed off to his right to reach the machine gun. The gunner, a corporal named Slade, knelt behind the Hotchkiss, right hand on the pistol grip, his finger outside the trigger guard to prevent accidental discharge. His loader, Private George Cunliffe, lay beside him, ready to feed in the metallic strips of ammunition. Gordon Ferguson was nearby, rifle at the ready.

"What the hell does he think I'm going to do?" snorted Slade. "He already told me twice himself to wait for his signal." Slade had the habit of whistling "Tipperary" through his teeth when he was nervous. He was whistling it now, getting on Tom's nerves.

"Didn't your mother know any other songs, Slade?"

Slade checked the rear sight on the Hotchkiss. "Sure, Sergeant. And you better hope this baby doesn't jam, or we'll all be singing 'Lili Marlene' in German and saluting Kaiser Bill in our next march past."

Tom turned toward the advancing enemy. At least Slade had stopped whistling. Tom was sweating in spite of the chilly March air; a fitful sun broke through but brought no heat. He forced himself to breathe, watching the oncoming Germans. After he had counted a hundred of them, he stopped. The Canadians were badly outnumbered; it was a question of holding up the enemy advance for as long as possible.

He lay prone behind the low ridge, just able to see over the stubble. His rifle was already at his shoulder, his left arm stretched out ahead of him, supporting the forestock. To his right Slade sat, exposed on the bare earth, both hands on the Hotchkiss, the vicious weapon on its portable mount between his knees, ready to pour 450 rounds a minute at the advancing Germans. Cunliffe was poised, set for action.

Tom glanced left, to where Flowerdew lay, glasses once more in hand, his revolver at his elbow. The Germans were closer. They appeared to be advancing in groups of a hundred or so, scattered across the horizon from left to right in front of the Strathconas.

God, Flowers, Tom screamed silently, let's give them a blasting and get the hell out of here! Somebody had told him Flowerdew was out of sorts because Lieutenant Fred Harvey, another Strathcona, already had a Victoria Cross, and Flowers was itching for a chance to earn one as well. Not now, Tom said to himself. Not now. Go for it when I'm not around.

Sweat beaded on his forehead and trickled down his nose. The nearest Germans were no more than two hundred yards away, a small group of twenty or so, the point men alert and cautious. Come on, Flowers, shoot that Webley of yours. Tom became aware of a bird singing, an incongruously cheerful song of ascending notes repeated over and over. His body ached with the strain of lying doggo, mortal enemies now only a hundred yards away. He lined up his sights on the nearest German.

Just as Tom thought Flowerdew must have fallen asleep, his Webley spoke and at once Slade opened up with the Hotchkiss, right in Tom's ear. Tom squeezed his trigger and fired, and his target went down. The Germans kept coming, advancing across the open field in spite of the hail of rifle and machine gun bullets slashing into them. Tom's nose twitched at the smell of gunpowder. Finally the Germans fell to the earth, ground to a halt in the deadly Canadian fusillade.

"Hold your fire," yelled Flowerdew.

Slade had already stopped firing, and the riflemen on the ground reloaded their magazines in the sudden silence. Tom's hands were shaking as he inserted the recharged mag and slapped it into his Lee Enfield. He kept one eye on the Germans, vague shapes hard to make out in the stubbled field. Too far away for them to hit us with grenades, he realized with relief.

Sergeant Quartermain scuttled along behind the troopers. "Steady, boys. Won't be long."

A group of Germans got to their feet and ran forward. Tom fired, everybody fired, including Slade and his machine gun. The Germans went down. Another group off to the left dashed forward and were met with a hail of lead. Just as they fell to hug the ground, another ten stood to run forward for a few seconds. Sudden movement behind the Germans caught Tom's eye. It was a team of horses that galloped straight toward the Canadians, then swung a hundred and eighty degrees and stopped, revealing a two-wheeled field artillery piece, a 77 mm, its stubby barrel peeking out between steel armour plates. Men leapt up to unhitch the team, which then trotted away.

Another wave of Germans was advancing, stolid and implacable. Tom fired. Answering fire ricocheted around him. He glanced toward the 77 in time to see it buck and recoil as a shell whistled overhead.

"Slade, get the gun, get the gun!" roared Quartermain from behind them. Slade redirected his weapon to fire steady bursts of .303 rounds in the direction of the German artillery piece, hoping to knock out the gunners.

The German infantry kept coming, going to ground within fifty yards of the beleaguered Canadians. Once again Tom saw the German 77 fire, and instantly there was a tremendous crash as the shell hit the earth right in front of Slade's Hotchkiss. Slade was flung backward, where he lay groaning. His Number Two, Cunliffe, didn't move, splayed face down.

From the other side of the machine gun, Ferguson threw himself into Slade's position and realigned the barrel to face the Germans. Tom crawled over and crouched beside him. "Do you know how to work this thing?"

"No time like the present to learn, eh? Feed it to me." He pulled the Hotchkiss's butt to his shoulder and bent over the rear sight.

Tom was startled by screams from the enemy and a flurry of bullets that hit the ground all around him, one ricocheting off the Hotchkiss's front mount. A half-dozen Germans were only feet away. Ferguson jerked the rear of the Hotchkiss down to elevate the gun and fired continuously. Tom, desperate, fed in a fresh strip of bullets then seized his own rifle, firing again and again. The Germans faltered and fell. Survivors crawled backward. The mortally wounded moaned among the silent dead.

Another whizz bang zipped overhead.

In a brief lull, Tom heard a low monotone raised in song. "It's a long way . . ." Tom looked around to see Slade, lying on his side, his helmet on the ground beside him. A pair of body snatchers rolled him onto a stretcher and dragged him away. ". . . to Tipperary . . ." Tom wasn't sure if he heard the words or if they were in his own head. He glanced left to where Flowerdew lay as bullets whined in the air. He was speaking to Quartermain, who ran, crouched, to Tom's position.

"Your section to hold on," he yelled. "One other section will hold to your left. We'll pull back the others a hundred yards, then give you covering fire. You," he pointed to Ferguson, "move back right now, with the Hotchkiss." Quartermain rushed away.

Tom swung his gaze from right to left, and back to the front again. The squadron was falling back, and any minute it would be his small section holding the line for as long as it took Quartermain to get dug in or at least into some sort of defensive posture to the rear. They'd have to hold off the Germans without the Hotchkiss. Then Tom and his boys would have to race back, covered by their comrades' fire.

Eight men, he thought. No, five. One was already in an aid station with wounds suffered the previous day and Johanson was away holding the horses. Ferguson had been ordered to the rear. Not good odds: mostly men newer to the regiment, although, like Simpson, many of those were proving their metal.

The field in front of him looked like an anthill with its top kicked off. Everywhere, grey-clad figures tramped and crawled. As soon as the Germans realized that the bulk of the Canadians had withdrawn, they would overrun Tom's section. He glanced left and right again. Ferguson still lingered with Slade's Hotchkiss. It would take two men to move it, one for the rifle itself and one for the mount. Simpson was crouched, ready to grab the mount once Ferguson unclipped the automatic gun, but Ferguson didn't look like he was in a hurry.

Somebody came up beside Tom, and he turned to see Lieutenant Flowerdew, inserting fresh cartridges into his Webley.

"Won't be long now," he said.

"No, sir." Tom pulled the magazine out of his rifle and refilled it, then smacked it back in and cycled a round into the breech. He spoke to the men lying or crouching to his left and right. "It's up to us, boys. Just a few minutes. Fifteen rounds per minute, like the book says."

Another whizz bang passed overhead, and there was a great shout from the direction of the German formation. They were on the move. Tom aimed at the first man he saw, only fifty yards away, and fired. Too bad we don't have the Hotchkiss, he thought, when there was a shattering wall of sound from his right. It was Ferguson and Simpson, still there, in spite of Quartermain's order, displaying the flexibility, even insubordination, to superiors' orders that was the bane of the officer corps and a major attribute of Canadian soldiers. The riflemen blazed away, putting up a furious rate of fire, kneeling or lying prone. Flowerdew was on his feet, revolver outstretched in his right hand, striding forward. Tom gulped, jumped up, and followed, shooting as he walked, bullets buzzing around him like demented hornets.

Flowerdew stopped firing, broke his weapon open, and inserted fresh cartridges. He wheeled back toward Tom and looked past him. "There's our signal." He shouted at Ferguson. "Pack that gun up and get back to the others. Now!"

Ferguson looked sheepish as he jumped up, grabbed the Hotchkiss in both hands, unclipped it and ran like a startled deer. Simpson was right on his heels, the gun mount over his shoulders. A rattle of covering rifle fire flared from the Strathconas who had withdrawn minutes earlier.

"Let's go, boys," Tom yelled, and the remaining men of his section leapt to their feet and ran pell-mell. Simpson stumbled under the weight of the Hotchkiss mount. Tom clutched him by one arm and Flowerdew got hold of the other to steady him as they ran toward the Canadians, who kept up a constant fire. Hope I haven't made any enemies, Tom thought, the covering fire whistling around him.

Just as Tom reached the line of Strathconas, the horse-handlers trotted up with their excited charges and his section scrambled into their saddles, jamming their rifles into their buckets. Toby snorted and stamped, caught up in the frenzy.

"Off you go!" Flowerdew shouted at Quartermain, who led the mounted troop away. Tom and Toby thundered after them. Flowerdew waited until everybody was clear, then brought up the rear.

◆ ◆ ◆

No sooner had Tom put his head down three nights later than he felt something clamp onto his ankle. He kicked out furiously, not knowing what was going on but sure he was in terrible danger.

"Whoa, Sergeant," said Ferguson, stepping back. "You've had enough beauty sleep, my boy. Time to rise and shine."

Tom groaned. "What time is it?"

Gordon Ferguson had been on sentry duty. "Oh four hundred, and there'll be no rest for the weary today. Word is we're to be saddled and stood to by 5:30. René Carbonnier is back in the line, in spite of your rudimentary efforts at first aid. And you'll be interested to know some mail got through. Here you go." He tossed a battered envelope at Tom, who recognized his mother's handwriting and stuffed it into his tunic.

He kicked off his slicker, rolled up his blankets, and stumbled off to feed Toby. He felt like he'd gone ten rounds with Tommy Burns, the Canadian former heavyweight champion of the world. Or maybe even Jack Johnson, who beat him.

Casualties and the resulting manpower shortages had changed the face of the 1st Troop. Sergeant Quartermain had been given a field commission and was in command of a troop of his own; Tom was now Troop Sergeant, under the command of Lieutenant Harrower, and he checked that his men were up and tending to their mounts.

He ate standing in a light drizzle, tea and bacon provided by tired duty cooks as icy water dripped off the rim of his helmet. It was March 30, 1918, Easter Saturday, and the Strathconas were bivouacked on an east-facing hillside above the village of Guyencourt. His family would be at the little church in West Kildonan, across the river from their home. Remembering his letter, he pulled it from his pocket.

"Dear Tom," his mother had written. It was a miserable spring in Winnipeg, too, he'd be sorry to hear. Father, brothers, and sister were fine. Oh, yes—an afterthought—a recent story in the *Manitoba Free Press* recounted that Bernard Inkmann, one of the Kravenko escape conspirators, had committed suicide in jail. Wasn't his brother also in the army?

Holy smoke. Tom shook his head. Cedric Inkmann was pretty crazy already; this would really set him off. And poor Bernie. Tom had never liked him, given Bernie's fancy clothes and slightly menacing air, but it had never occurred to him that Bernie wouldn't be out of jail in due course. He would hardly be the first man to do hard time, then make something of himself afterward. Tom resolved to keep an eye out for Cedric. Maybe he should say something sympathetic to the captain when he next saw him. If he'd listen, that is, given his antipathy so far.

Dawn approached, the cloud cover slowly growing brighter, now a lighter but cheerless grey. The regiment was camped in a slight hollow, lines of horses feeding, smoke from makeshift cook stoves hanging like a fog. Tom found his saddle and bridle, walked to the picket line where Toby waited, and dried his back with a spare blanket. He settled the saddle onto Toby's dry blanket and was bent over to reach for the girth when his horse arched his back and crapped, a great steaming pile. Pungent steam arose, and Tom straightened.

"Nice work, old boy," he said, and felt his spirits lift. Against all odds, he was coming through the maelstrom of a world war. His luck was holding—not a scratch to speak of in nearly three years on the battlefield, much of it in the man-killing trenches. Now the cavalry brigade was actually being used in a mounted role, the one they had been trained for.

He bent again to finish saddling Toby. Some of the men had stopped naming their mounts, afraid of an emotional bond that was inevitably shattered if horse was killed or rider was wounded. Worst of all was when a horse was badly injured and had to be put down. Cavalrymen hated performing the *coup de grâce* on their horses, but the inevitable suffering of the animal if they failed to do so was no alternative. They would never ask another man to do it for them, as the approach of a stranger would be upsetting for an already stricken horse.

Tom grasped the reins in his left hand, the front of his saddle with both hands, and swung up. He rocked in the stirrups, walked Toby around the camp, checked his attached sword, rifle, and ammunition bandolier. When they moved out, the bandolier would go over his own shoulder. A day's iron rations, food for times when they were away from cooking facilities, with its preserved meat, cheese, biscuits, and tea, as well as oats for Toby, would be buckled to his saddle.

Returning to the horse lines, he dismounted and tethered Toby. He loosened the girth, then unbuckled the spare saddle wallets, the leather bags that were strapped to the front of his saddle. Draping them over one shoulder, he headed for the camp kitchen—a tarp hung between trees, over a cook stove hastily constructed of found sheet metal and banked-up earth. He found the sergeant cook supervising breakfast cleanup, inhaling tea and cigarette smoke in equal parts. Judging by the scant breakfast that morning, Tom knew the supply wagons had once again not caught up to the regiment.

"I suppose you're here to complain, too?" the cook barked.

"Nope. I wouldn't do that. I know better than to bite the hand that feeds me—even if what it feeds me can be a little thin at times."

"Well, I'm all out of coffee and I'm all out of time. Don't you have horses to attend to?"

"We're standing to, that's all I know. Could get the word to take off any time."

Tom casually slid the wallets off his shoulder and lifted the flap on one of them to show the cook a bottle of French brandy. "Would this improve your mood any?"

The cook's eyes lit up, but his face stayed neutral. He was known as a good bargainer. "What do you want for it?"

"I could use some extra grub. No telling where we'll be by tonight."

"Maybe we can do business."

The cook prodded a wooden crate with his boot, turning it so Tom could read the label. Cans of Argentine corned beef, a staple of iron rations and their main source of protein. Tom figured he had eaten a thousand pounds of bully beef, but it was a lifesaver for hungry soldiers.

Together they broke the crate open, and Tom stuffed his wallets until they were stretched tight as drumskins, lumpy and angular-looking. He whistled as he made his way back to the horse lines and secured the bags to the front of his saddle. He felt as rich as a British lord, his future assured.

The rain had let up and the sun was trying to break through, the sky patchy with light. While faraway artillery drummed from time to time, Tom made the rounds of his troop, checking rifles and ammunition, swords and water containers, rations of oats and feedbags for their horses.

Young Simpson's face looked haggard. "You ready for another day of fun, trooper?" Tom asked.

"Didn't get much sleep, Sergeant."

"Neither did anybody else. You'll be all right once we get on the move."

"I reckon."

Simpson would be fine, but Tom was worried about the other younger men, recent replacements not yet hardened to the demands of battle and the deprivation that was the lot of the soldier. They could bounce back if they got some rest, but when they spent all day in the saddle and had only three or four hours of sleep for days on end, they got run down fast. He would make sure old hands like Ferguson, Johanson, and Carbonnier kept an eye on them.

He reported to Lieutenant Harrower. The troop was ready.

AT THE GALLOP

♦ ♦ ♦

"Stand to your horses." God, if there was any order that would stay in his mind, it was that one. They had been hanging around for three hours, with no word yet on what the day would hold, just like so many days, weeks—hell, years—before. Tom thought again about Strathconas who had tired of standing to their horses and transferred elsewhere. Some were dead already, victims of the war in the trenches or in the air. Maybe some were among the pilots in the aircraft that, incongruously, whined and roared overhead, looking down as cavalrymen, symbolic of military strategy for centuries, galloped across the European landscape.

Tom's mind snapped back to the present as he heard hoofbeats pounding in from the east, up the hill toward the camp overlooking Guyencourt. Two riders came into view, a corporal and a private, the corporal in the lead by fifty yards. Their horses were sweating and lathered, foam dripping from their forequarters. Tom recognized the corporal, a member of General Seely's signal troop, as he swept past and reined to a halt at the headquarters tent. A minute later a trumpet call rang out—"Mount up."

Tom hurried to Toby, freed him from his tether, and climbed aboard. Mounted men milled around, forming up. They had responded to the bugle on countless occasions, but each time sent a shiver of excitement through Tom and, it seemed, the horses as well. They were all business as they awaited further orders: orders that could mean standing to, or thundering into battle, or any variation in between.

At Tom's signal the 1st Troop formed behind him in a paired column, side by side, that would straighten and line up when they moved out. He reported to Lieutenant Harrower, who took his place at the head of the troop while Tom rode Toby to his station at the rear of the formation.

Flowerdew trotted over. "C Squadron, walk—march!" he ordered, and turned his horse east.

Lieutenant Harrower passed on the order to the 1st Troop, and they followed behind him and Flowerdew, heading down the hill toward the Noye River. Once the whole troop was on the move, Tom spurred to catch up and stay close. It was his job to make sure horses and riders maintained the pace and to be ready to lend assistance if there were problems.

The remaining troops of C Squadron followed, along with the rest of the Strathconas. The whole of the Canadian Cavalry Brigade was under way. They forded the Noye at Remiencourt, where they watered the horses and the men filled their water bottles.

The Dragoons were leading, so the ground was well chewed up by a myriad of hoofs when Tom and the rest of the Strathconas climbed up the slope from the valley of the Noye. The brigade moved northward, staying off the skyline of a prominent ridge to their right. An hour out of camp they swung east, around a shoulder of the high ground, riding on a winding, hard-packed road that gave them better footing, and increased their pace to a steady trot. The promise of sunshine had faded, a uniform layer of high cloud covering the sky. Tom kept one eye on Lieutenant Harrower at the head of the troop, and one eye on the riders between him and the lieutenant. The 2nd Troop was right behind Tom, with the Fort Garrys in the rear of the Strathconas.

As they crested a small hill Tom caught glimpses of a motorcycle coming from the south to intercept the brigade. The lead horses paused while the Dragoons took in the message, Tom assumed, then abruptly wheeled south, the rest of the brigade following.

An hour later the troop topped a rise and Tom had a clear view of a broad valley, with fields and woods in a random pattern. Lieutenant Harrower showed Tom his map. Directly below them, the road led to the village of Castel and a bridge over the Avre River, which flowed roughly south to north. On the far or eastern side of the Avre was the village of

Moreuil, a mile or so away, and on top of the ridge east of the village was a large wood, the Bois du Moreuil. The lowering sky lent a gloomy atmosphere to the scene, made more sombre by the rumble of desultory artillery.

Movement at the north end of Moreuil Wood caught Tom's eye, directly across the valley. He could just make out a group of horses and men, tiny in the distance, and perhaps even a red pennant. The pennant would be the flag of the Canadian Cavalry Brigade, marking General Seely's position.

The Dragoons led the way down the slope toward the bridge at Castel, the Strathconas and Garrys clattering down the cobbled road behind them. They crossed the stone bridge and started up the eastern hillside toward General Seely's headquarters at the northern edge of the wood. The horses worked hard, pushed by their riders. Suddenly, a trumpet sounded and the brigade thundered ahead at the gallop as they came under fire.

Bullets whistled by Tom, seeming to come from his right, the general direction of the forest. Out in the open, he felt like a target in a shooting gallery. Bending low over Toby's neck, he tilted his helmet to protect his face from the flying clods of earth and stones thrown up by the hoofs of the horses ahead of him.

Something to the right caught his eye. He turned his head and saw a horse down, not moving. A soldier sat on the ground, legs stretched out in front of him, back against the saddle still on his horse's body. The trooper waved an arm as the riders swept by.

Tom concentrated on the horse and rider ahead of him as fear rose in his belly, clenching tight. A bullet could find him at any moment, and he'd be down on the ground, trampled by the following horses. There'd be no stretcher-bearers on this open hillside, raked as it was by enemy fire.

He heard a cry behind him and looked back to see a horse and rider break ranks and quickly fall behind. He didn't know who it was, but he thought of the new men in the troop and the fear they must feel, with no experience to fall back on. Tom, Toby, and the brigade spurred on, up the hill, following the lead riders toward Moreuil Wood.

Nine days before, German forces had broken through where the French and British lines intersected. They were advancing in a south-westerly direction, looking to take the key city of Amiens, which was so close it could be seen from Seely's headquarters. One hundred kilometres south of Amiens by arrow-straight railroad was Paris, the grand prize. The Canadian Cavalry Brigade—Dragoons, Strathconas, Fort Garrys— had been ordered into the breach.

For those nine days the cavalry had fought skirmishes and delaying actions, usually in formations of a squadron or troop. A hundred, or thirty-five men and horses, or even fewer. The nimble cavalry could dash in, fight, and retreat. But this time the whole brigade was committed, and they were already under fire.

♦ ♦ ♦

Ellen sat in the foyer of her father's house, her blue coat on, one knee crossed over the other to allow a black, low-heeled, fashionable walking shoe to bounce up and down. Confining her hair was a matching blue bonnet that she thought of as jaunty, but she didn't feel at all jaunty as she drummed her fingers on the arms of her chair. The otherwise som-nolent house was disturbed only by the ticking of the tall clock down the hall and the vague scent of bleach and furniture polish, a leftover from the cleaning lady's ministrations earlier in the day. She tried to calm her chaotic thoughts, impatient for Harry to arrive.

Just when she was ready to leap from her chair and throw some-thing at the wall, she heard approaching footsteps. Confident steps, that crunched on the frosted front walk. She waited until the knocker banged, counted to ten, rose, and opened the door.

"Harry," she said. "I was waiting for you." Annoyed that he was late but relieved he had showed up, wanting to bring things to a head.

Harry gave her a hug, but she turned her head as he tried to kiss her, so his lips brushed her cheek.

"Let's go. I've been looking forward to seeing you." Harry had a broad smile on his handsome face, his eyes dancing.

They set off on their walk. Ellen had agreed to see Harry yet again; he was fast becoming part of her life. Since their first kiss Ellen had melted. She was torn by Harry's ardent attentions and the fading memory of Tom. She had a picture of Tom in her room, where she kept his letters. She gazed at the picture and reread the letters when her mental picture of him faded, but it was harder and harder to relive the joy she had felt with him.

Harry held Ellen close, one arm around her shoulders. She kept her hands in her pockets as if they were cold, refusing to let her body relax against his.

Only the night before, during the night shift at the Winnipeg General, Ellen had been taking a tea break with her friend Winnie when they were joined by two other girls, Sharon and Carol. They volunteered on another ward, though they had jobs elsewhere, and Ellen had come to know them at the hospital.

Sharon had the reputation of being a bit fast but she was always good company. "Guess who has a new boyfriend?" she asked, glancing sideways at Carol.

Carol was a short, curvaceous blonde. "He's not a boyfriend. I hardly know him."

"Tell them about it," teased Sharon.

"Never mind."

"Then I will. Carol was working last Saturday and had to stay late to put away some stock. She was bending over a shelf in a storeroom when a man came up behind her—and when she straightened up he grabbed her and kissed her."

Carol was beet-red. "He didn't grab me. I wouldn't stand for that. But he did kiss me, and I kissed him," and she shot a venomous look at Sharon. "And you'd better not tell anyone else."

"And just who is this new man of yours?" asked Winnie.

"I wouldn't call him my man, but I can't wait to see him again. He works for the Bay too, in the accounting department. He's really good looking. Harry something."

Ellen had somehow kept her composure, as blood rushed to her face and her hands shook. She wanted to reach across the table and slap Carol, the lying little . . . little . . . hussy. My God, what if it's true? She could hardly bear to sit and drink her tea, and as she finished her shift, she kept her mind busy with work.

Now, as she walked with Harry, her feelings welled up again. It wasn't that she had totally made her mind up about him, but she didn't want to be made a fool of, either. She planted her feet. Harry, surprised, stopped and looked at her. She stood, tall and rigid, chin elevated, searching his face.

"What? What is it?" he asked.

"Do you know a girl named Carol?"

"The only girl I know named Carol works at the Bay."

"Did you kiss her?" Ellen's voice cracked. "What does she mean to you?"

"Did I kiss her? Did *I* kiss *her*? Absolutely not."

"That's not what I hear."

Harry looked like a dog that had been kicked. "I don't know who you've been talking to, Ellen." His voice got stronger as he went on. "All I know is some girl named Carol, who's a part-time salesgirl, has a crush on me. She left me a note, for heaven's sake. Of course I threw it away. I've never been near her."

"You didn't kiss her and hug her in the stockroom?"

"Is this some kind of joke? Is someone out to get me, making up stories like that?" Harry ventured to put his arms around Ellen to give her a brief hug. "Come on. Let's walk."

Ellen stalked beside him, hands still in her pockets. She wanted to believe him, and it was hard not to. He had looked her in the eye and was genuinely upset, she could see that. She knew some girls could make up stories about relationships. But yet . . . They went west along streets lined with elm trees, naked of leaves. Patches of snow clung to the dead grass on the river's banks.

As they came to a cul-de-sac with a small clearing that looked out on the river, Harry fumbled in his pocket, then grasped her left hand. "This may not be the best time for this. But the fact is, Ellen, no other girl means anything to me. I love you, and only you."

He turned her hand palm down, and produced a ring which he slipped over her third finger.

Ellen was in shock. Her mouth flew open, and she covered it with her right hand.

Harry still held her hand. "Marry me, Ellen. I know there was someone else—I know all about him. But you know we have so much in common. Together we could make a home, move anywhere we want. We can raise a family. I can afford it—I have a promotion coming . . ."

She put her right hand up in the air, palm toward him. "Harry. This is too much. I need to think." She took off the ring and held it out to him.

Harry took her hand in his, folding her fingers over the ring. "Keep it. I am going to convince you. You are going to put it on one day soon, and I'll be the happiest man in the world. Keep it."

Once again, Ellen found herself searching Harry's open, assured face. The blue eyes, dark hair, elegant nose, and broad mouth. There was a lot to like.

Harry walked her home and kissed her at the door. Ellen was glad her father was not at home. She knew he approved of Harry, but she was in no mood to listen to his advice. She ran up the stairs, put the ring in a drawer, and sat on the bed, her face in her hands.

After a while she straightened and shook her head. When Ellen felt at a loss she always turned to the memory of her mother, wondering what she would have done in her place. This time, her mother had no answer for her.

◆ ◆ ◆

When the Strathconas arrived at the northwest corner of the roughly triangular Moreuil Wood, the Dragoons were already engaging the enemy on the west side, between the forest and the village of Moreuil, and had swung into the wood itself. Lieutenant Harrower ordered a halt and gathered the men and horses of his troop in a rough circle around him. He and Tom walked their horses from man to man, checking that none of them had been hit, that they were ready for action.

Tom stopped his horse in front of Reg Simpson, who was pale and staring at the ground. "You okay, Simps?" he asked.

Simpson didn't answer. His eyes slid from side to side, not focussing on Tom.

Tom pushed Toby ahead so he was right beside the private, reached out, and gave him a punch on the thigh.

Simpson jumped and met Tom's eye. He looked surprised.

"Okay, Simpson?"

Simpson swallowed. "Okay, Sergeant."

Tom and Toby trotted back to where Lieutenant Harrower waited at the head of the troop. As they got there, a messenger galloped over from the general's headquarters a hundred yards away.

"Lieutenant, you are to report to General Seely immediately for a scouting assignment. Sergeant, you are required as well."

Tom was surprised at the request if it meant that both he and Harrower were to be sent off on tasks away from the men of their troop, depriving them of experienced leaders. The brigade was stretched thin, with the Strathconas in reserve, expecting to be thrown into the battle at any moment. Even as he and Harrower trotted by, A and B Squadrons of Strathconas were receiving orders to join the battle in Moreuil Wood. Tom could hear rifle and machine gun fire from the south, where the trees of the wood approached the village of Moreuil. In the distance, aircraft buzzed and droned, circling the forest like buzzards around a sick animal.

Tom and Harrower dismounted at the corner of the wood where General Seely's temporary headquarters had been set up. The general's signal troop and adjutant were in attendance, along with the command-ing officers of the three regiments. Messengers were constantly pounding up while others were being dispatched. The general spoke to Harrower and sent him off; he was to take eight men and reconnoitre to the east, to try to gain intelligence of German movements.

With Lieutenant Harrower away leading a scouting party, Tom, as troop sergeant, would take over as troop leader in his place. But it seemed he also was to be sent somewhere, so the next senior noncom, Corporal Dunnett, would assume command. Perhaps this meant the troop would be held in reserve until Tom and Harrower returned to refill the gap in leadership.

Tom didn't like leaving Dunnett in charge. He was a conscien-tious soldier but too inexperienced to be senior man in a troop of independent-minded men and horses, even if their numbers had been reduced to fewer than thirty by casualties suffered in previous days.

General Seely was gesturing at a map and then at the wood to the south, while the brigade major and Lieutenant-Colonel Macdonald looked over his shoulder. Macdonald turned to Tom.

"Look here, Sergeant," he said, and pointed at the map. "That's Moreuil Wood, and down to the right of it, at the bottom of the hill, is the village of Moreuil and the Avre River that we crossed to get here. The Dragoons are already engaging the enemy in the wood. We need intel-ligence, Sergeant. We've had no word back from the Dragoons. How bad is it? Can they drive Fritz out the far end? How many Germans are in there, and what artillery or other support do they have?" He gestured at the general, who was speaking to a private manning a radio. "We can't get a clear picture from the flying corps—radio's not working worth a damn. And they can't see much from the air anyway, given the thick woods. You are to get into the woods and make contact with the men in there, preferably some of the Dragoon officers. Find out what you can, and get back here fast. The general needs to know whether to commit more troops or hold onto a reserve. Understood?"

"Yes, sir."

"Off with you then, Sergeant."

Tom leapt into the saddle and urged Toby into a canter toward the main part of the forest, only a quarter mile away. The field around him was marked by the passage of horses and men, but he could see breaks in the trees where the Dragoons had pushed into the forest. He slowed Toby, and reined him along the nearest face of the wood until he came to an opening, a slot between the trees.

They entered a world of dim light, beech trunks, fallen trees, and scattered undergrowth. Ahead of him he heard a furious battle, small-arms fire forming a wall of sound that rushed at him like a cyclone-driven hailstorm. Stray rounds spattered through the leaves overhead or thunked into branches and trunks.

As he advanced he could hear the shouts and cries of his fellow caval-rymen engaging the enemy in the gloom ahead. A milling mass of horses appeared in front of him, their eyes rolling, great muscles trembling. Handlers struggled to hold them, their riders somewhere ahead in the battle.

Tom seized his Lee Enfield from its bucket, dismounted, and tied Toby to a tree. He nodded to the handlers, and crept ahead. Almost immediately he came upon a corporal of the Dragoons lying against a tree trunk, pale faced, a private bandaging his arm. Blood seeped through the bandage.

"Fucking Huns," said the corporal, to no one in particular.

"Where's your troop? Up ahead?" asked Tom.

The corporal's eyes flickered, registered. "Yeah—just ahead. Lots of Germans. Watch out for the machine guns."

Tom crouched, rifle ready, and moved cautiously toward the sound of firing. He almost tripped over a lieutenant, whom he recognized as a Dragoon squadron leader. He was lying prone, aiming his Webley into a clearing. It was almost quiet as the firing simmered down to an occasional rifle report.

Tom threw himself to the ground beside the lieutenant. "The general needs intelligence, sir. How many Germans? How are they armed?"

"There are one hell of a lot of them, I can say that for sure, and they have some automatic weapons. As you can see," and he gestured left and right at his troops, lying along the edge of the clearing, "it's heavy sledding. We had to dismount. It's been hand-to-hand fighting at times. We need any help they can send."

"What about the other squadrons?"

"They've got their hands full too. They're off to the left. They sent a man over a few minutes ago to see if we could assist. I told him no can do."

Just then a machine gun opened up from the other side of the clearing, and Tom and the lieutenant buried themselves face down in last year's leaves. The devastating German Maxim's deafening chatter sounded like it was ten feet away. Slugs ripped trees and branches just over their heads, then the impacts traversed to their left. A fusillade of rifle fire crackled, and the woods on the other side of the clearing seemed alive, leaves shaking as the steel-jacketed bullets spewed toward the Canadians. A soldier screamed and scrambled back, blood streaming from the side of his head. He writhed in the undergrowth, moaning, both hands to his head, but still had sufficient sense to stay flat.

Tom wondered if the gunners were close enough to be taken out with a grenade. Suddenly the rifle fire stopped and fifty Germans came roaring out of the woods straight toward him, lobbing grenades, firing as they came, then abruptly falling flat.

"Down, down," shouted the lieutenant, and Tom hugged the earth even tighter, as grenades exploded all around him. There was an instant of silence, then the lieutenant was on his knees, waving his revolver. "Let's go, boys!" and he jumped up.

Tom was right with him, as all around them the Dragoons leapt to their feet and charged, yelling like banshees. The Germans, too, were up and running forward, trying to get their long Mauser rifles into play.

The Canadians were on them, clubbing, shooting, stabbing. From the corner of his eye Tom saw a man to his left flung back as blood sprayed from his neck. In front a grey-uniformed, heavy-set German, not ten feet away, screamed and charged, bayonet aimed at Tom's face. Tom fired, and the man's legs gave out. He slid forward, face down, rifle still out in front of him.

Tom worked the bolt on the Enfield, his rifle again ready to fire. Something hit him from behind and he went down, a Canadian soldier across his legs. Struggling out from under the man, he looked up to see a German sergeant directly in front of him, bringing a Luger to bear. With no time to do anything except violently swing his rifle, he caught the man across the head, felling him like a pole-axed steer. The lieutenant pointed his Webley and shot the German where he lay.

As abruptly as it had started it was over, the surviving Germans melting into the undergrowth. The Dragoons moved into the woods at the south side of the clearing where the Germans had been two minutes before. Sweating corporals and sergeants detailed men to tend to the wounded and set up perimeter guards.

"Bastards," the lieutenant muttered. "But I have to hand it to them. They fight like cornered rats. Tell the general it's hard going and we can use some help. It's been like that the whole way. Fritz is not rolling over."

Tom scrambled back to where he had left Toby, who seemed unusually nervous, high-stepping and prancing as Tom untied him, then jammed his rifle into its bucket and climbed aboard. The horse-holders were still there. One of them was a man he recognized, an old hand who had been with the Straths before being transferred to the Dragoons.

"Keep your head down, Sergeant. There's still lots of Germans around. We pushed past a bunch of them as we came through."

"Obliged," said Tom. "See you later." He spurred away, wondering if he'd ever see the man again. Casualties were piling up and the Dragoons were paying a heavy price for the ground they won. But now it was vital that he get back to Seely to report on the ongoing fight in the wood.

Tom pushed Toby to a fast walk, about all they could manage in the forest, blasted as it was by artillery shells and bombs. In places the forest floor was a maze of downed limbs and shattered trunks, with huge, jagged splinters protruding into the air. He let Toby pick his own way but kept him heading north toward Seely's headquarters. Tom swept his gaze from side to side, keeping a lookout for a flash of German grey.

A rider appeared ahead and to his right, only forty feet away through the undergrowth and coming toward him. Tom tensed, but recognized a British uniform. The man waved, and Tom pulled Toby to a stop to let him come closer. He was looking around to his rear, then up the left side, watching for Germans, when a heavy blow smashed him from his saddle and drove him to the ground.

He hit hard, face first, his helmet jammed back, chin strap choking him. Dazed, he struggled to get his hands under him, pushed himself off the ground to his knees, and pulled his helmet off. A tall figure approached. A second blow stunned him again, and he collapsed onto his left side.

◆　◆　◆

As Tom shook his head to clear it pain shot through his skull to land somewhere behind his eyes. He groaned, realizing that his hands were tied behind his back and he was being dragged backward by the shoulders. Twisting his neck, he looked up into the distorted features of Cedric Inkmann.

"Awake, are you? Good," said the captain, red-faced with exertion. "Stand up, damn you," and he propped Tom against Toby, who shied away. Tom's knees buckled, and he fell to the ground.

"Have it your way, then," Inkmann said. "Stay there. Behave yourself. I have plans for you, Macrae."

He walked to his own horse, reached into a saddlebag, pulled out a rope, and threw one end over a tree branch. The knotted end landed a few feet from Tom. He stared, and his guts roiled, seeing the hangman's noose. The man was mad.

Tom glanced down. His Webley was gone from its holster; Inkmann must have taken it. I need a weapon, he thought frantically. I need a weapon.

Inkmann came and stood over him. "Thought you'd get away with it, did you, you lying swine?"

"I'm not trying to get away with anything, you idiot. I've got to get back to the general," Tom screamed.

Inkmann did not react in any way, his blank eyes on Tom. "Mother has been writing to me, you see. I know what went on. You and that bastard Zink thought you could frame my little brother, didn't you? But Bernie . . . Bernie . . ."

To Tom's amazement, a single tear coursed down Inkmann's cheek. Then the man's face changed again, hardening and twisting into a furious mask. "You lied to the police, you lied to everybody, but you can't lie to me. My little brother died in prison at the end of a rope, you bastard," he spat, "and you will too." He bent, grabbed the noose, loosened it, and dropped it over Tom's head. Pulling hard on the knot, he slipped it down to rest under Tom's left ear.

Christ, Tom gasped, this madman is going to hang me if I let him. He struggled, looking around desperately. There had to be something—then he remembered he still had his bayonet by his right hip. But what good was it? His hands, already going numb, were tied firmly behind his back.

Inkmann turned, froze in an alert posture, then clamped a sweaty hand over Tom's mouth, his right hand in the air as if to command silence. Tom became aware of slow hoofbeats approaching from the northwest. Inkmann slithered away, and Tom fell on his side. He pushed his hands down and away, trying to get them past his buttocks and around his feet so they'd be in front of him. He felt his bayonet handle against his forearm, and tried to think. Getting his fingers on the bayonet, he was able to slide it up and out of its scabbard so that it dropped to the ground.

Inkmann had disappeared.

Forcing his hands as far apart as he could and jamming his right one lower, Tom dropped his shoulder enough that he was able to get his hand down past his buttock. His chest was constricted; he couldn't breathe. The noose around his neck was choking him and he reared back to ease the tension on the rope.

Fighting hard to expel yet more air, he scrunched his body even tighter to allow more play to his arms. His bindings were cutting his wrists; his hands felt as though they were going to fall off. Another hard exhale—and then his hands were down to the backs of his knees. He lay still, cramped in the fetal position. Where was Inkmann?

He could still hear hoofbeats plodding slowly, branches snapping as an unknown rider moved through the wood. Then they stopped. He pictured someone out there, maybe scratching his head, trying to figure out what was going on, when he heard a roar from Inkmann, a yell, and pounding as a horse was spurred into action. The shouting continued as Tom struggled to his knees in time to see a mounted René Carbonnier, sword extended straight at Inkmann, who rose from behind a log and aimed his revolver. René's horse plunged ahead as Inkmann fired. René was flung backward off his saddle, his sword flying up, raking Inkmann's face.

Inkmann screamed and clasped his left hand to his face, blood flowing between his fingers. René's horse galloped away. Tom could no longer see René anywhere. He struggled to get his right foot through the bindings on his wrists; they caught on his spur. Squeezing the last breath out of his lungs, he freed his right foot. The left one was easy. Now his hands were in front of him. He heard Inkmann stumbling back toward him.

"Redskin bastard. Red-bastard-red-bastard-red-bastard. You're all the same. But I got him, and now I've got you, you son of a bitch," he sobbed.

Tom lay still on his right side, hunched over. He hoped the berserk Inkmann wouldn't notice that his hands were now bound in front of him and not behind. Inkmann threw his revolver to the ground, reaching for

Tom with both hands. Blood poured from the wound that split his face as he started to drag Tom toward the tree. Gathering his feet under him, Tom surged upright, catching Inkmann in the chest and knocking him to the ground. Tom landed on top of him, pounding as hard as he could with his clasped hands. He gasped for breath. Inkmann was down but not out, both hands up, protecting himself. Tom swung again and blood spattered from Inkmann's lacerated face. Inkmann's right hand snaked out and snatched up his revolver.

Tom dived for Inkmann's gun hand, but only got his wrist. Inkmann slowly won the battle, as the barrel of the revolver, which looked like a 15-pounder to Tom, angled closer, closer—suddenly exploding with a thunderous report.

Tom's left arm lost all strength. He fell back, stunned, a numbing pain in his arm. Inkmann knelt upright, mumbling to himself, oblivious to the gore that streamed from his face and covered the upper half of his body. As he got to his feet he clutched Tom's tunic, again dragging him closer to the tree. Suddenly Tom caught sight of his bayonet where it had fallen to the ground, grasped it with both hands and twisted hard to the left. Inkmann was caught off guard, reaching for the rope still around Tom's neck and pulling on it.

Off balance, Tom swung the bayonet wildly with a scything motion, slicing into Inkmann's tunic. Inkmann looked down, blank-faced, at the cut in his uniform where blood was already seeping. With a bellow he threw himself at Tom, who was struggling to get to his feet. Tom thrust blindly, sinking the fifteen inches of steel bayonet to the hilt in Inkmann's throat. Inkmann lurched backward, clawing wildly at the bayonet as arterial blood spurted. Finally he lay still, his upper body covered in blood.

Tom struggled with the hangman's noose, slackened it enough that he could get it off over his head, then lay back, gasping for air. After a moment he yelled, "René, René," but heard no response. He clambered to his feet, aware again of the wound in his upper left arm, and floundered in the direction he had last seen René: René, who had saved his life. He found him, flat on his back, eyes open, staring up through the trees at the cloudy sky. Tom knelt and bent over him.

"Where did you come from?" Tom asked, his voice husky.

René looked at him. "That bastard came over to our troop and asked where you were. He was damn near foaming at the mouth. Looked like a dog with rabies." René laboured, his breathing shallow. "Soon as he heard you'd been sent into the woods he chased after you."

A fleck of blood appeared at the corner of René's mouth. He spat. "Too many officers around—I couldn't get away 'til just now." His tunic was soaked in blood. He coughed, and blood bubbled at the corner of his mouth.

Tom cradled René's head awkwardly in his bound hands and forearms. "Hang on, René, hang on." Raising his head, Tom couldn't see any living thing except Toby, but the incessant sound of the furious battle in the wood continued. "Help is on the way," he said. "Don't die." Tears coursed down his face.

"Don't bullshit me." René's eyes rolled away from Tom as he shuddered, groaned, and took a breath. Tom waited, but there were no more. René's body relaxed in Tom's arms, and the light in his eyes faded.

Tom held René for a moment, then eased his head to the ground. He gently closed René's eyes and crossed his arms on his torso. "Goodbye, my friend." Still kneeling, he rocked back and forth on his heels, hands clasped.

Another comrade gone. A man Tom had once thought of as less of a soldier, but a man with a code of honour all his own. Killed by Inkmann, for God's sake, a Canadian officer. But it was the war. It could as easily have been a German bullet or chunk of shrapnel or Krupp steel through the guts. He looked down at René. René had known what had to be done when the colonel was shot. René would know what to do now.

Tom jumped to his feet, hurrying to where Inkmann lay. He grasped the bayonet, still stuck in the corpse's neck, planted his boot on Inkmann's chest, and jerked the weapon free. He wiped it on Inkmann's tunic, then knelt with one knee on its handle, manoeuvring so he could saw the cord that bound his hands back and forth against the blade. It was awkward and painful, but eventually the fibres gave way and his hands were free. He tore the remnants of cord off his wrists, then chafed at them to restore circulation and jammed the bayonet into its scabbard. Looking around, he rubbed at his face where the tears had dried. He wasn't doing René or anybody else any good wasting time here; he had to get back to the general. As he turned to go after Toby, he spotted his revolver on the ground where Inkmann must have thrown it. He snatched it up, holstered it, and hurried to where Toby waited a few yards away.

He looked once more at René, muttering a silent prayer and becoming aware that blood was dripping from the fingers of his left hand. Stumbling, Tom threw the reins over his horse's head and hauled himself into the saddle. He was able to hold the reins in his left hand but kept his right on his upper arm to slow the bleeding. The wound needed attention, but that could wait. Together, man and horse weaved their way through the woods in the direction of General Seely's headquarters.

Clearing the trees, they cantered across the open field to the cluster of officers, who looked up expectantly. Two hundred yards away, his troop and the rest of C Squadron still waited, in reserve. Off to his left an artillery round exploded, throwing up clods of earth.

The colonel reached up and gripped Toby's bridle.

"Quickly, Sergeant!" barked Seely, who had hurried over.

"Heavy fighting a mile into the woods, sir. The Dragoons are making some progress but it's all on foot, hand to hand. They're taking casualties. The lieutenant said any help would be much appreciated."

"What did you see by way of German arms, Sergeant?" asked the colonel.

"Machine guns and small arms. Lots of grenades."

"That will do, Sergeant. Best get yourself attended to," said Seely. He turned to the colonel. "The only reserve force we have is your C Squadron. Tell them to mount up."

Tom dismounted and led Toby toward a group of men standing by a stack of stretchers. "Hey, you body snatchers," he called out. "I have a wound that needs dressing." He tied Toby to a stretcher.

A medical orderly named Blanshard sat Tom down on a box of supplies and helped him take off his tunic, right arm first. His left shirt sleeve was soaked in blood from the shoulder down, but most of it had congealed. Blanshard cut away the arm of his shirt with surgical scissors. "Can you move it?" he asked.

Pain shot up into his shoulder as Tom flexed his left arm a few degrees, and he cradled his left wrist in his right hand to take the weight off it.

Blanshard grunted. "You're lucky. No bones broken, that I can see. The bullet passed clear through." He cleaned the area with alcohol and added a dollop of iodine, as Tom flinched. The medic picked up Tom's tunic, ripped loose the dressings sewn into it in the factory and pressed them to the wound, then topped it all off with a bandage wrapped around the upper arm.

Tom felt dizzy. Get hold of yourself, he thought, as his mind wandered back to the death of René just minutes before. He tried to push it out of his mind, but couldn't. René—dead. René, who could have gone to an aid station, maybe even to hospital, with his leg wound. But René had stayed behind and fought on, and now he had died, on Tom's account. He'd get help, go and bring René back once the battle eased off.

"Aren't you the lucky one."

"What?" asked Tom.

"I said aren't you the lucky one," Blanshard repeated. "You'll have to sit tight here, though, until things settle down. Walking wounded. There'll be lots more coming in, by the sound of that . . ." and he gestured toward the wood, where the battle was growing louder by the minute. "Then we'll get you away, maybe even to hospital."

Maybe even to hospital. So *he* had a Blighty, courtesy of Inkmann, for god's sake. Something many a man, maybe most of them, dreamed of when the shells were flying and the German bullets were zipping past. He'd be out of here in no time. Maybe the war would end before his arm recovered—a happy thought, but probably a forlorn hope; it looked as though the war would go on forever.

Blanshard interrupted again. "Here you go, Sergeant. First today, I expect. Courtesy of the colonel." He held out a tin cup, half full of rum.

Tom tried to reach with his left hand, winced, and grabbed the offering with his right. He drank. The wooziness passed as he gazed around. Toby was standing patiently a few yards away, still tethered to an unused stretcher. The world was full of possibilities. He would go home, might never see action again. He'd write to Ellen with the good news; he had a wound, not a major wound but a real one. She'd come around, see things his way. If there was someone else—well, leave that for another day.

Tom realized he was smiling: sitting on a wooden box on the outskirts of a battle and smiling. He glanced down at the tin cup in his hand—nearly empty. He tossed it back. Maybe he could get some more from Blanshard. Looking around, he saw C Squadron, his squadron, showing a flurry of activity. The men were tightening girths, checking equipment, mounting up. As he watched, the confused mass of men and animals took shape, formed up in double ranks, and walked toward him.

The squadron was led by Gordon Flowerdew, former farmer, sergeant, and now lieutenant. Right behind him was Dunnett, acting as troop leader for the 1st Troop, with both Tom and Lieutenant Harrower away. Tom stood up, his bare left arm cold in the biting March wind.

Two by two the mounted squadron passed by, Tom watching as his comrades followed Flowerdew, faces set. Beside Flowerdew was Longley, the boyish bugler who had lied about his age to get into the army. He saw Tom, and waved.

Bruce Johanson went by, touching two fingers to the rim of his helmet when he saw Tom. He looked drawn, like all of them. Haggard, with lines etched in their young faces. Exhausted. A lot of them were just boys going in over their heads, beaten up, ranks depleted. A lot of the senior noncoms were dead, or wounded, or away at officers' school. Or standing and watching.

"Blanshard!" Tom's tunic was on the ground where it had been tossed. "Help me." He struggled to hold the tunic with his right hand and get it up over his left arm.

"What do you think you're doing, Sergeant?" Blanshard hurried over from where he had been unpacking medical supplies.

"Get this goddamn tunic on me."

Blanshard pulled the tunic from Tom's hand as he clenched his teeth with pain. He eased it up Tom's wounded arm, then held it so Tom could get his right arm in and do up the seven buttons, one-handed. Tom hurried to Toby, freed him, and clutched the reins and the pommel of his saddle with his right hand. Another bout of dizziness engulfed him. He didn't know if he could mount or not.

Blanshard came over and bent close to him, hands clasped in front. Tom nodded, put his left boot in the proffered hands and pulled on the saddle as Blanshard boosted him. He settled into his seat, right behind the saddle wallets still crammed tight with tins of bully beef. He took the reins in his right hand, left arm slightly bent, the weight of his left hand on his pommel. He touched his spurs to Toby, who broke into a trot, then a canter, and they followed in the tracks of Flowerdew's squadron.

With Tom urging Toby on, they quickly cut down the half mile that had opened up between them and the last of C Squadron. Too quickly, maybe. Toby seemed reluctant, but the die was cast, and Tom struggled with a feeling of foreboding, accentuated by the dark wood, the gloomy sky, and the carnage he had witnessed with the Dragoons in the forest. He swung to the left of the double column as he closed the gap and kept going, passing his friends and troopmates. As he neared the head of the column, Flowerdew turned in his saddle and nodded at him.

Tom slowed to a trot, transferred his reins to his left hand, gave a casual salute. "Reporting back for duty, sir."

"Take your place, Sergeant."

Tom reined to the right, signalled Dunnett to move to the rear of the troop, and settled in to the troop leader's position behind Flowerdew. His left arm was more painful by the minute, but if he kept it slightly bent at the elbow and rested his hand on his thigh, he could at least cushion it from the shock of the awkward trot set by Flowerdew.

The column now had Moreuil Wood on their right. The forest resounded with the noise of the ferocious fight raging out of their sight. A constant staccato background of rifle fire was overridden at times by the stutter of machine guns and the thump of artillery. An aircraft circled overhead, pistons hammering.

Flowerdew sat bolt upright in the saddle, his gaze straight ahead. Tom did a quick count. The squadron was down to well under a hundred riders, his own troop at less than thirty. He slowed Toby a little so he could drop back to talk to Johanson. "Where is Harvey's troop?"

"Flowerdew detailed him and the 2nd Troop to reconnoitre, occupy the northeast corner of the forest."

Not good news. With Lieutenant Fred Harvey and his troop gone, the squadron was down to only three out of four troops, and even they were below strength. They had been fighting constantly for days, their ranks thinned out by men wounded and killed.

A rider cantered up on his left and Tom realized with a start that it was General Seely himself. Seely slowed his horse to match Flowerdew's pace and rode alongside him. The two men talked briefly, then Seely wheeled away and rode back the way he had come.

Flowerdew was considered a good officer by the troops, thoughtful of their welfare and a motivated leader. The men had heard that he had told the colonel, the regiment's commanding officer, that if necessary he and his squadron would stand fast in the face of the German breakthrough—fight to the last man or last bullet.

The three remaining troops of the squadron trotted parallel to the side of the wood toward its northeast corner, a half mile ahead and to the right. All around the wood were farm fields, some dark and fallow, others with yellow stubble from last year's grain crop. Jutting out from the corner of the wood was a gradual embankment some thirty or forty feet high; the squadron would have to climb it to get around the corner of the wood. A shallow draw led from their present position to the embankment. As they neared the mouth of the draw Tom saw Lieutenant Harvey and his 2nd Troop, off to the right. They were dismounted and exchanging fire with unseen forces in the trees, fighting their way into the wood. Flowerdew led his troops over in Harvey's direction.

"Hello, Flowers," Harvey shouted over the noise of the battle as the squadron trotted up. "Bunch of Huns just inside the forest but I think we can deal with them."

"Go to it, Fred! Drive them out the other side if you can. We'll catch them when they come out."

Harvey nodded and turned away to join his men, pushing into the trees in the face of German fire. They were soon swallowed up in the forest. Constant small-arms fire and even sporadic artillery reverberated, and bullets whistled around the mounted men of the squadron as Flowerdew led them, now at a canter, toward the corner of the wood.

Tom followed right behind Flowerdew into the draw, the ground rising on either side of them. They were out of sight of the trees, and gained a welcome respite from the random but deadly small-arms fire. Tom noted with alarm that Toby was snorting and shaking his head, just as he had done when René's Gabriel had been shot out from under him, but he couldn't worry about that now. He patted his horse on the neck, turning in his saddle to check on his troop. The horses were coping well, riders concentrating on staying formed up.

Flowerdew put his horse to the upward slope at the end of the draw, and Tom spurred Toby, who lunged at the embankment. Tom leaned forward to transfer his weight, shifting his reins to the more familiar left hand. His left arm still hurt but he could handle it. He could hear the men behind him urging their horses on.

As the slope eased Tom could see the corner of the forest to the right, and a broad field flattening out in front of them with a narrow road angling across it. Flowerdew, two lengths ahead, suddenly turned in his saddle and past him, around the corner, Tom saw a mass of grey uniforms not three hundred yards away. Christ, we're into it now! He turned, bellowing at the men following, "Sections right! Sections right!" He waved his right arm to try to get the men and horses spread out to the side so they'd be a more dispersed target. Toby tossed his head and veered. Tom reined him back on course, the pain in his arm forgotten.

Flowerdew ripped his sword from its scabbard and waved it overhead. "It's a charge, boys, it's a charge!"

More horses and men tore up the embankment and into the open. Riders shouted and cursed, struggling to control their excited mounts and get into parallel lines, stirrup to stirrup. Horses spread out, some flinging their heads, nostrils flaring. The mass of men and horses plunged ahead.

Tom reached across his body for his sword and jerked it from its scabbard behind his left thigh, pain stabbing at his left arm. Over the pounding of hoofs he heard the scrape of swords as the three troops of cavalry drew their weapons, their horses' eyes rolling as they thundered on.

A hail of bullets came at the Canadians, and some went down. The men roared as they leaned low over their horses' necks, bolting toward the Germans. From the corner of his eye Tom saw the youthful trumpeter, Reg Longley, pull up his trumpet to sound the charge, then disappear, his horse cut from under him.

It's not a charge, it's a stampede, and Tom bent forward, reins in his left hand, sword reaching, Toby pounding close behind Flowerdew's horse.

Rifle bullets buzzed all around, like a thousand hornets streaming from a hive, and Tom heard the sickening thud of lead hitting living flesh. To his right another man went down, shot out of his saddle. Toby had his bit in his teeth, stretched out in a full gallop. The Germans were now only a hundred yards away. A machine gun opened up ahead, another from the right. Grey-clad figures were bent over their automatic weapons as they spat out five hundred rounds a minute, riflemen adding to the fusillade.

Flowerdew rocketed out of his saddle, falling backward off his horse, which stumbled and collapsed. Tom was now lead rider, fifty yards from the Germans. Christ, there's a second line of them behind the first. Toby missed a step and kept going. Tom felt a hammer-like blow and flinched as a shocking pain seared his right leg. I'm hit, by God, and so is Toby. He glanced down. More bullets thudded into Toby's chest, Tom's saddlebags, and both his legs. Blood spattered, flecked with flying shreds of uniform and leather. He screamed in pain and fury as he levelled his sword. Sergeant Quartermain's instructions flashed through his mind. "Sword horizontal. Arm straight. Let your shoulder take the shock . . ."

Toby was grunting in pain as the bullets took their toll. Ten yards to go, and a grey-coated figure, rifle at his shoulder, fired, lifting his eyes to Tom's at the last instant. Tom's sword-thrust took the man high in the chest and he fell over as Toby swept by. Tom kept his grip on his sword and let his arm swing back, Toby's forward motion dragging the weapon from the slumping body.

Tom knew they'd never make it to the second line of Germans. Toby barely responded as Tom reined him hard to the right to get back to the first line. The horse stumbled and crashed to the earth amid the German soldiers and, as Tom went down, he reversed his sword and drove it two-handed through a prone gunner, like a man driving a crowbar into hard ground. What was left of the squadron pounded past Tom, men yelling, stabbing, dying as the German barrage continued.

Tom's right leg was pinned under Toby, the big horse thrashing and screaming as he tried to get up. Tom grabbed tufts of grass, slippery with blood, and pulled himself clear. More bullets thudded into Toby's body, even after he lay motionless.

Horses, some to Tom's amazement still with riders up, milled around. Withering fire poured from the second line of Germans. Tom was desperate to get clear of the ongoing hail of lead and trampling horses but he couldn't get up. His legs were in agony, felt as though they had been hit with sledgehammers. He tried to crawl on his belly closer to Toby's body, but his holster and ammunition pouches caught in the grass. Undoing his webbing, he let the Webley and other gear fall away as he pulled himself in close behind Toby's mercifully still form and hunkered down, tin helmet pulled low. Peering from under the brim, he saw a few surviving Straths ride or run on foot into the woods to escape the hammering German guns.

Gradually the volume of fire eased and the surviving Germans withdrew to their second line. The sounds of battle gave way to the moans and shouts of men calling for help, the halting hoofbeats and pitiful neighing of horses wounded and bleeding and falling. Tom felt rather than heard the moan deep in his own chest as the pain in his legs intensified. His left arm throbbed with the grinding quality of a toothache. Blood oozed from his shredded trouser legs and puttees.

Tom heard a groan and a muffled curse. Gus Dunnett, pale and sweating, hitched his way through the churned-up earth to join him. "Hope those bastards don't come back," he mumbled, jaw clenched. "How bad are you hit?"

"My legs," said Tom.

Dunnett was holding a hand to his belly, blood coursing between his fingers.

Above the racket of shooting still going on in the wood, Tom heard shouted commands from the direction of the second German line. He peered over Toby's withers and saw a detachment formed up with fixed bayonets, marching toward him, close enough that he could make out the rank insignia on their grey uniforms.

He dropped down. "Buggers want to finish us off."

Wishing he had held onto his Webley, he turned to see Dunnett crawling away. Tom wondered where he was going, then saw what Gus was up to. A German Mauser lay on the ground ten feet away. Dunnett stayed flat, propelling himself with his legs and one arm. Finally he stretched and managed to reach the rifle, pushing it stock first toward Tom who leaned out to grasp it.

Tom quickly checked the weapon over, sliding back the bolt and inspecting the chamber. Empty. But the magazine had at least two rounds in it, maybe more. Muddy but serviceable. Hoping for the best, he looked over Toby's body.

The German detachment had covered much of the intervening ground and was no more than fifty yards away. Tom tried but failed to get his left arm up on Toby's body to form a rest and grasp the forestock of the rifle. Dropping the weapon to the ground, he lifted his left arm with his right, placing it on Toby's rib cage. Everything went black for a second or two as pain shot into his shoulder and neck.

Picking up the rifle with his right hand, he lodged it in his left and pulled the stock to his shoulder. Open sights. He cycled a round into the chamber, focussed on the first enemy soldier that came into his line of sight, and fired. The man dropped. Tom pulled back the bolt to eject the empty shell and cycle in another round. He fired again. He missed. Slow down, he said to himself. Slow down, or you'll soon be dead.

God, get us through this, he thought, working the bolt one more time. Was this the end? He saw one of the Germans pointing at him, waving a pistol. An officer, or a noncom. Got you, he thought, and fired. The man went down, spun backward by the force of the bullet.

The German patrol wavered as another soldier fell. Someone besides Tom was firing at them, someone to his right, maybe from the wood. So at least some of the boys in there were still alive. The Germans turned and hurried back to their second line. Tom watched as they formed up and withdrew to the southeast, away from the forest, away from the scene of the battle. He shot once more, fearful that the enemy would yet return to finish off the wounded Canadians, and hit a man in the back. His companions left him where he fell as they marched away.

Left arm and shoulder on fire, legs numb and blood pounding in his brain, Tom let the Mauser drop and turned to lie with his back against his dead horse, his left arm cradled to his belly. Horses and men—his comrades—lay dead or dying, scattered across the grassy field. The battle in the wood continued, and stray rifle bullets still whined through the air.

How many dead? Not many survivors. He felt light-headed, but then the pain flared up through his legs again, pulling him back to his own terrible reality. Maybe he'd die right here, bleed to death in a Picardy field beside poor Toby.

His mind wandered to thoughts of home, Winnipeg, his family. Images of Ellen flared and faded, along with thoughts of jail and the Kravenko jailbreak. For some reason the young face of the blond German boy he had killed outside the listening post flashed in front of him.

It's over for a lot of the boys. And for me. I wasn't happy with one wound—now I've got more than enough. Dazed, he looked around for Dunnett. Gus was right beside him, turned on his side, facing Tom. His hand was no longer on his belly, and the blood no longer flowed. He was dead.

Poor bastard. He looked down at his own legs, splayed out in front of him, at Toby, lying still, at the other huddled shapes on the ground, men and horses. Poor bastards.

BLIGHTY

◆ ◆ ◆

"This one's gone," said a laconic voice.

"Leg wounds here. Give me a hand," said another.

Not sure if he was dreaming or conscious, Tom felt hands push him onto his side and roll him onto his back. Everything went black and silent; then he felt dizzy, as if he were in a bunk at sea, swaying and lurching—was he back aboard the *Cape Wrath*? Sudden agony in his legs made him try to move them, to sit up.

"Hold still, Sergeant," barked one of the voices.

Tom was on a stretcher, four men carrying him. He lay face up, fully booted and spurred. Spurred for sure—whenever the men at his feet let the sides of the stretcher sag together, the canvas bulged down with his weight, his legs dropped and his spurs dug into the ground, sending pain shooting through his calves.

The stretcher-bearers bent double as bullets still whipped through the air. As they passed a tree with a cluster of men around it, Tom could make out Lieutenant Harrower, back from his patrol, bent over Gordon Flowerdew who was slumped, back against the tree. He was waving off the men, who seemed to be urging him to get onto a stretcher.

"Wait," called Flowerdew. He lifted a hand. "Macrae—you'll be all right? You finished the charge?"

"Yes, sir. I finished the charge."

"A lot of the men didn't make it, did they?"

"No, a lot of them didn't," Tom almost sobbed to himself. He couldn't summon the strength to reply or to hold his head up to look around anymore, but as the bearers pushed on he saw tears streaking the battlefield grime on Flowerdew's face.

They took him to a horse-drawn wagon, pressed into service as an ambulance. The iron wheels and wooden spokes had no give to them, causing the other wounded stretched out beside him to groan with every bump. Two hours later he was in an aid station on yet another stretcher, a doctor in a blood-stained gown bending over him.

"Get the trousers and puttees off him. I'll be right back." A soldier cut away the field dressings that had been applied right over his clothing by the bearers. Next came puttees and trouser legs, followed by boot-laces, and then he eased off Tom's boots. They joined the heap of bloody clothing on the ground.

"You'd better look at my left arm, too." The sleeve of his tunic was added to the pile.

Tom shivered, his torso and right arm still in full uniform as it were, his other limbs exposed to the elements.

"Couldn't stay out of it, eh, Sergeant?" the orderly remarked.

"Guess not. How do my legs look?"

"Bad. Lots of wounds. What did you run into, a buzz saw?"

"Kaiser Bill's buzz saw."

The doctor returned and, after a quick look, called for disinfectant and bandages. A grimace flashed across his drawn face. Tom could see that his legs were masses of raw, torn flesh, the bandage on his arm blood-soaked. He lay back while the doctor cleaned his wounds, the pain worse by the minute. He gritted his teeth, but a moan escaped his lips.

The doctor looked at him sharply. "Morphine," he ordered.

As the drug took hold, Tom knew the pain was still there but felt less concern. In fact, there was really nothing to worry about. He drifted off, picturing himself paddling down the Red River in a glowing sunset.

"Strange thing, Sergeant. Lucky," said the doctor, snapping Tom back to Picardy. "Large number of wounds. Didn't actually count them. But they're all in the flesh, the outside of your thighs and calves. No bony injury."

"Bully beef," said Tom, smiling to himself. He never wanted to eat the stuff again as long as he lived, but those cans of beef in his saddlebags had saved his legs.

The calm river scene slowly changed. The night grew darker. Tom was still in his canoe. Ellen was in the bow, facing away from him. He called her name, but she did not turn. Looking down, he saw stumps of legs. He muttered, fighting the oncoming darkness in his mind, forcing his eyes open, to face the darkness of the night in northern France. The morphine was wearing off, and Tom lay sweating under a canvas roof.

Tom remembered Ellen's words about the war-shattered, armless sergeant, spoken so long ago in Winnipeg: "I don't have to spend my life with Sergeant Grey. A few hours a day is one thing—a lifetime is another."

He was conscious when they moved him to an ambulance forwarding station, and later loaded him on a train. Hope they stopped the bleeding. Don't want to bleed out. In spite of himself he dozed whenever he was left alone, dreaming of advancing Germans. He had the Mauser in his hands, but it was empty.

◆　◆　◆

Within days he was in England, at Number Four Canadian Hospital, Basingstoke. They had sedated him again on arrival and when he came out of it he was feverish, with nerve-shattering pain in his legs. A uniformed nurse with a clipboard and pencil waited while a white-coated figure inspected his wounds and sniffed.

"Gas gangrene," said the doctor. "Surgery this afternoon."

Tom struggled to sit up. "No surgery."

"I'll be the judge of that, Sergeant. Your left arm will be all right for now—don't know what the final condition will be but it's not infected. Lucky there. But," he went on, "your calves have numerous wounds, and the flesh is virtually stripped from the outside of your thighs. Your right leg is particularly bad. It may have to come off if we're to save your life."

"Then no surgery. I'll not go back a legless man. You'll have to fight me to get me under."

"Let me explain things to you, soldier. When you get shot on the battlefield, the bullets carry with them bits of clothing that get left in your body. Your uniform is caked with mud and animal and human excrement—shit, Sergeant—that carries with it the bacteria that cause gas gangrene. Those bacteria are multiplying in your legs even as we speak. The only way to beat it is to expose it to air—to cut into your legs and debride—gouge out the infection."

"What if it's in deep?"

"Doesn't matter—the procedure's the same. We make a hole right through the limb if we have to, keep it open for days to try to kill the bacteria. Then we cut out the infection and try to heal the wound. Amputation is a last resort, but it might be the only choice. We'll decide once we're in there. You're lucky," he added. "If your wounds were in your torso you'd be dead, because then we can't cut out the infection without doing more harm than good."

"You'll not take my legs."

The doctor turned to the nurse, who looked tired. "He knows the score. Surgery this afternoon. If he fights it, put someone else in his place. We have plenty more where he came from." Turning on his heel he left the room, the nurse trailing him.

♦ ♦ ♦

Tom was adamant. They had him in the operating room, the surgeon had his mask on, and an anaesthetist waited with his bottle of ether and pad of gauze. But Tom wouldn't let anyone near him, for fear they'd put him out and he'd wake up a legless man.

The surgeon's eyes narrowed. "All right. We'll do this the hard way." He spoke to two orderlies who stood with arms folded. "Strap him down. Can't have you jumping around, can we, Sergeant?"

They strapped him down, securing his torso, feet, and arms with wide canvas strips and leather cinches. The surgeon sliced Tom's bandages from ankle to crotch, then peeled them back, first one leg and then the other. Tom groaned, teeth clamped, lips apart in a grimace.

"Give him something to chew on, or he'll break his teeth." The doctor nodded at a nurse.

The nurse put a hand on Tom's brow, calming him. "Open wide," she said, reminding Tom of his mother when she fed his younger brothers. She put a short piece of thick rubber tubing between his teeth.

Tom's body jerked, muscles seizing up, as the doctor cut away at green flesh. "The sooner he passes out, the quicker we can be done," the surgeon commented.

But Tom didn't pass out. He tried to concentrate on dots on the ceiling, anything other than the reality of the present: the smell—blood, ether, rotting flesh; the doctor's monosyllabic demands—scalpel, suture, gauze; his teeth—making the rubber tubing squeak; his grinding jaw muscles, which spasmed with a pain that was like a flea bite compared to the pain in his legs. That felt as though a bear was tearing at his living flesh.

It was an hour before he was back on the ward. A nurse gave him a shot of morphine, and he slept.

◆ ◆ ◆

Tom had a second surgery, and a third. He accepted anaesthetic, for the last one, because the surgeon, Smythe, told him he thought the infection was beaten and they were trying to promote healing of the wounds themselves. For now, at least, amputation was not part of the equation. Tom had skin grafts. A new technique, he was told. He couldn't tell where the skin came from, although a nurse told him it looked like pigskin, which made him wonder if in fact it had come from a pig. That would make a good story, if he ever made it out of there.

A wound on his right thigh up near his hip would not heal. They put him out again, and when he came to he was in agony, which became unbearable over the next four hours. Dr. Smythe was summoned, and he pulled back the dressing.

"Thought I'd try something different," he explained in his clipped fashion. "Gunshot wound, debrided earlier. Insufficient skin. Used catgut to stretch the remaining skin to cover the gap. Long stitches, then pulled tight. Much like lacing up a boot, really." He ran his fingers over the area where he had operated. Tom's pale skin was as hard as a drumhead. The surgeon flicked it with a forefinger; Tom jumped.

"Infection's back, and that's not going to work." Smythe grasped a loose end of the catgut, wrapped it around his middle finger, and pulled sharply. Tom's hip lifted two inches off the bed; infected skin and surrounding flesh tore loose. Sweat popped out on his forehead, and he fell back, quivering, lips clamped.

"Tough guy, eh?" said the surgeon. He peered at the mass of yellow pus and red flesh that dangled from the catgut in his hand. "We'll do what we can for the infection. This got some of it," he said, and looked approvingly at the oozing gap in Tom's hip.

◆　◆　◆

Ellen sat in front of her dressing table and regarded the face that looked back from the mirror. No longer a girl, but a young woman in her early twenties. Blue eyes, brown hair with golden highlights when the sun shone on it, pleasant features, if she did say so herself. Good posture, healthy as a horse. She should be happy.

She sat, irresolute. Her father was pushing her to make a decision about Harry. Harry was persistent, insisting they had a future together. She had held him at bay for months now but wondered if she had it in her to continue to do so. Tom's letters had nearly stopped, once she had told him she didn't know what to do. And she truly didn't; she was only trying to be honest with him. They had had such a brief time together. Her one photo of him, taken in uniform just before he left for England, was right in front of her, tucked into the frame of her mirror. Even with that to help, after nearly four years she had trouble conjuring up the sound of his voice, the feel of his hands on hers. The right upper drawer of the table was open, and in it she could see Harry's ring, still lying where she had placed it.

Male voices drifted up from the ground floor where Ned, Ellen's brother, was grumbling at his wife, Joan, and their infant daughter. It was late afternoon but even so, his voice was already slurred. The little girl started to cry, then fell silent. Ellen could picture Joan comforting the child.

A few moments later she heard footsteps approach, followed by a tentative knock on the half-open door.

"Come in," she called, closing the drawer as Joan entered. Her sister-in-law walked over to put a hand on Ellen's shoulder. Ellen moved over on her bench, patting the seat beside her. "Sit down, Joan. Am I holding everyone up?"

"Not so anyone would notice." Joan's face was prematurely etched with deep lines, her often-grave mien even more pronounced than usual.

Now what, wondered Ellen, just as she noticed Joan had a folded newspaper in her hand. "What's that?"

"Not good news, I'm afraid." Joan handed the paper to Ellen, who hesitated but took it in her hands. The paper had been folded to the second page, displaying a photo of Tom, a copy of the one on her mirror. The caption screamed at her:

WINNIPEG SOLDIER WOUNDED

Mr. and Mrs. Wm. Macrae of East Kildonan have been informed their son Thomas has been severely wounded in France. Sergeant Macrae, pictured above, was injured at Moreuil Wood while serv-ing with the Canadian Cavalry Brigade.

Ellen gasped as she clenched the paper in her hand, shaking it angrily. "It can't be true. It can't." She flung it from her, knocking bottles and jars from her dressing table. Joan put her arms around her.

201

Ellen let herself be held for a moment, then broke loose and stood to pace the room. The anger eased, and guilt rocked her. My God, how could I lose faith in Tom, how could I think about not waiting for him? I haven't written, I've left him alone. Now he may be dying. She stopped her pacing and stared out the window, where a late spring threatened snow.

Joan rose, once again putting an arm around the younger woman. "I'm sure Tom can fight his own battles, Ellen. There's nothing you can do for him, so far away. You may not want to hear this, but really, you should think about yourself. Your father has your best interests at heart. He jokes and says he wants you to settle down before he's too old to enjoy grandchildren. God knows he won't get any more from Ned and me."

Joan walked to the door, then stopped and turned back. "I'm going downstairs, Ellen, and I'll just say this once. Before this damned war, I saw a world-beater of a man off to England. You remember what Ned was like. But it wasn't Ned who came home to me, it was a shadow. Don't let that happen to you." She left, softly closing the door behind her.

Ellen knew Joan was right about Ned: he was not the man he had been. He had not been able to work once his wounds healed, nor had he adapted to the fact that he could no longer walk. An air of self-pity pervaded all his thoughts and conversations. Wheelchair-bound, he was less than a man in his own mind and he was drinking far too much for his own good. The family's efforts to make him face up to his problems with alcohol had been shrugged off.

Ellen resumed her pacing. She had to decide. She thought she had done the right thing, telling Tom about her indecision, but perhaps that had been wrong. She simply must face up to the decision that only she could make. Harry was everything she could want: handsome, good prospects, as her father reminded her on numerous occasions, up-and-coming in society. He'd be good to her. So would Tom, if he was able, if he was the same man, in spite of his wounds. Assuming he survived.

She walked absently to her window, where she saw bright crystals of snow floating from a partly blue sky. Unconsciously clasping her hands, she stared at the falling flakes, lit from the side by late rays of sunshine. She smiled, her mind turning to a nearly forgotten earlier snow shower, just before Belle had unceremoniously dumped her, face down in the snow.

Her brother's querulous voice, expressing some complaint that she could not make out, was enough to distract her. She frowned, then, purposefully returning to her dressing table, she picked up her fountain pen, placed her stationery squarely in front of her, and began to write. She didn't stop until she had completed two letters, which she sealed in envelopes and addressed, one to Harry and one to Tom.

◆ ◆ ◆

Through the window, Tom saw larches waving in the Hampshire breeze. He looked around the ward and counted twenty beds, mostly men with missing limbs or other severe wounds. The man on his left, who was named Sykes, had no right arm. Sykes would sit, if the orderlies propped him up, but he wouldn't respond to questions and would not feed himself.

In charge of the ward was Clara Duncan, an English girl, although most of the nurses were Canadian. Clara was only twenty, a young woman with an open, freckled face who did her best to be reserved with the men.

Tom asked Clara about Sykes, and she told him Sykes, who was from rural Ontario, had been wounded in an artillery barrage. "He's only spoken once since he's been here," Clara whispered. "Said, 'How am I going to milk the cows?'"

Tom thought back to Sergeant Grey, who had lost both arms. "Maybe he could do something else."

"We get a lot of them," said Clara. "Sometimes they're not even wounded. 'Shellshock' they're calling it, from all the explosions. It's almost as if they're not here anymore."

She looked around, leaned close to Tom, and said, in such a low voice that he could hardly hear her, "It drives some of the senior officers crazy. They think the men are faking."

Tom remembered his first time in the trenches, when the artillery pounded without letup, the terror that blossomed like a poison, clinging even after the barrage had lifted. Sykes reminded him of some of the troops they had replaced, men who had been under constant shelling for days. He had wondered at the time if they'd be able to force themselves back into the front lines when their turn came up again; he had wondered if he himself would be able to face it again.

Clara told Tom what she had read in the newspapers about the Canadian cavalry during the days and weeks he had been convalescing. Moreuil Wood had changed hands several times after the Canadians had fought the Germans to a standstill; the area was still the scene of heavy fighting days after Flowerdew's charge. Flowerdew had been awarded a posthumous Victoria Cross, the Empire's highest award for bravery. It was said he would not leave the field of battle until his men were looked after. Tom remembered his last sight of the lieutenant, waving off assistance that might have saved him, grieving over the staggering number of men killed or wounded in the charge he had led.

Tom had never aspired to a commission, had always identified with the common soldier, but at times he felt a grudging respect for the commanders at all levels, who accepted their role in this ugly war, leading or pushing men to their deaths. "Generals die in bed" was the common expression, but junior officers seldom did.

When Tom arrived on the ward the soldier in the bed to his right had moaned constantly. The nurses were feeding him morphine like there was no tomorrow, and maybe for him there wasn't. After a few days the moaning eased off. The soldier told Tom his name was Romeo, home town Toronto. He talked as if his mouth was wired shut.

"You don't look much like a Romeo," remarked Clara Duncan, who happened to be walking by.

"You want to try me out? Want to play Juliet?" Romeo had mumbled.

"Now, soldier, don't get yourself excited," Clara laughed as she left the room.

Romeo's head was bandaged. Only his right eye peeped out and he seemed to have a stiff neck. When he sat up he swung his whole body hard left so he could see Tom. "Don't get any smart ideas, Macrae. I been asked 'How is Juliet?' more times than you've been to the can. Hey—where you wounded?"

"The legs."

"Lucky. Damn Fritz got me in the left side of the head. Bullet went in my earhole and out my eye. Could have been worse—could have been my asshole." Romeo shook with laughter, then groaned. "Hurts when I laugh," he said, his voice pinched between gritted teeth. "Where's that nurse gone? Nurse!"

A nurse came and administered an injection. Romeo muttered to himself from inside his bulky dressings and dozed off.

A few days later, Tom was awakened from a troubled sleep by Clara. "You have a visitor."

It was Bruce Johanson. Tom had last seen him in the charge, way off to the right, close to the wood itself. He had to blink back tears at the sight of his comrade.

"How you doing, Tommy? They say you got a lot of holes in you."

"Yes. I do, for sure. I'm still fighting infection. They scrape it out of one place and it pops up in another. What about you, Cowboy?"

"Well, I got through the charge in one piece. I swerved into the bush. No sooner got there than Fritz popped up from behind a log and shot me clean through the left hand." Bruce held up his hand for Tom to see. It was misshapen, the skin scarred and puckered, but he wiggled his fingers. "It got infected and I've just been cleared to go back. Not too bad. Say—have you heard about Seely?"

"No. Nothing."

"He's out of it. Got gassed. And the regiment has been moved into reserve again." He leaned closer to Tom. "Word is there'll be a major breakout soon."

"There's always going to be a major breakout."

"Yes, but this time they figure Fritz has shot his bolt. Maybe there really *is* an end in sight."

"I'll believe it when I see it. What about the other boys?" Tom asked.

Bruce frowned. "Right after the charge I was sent off with the other wounded, too, so I'm not totally up to date. But what was left of the regiment attacked Rifle Wood, just a couple of miles from Moreuil. They were awful battered and shorthanded, as you can imagine. They went in dismounted, along with the Fort Garrys. Quartermain was somewhere out in front when he caught some shrapnel. They say he'll survive."

Tom hesitated. He didn't want to ask. "Ferguson?"

"You won't believe it! Fritz got an artillery piece into play during our charge, and they fired off a couple of rounds in the midst of the confusion until they were put out of action by rifle fire from our boys in the wood. One of their shells hit somebody bang on, right next to Ferguson. Blew Fergie right out of his saddle. They found him later, unconscious. Not a mark on him. One boot torn off and his uniform burned black in spots. He didn't know what had happened."

Relief flooded Tom. Better than a shot of morphine after a bad night. "Where is he now?"

"He said he was sick and tired of being shot at, so he volunteered for the machine gun brigade. He's there now, riding around on a truck with a Vickers machine gun, doing the shooting!"

"Hard to picture him in a truck and not on a horse. What's next for you, Bruce?"

"I'm back to the regiment tomorrow. I'll say hello to the boys for you."

"Speaking of boys, did Simpson make it?"

"He was real lucky. Took a piece of shrapnel in the ribs. He was knocked off his horse and would have died except that one of the 2nd Troop, Lieutenant Harvey's bunch, dragged him into the woods in spite of the German fire and stopped the bleeding. He's somewhere in England in hospital, too."

Damn few of the troop left, but Tom didn't pursue the issue. He had heard earlier that Reynolds, who had been wounded in the listening post, had been invalided back to Canada. He tried to avoid thinking about the carnage in specific detail, and he knew Johanson didn't need reminding about numbers killed or wounded. He'd be back in that brutal reality within days or even hours.

Bruce looked sombre, then brightened. "Hell, I'll get another crack at the Boche. Damn glad I don't have to hang around here and play pinochle like some people. I've got to go. My train awaits me." He smiled, clapping his cap on at a jaunty angle and sticking out his good hand. Tom shook it with both of his. Bruce swallowed and nodded once, turned on his heel and left without another word.

I wonder if I'll see him again. Maybe Bruce was thinking the same thing. For a moment Tom felt a pang of guilt, lying in a bed in England while the regiment's survivors carried on the war.

Nurse Duncan bustled into the ward and pulled back the blanket. "Dressing change!" she announced, and Tom watched as she peeled off the sticky bandages. He still had a few battles of his own to fight.

♦ ♦ ♦

Tom's wounds slowly improved. The smaller ones healed over, and his skin grafts finally took hold. Day by day the gangrene and the nightmare of surgeries with no anaesthetic faded from conscious thought, although he still had great raw gashes below his right hip, on his calves and left thigh. My very own craters, he thought. The same shape as the ones that dotted France, eighty-metre-wide holes that marked where tunnellers had blown up enemy dugouts, trenches, and soldiers.

Tom wrote to his parents. He passed on what the doctors told him: that he'd be wheelchair bound for years, perhaps walk again but maybe not. His father wrote back to say he had given up the option the family had obtained for a fresh start on a farm in the Peace River country. He no longer had the stomach for new ventures if his eldest son could not be at his side. Tom's mother was not well, but she was coping. There was no mention of Ellen.

"Hey, trooper. It can't be that bad." It was Clara, a smile on her face. The hospital staff put on cheerful countenances for the patients and Tom sometimes wondered what it cost them, given the dire condition of many of their charges. Patients like poor armless Sergeant Grey in the Winnipeg hospital, so long ago. A painful memory of Ellen, putting on a brave face as she ministered to him, came flooding back.

"No, it's not that bad," said Tom, "especially when I think of some of these other poor buggers."

"Well, whatever it is, my guess is it could be helped by a pint of bitters. Are you up to it?"

"Do bears have claws?"

"I'll be back at shift change. Get ready for some excitement, soldier. We're off to the local. I'll be here with your chariot."

An orderly, Herbert, appeared right after supper was cleared away. "I hear you have an appointment. Let's get at it then." He hauled Tom's greatcoat out of the storage locker.

"I'm not going out in this," said Tom, pulling at his gown. "Get me some trousers and a shirt."

"You're crazy, Canuck. Doctor would not approve."

"Doctor's not here. Get me some trousers."

Herbert came back with an oversized pair of khaki trousers and a checked shirt he had found somewhere. Tom wrestled his gown off. When he glanced down he was appalled at the sight of his emaciated body—his muscles atrophied, flesh sagging; he looked like his bloody grandfather.

Tom put on the shirt. Herbert helped ease his legs off the bed and with much headshaking and tut-tutting, guided the pants on. Tom hoisted his buttocks up off the bed by pushing down with his hands, and Herbert slid the trousers under him and up to his waist. As Tom did up his buttons sweat broke out on his forehead.

Romeo, now with some of his bandages removed, boosted himself upright in the next bed and cackled through his wired jaw, "Hey, Tommy-boy, you better behave yourself with our Clara."

Herbert brought the wheelchair alongside the bed and once again took part of the weight as Tom shifted to the chair from the edge of the bed.

Someone from down the row of beds yelled, "I've got seniority here. I saw her first, you Red River bastard."

"Maybe, but I'm going to be on my feet first."

"Now why would you want to be on your feet?"

Raucous laughter broke out and came to an abrupt halt as Clara walked into the ward, wearing a green civilian coat over a long brown skirt.

"What's the joke, boys?" she asked.

"Just enjoying the camaraderie of the common soldier, Nurse," Romeo replied.

"Mind your manners, Mr. Romeo," said Clara. "Perhaps you too will get out of your bed and off to the pub one of these days."

There were whistles and barely heard comments from the ward as Clara wheeled Tom toward the door, and he gave a wave over his shoulder to the catcalls of the remaining patients. All except Sykes, who never looked up.

Tom wheeled himself, with a lot of help from Clara, to the steps outside the public bar of the Iron Duke. It had been a rough ride for Tom and a hard push for Clara, bouncing along the cobblestones of the High Street.

"Hang on, love. Shan't be long." She went in through the door and was back a moment later with two older men.

"This him, then?" asked one. "Ready for a lift, Canada?"

Clara held the door open while the men each took a side of the chair and lifted Tom up the stairs. He wheeled himself in through the door to breathe deeply of the marvellous, pungent aromas of pipe tobacco and freshly drawn beer.

Clara pulled a chair out of the way so Tom could manoeuvre his wheelchair alongside a battered oak table, yellow with age, and then went to the bar while he looked around. The pub was dark, the windows few and small, its walls decorated with bits of harness and paintings of horses. Tom's mind flashed to the horses lost to the war, hundreds of thousands of them. He felt a sadness and a bitter edge that was new to him. A few men stood at the bar, and six or seven others were seated at tables nursing their pints. All the men were middle-aged or older.

Clara returned with a pint of dark ale for Tom and a small lager for herself. She sat and raised her glass. "Here's to a quick recovery," she said, clinking her glass against his.

Tom sipped the dark liquid, his first alcohol since Blanshard had given him a shot of rum just before the charge. A familiar feeling of warmth flooded through him. Maybe he *was* on the road to recovery.

He slowly became aware that he was the centre of attention in the pub. The last time he had been in an English pub, he and his mates had also been the centre of attention. They were big and boisterous, loud and confident. Somewhat exotic. Colonials, the Brits called them. He didn't feel boisterous now, or exotic.

Clara looked at him, touched his hand where it clutched his glass. Tom saw a figure approaching, and glanced up to see the "governor," the owner of the pub, out from behind the bar, a pint in his hand.

"Compliments of the squire." The governor nodded toward the saloon bar in the adjoining room where the gentry and their ladies sat and were served. As he put the pint on the table, Tom saw an elderly man in a tie and tweed jacket, who raised his glass and nodded.

Tom lifted his glass in return, and drank.

"That's Squire Barkley. He owns half the town," said Clara.

"That's decent of him."

"He lost his only son in France. He'd likely buy for anyone in uniform, but your Canada badges help, I expect. Coming to the rescue of the Old Country and all."

A painting of the Duke of Wellington on horseback hung over the bar. The duke gazed, stern-faced, at a field where a square of red-coated British infantry was surrounded by the blue and grey of a Napoleonic horde. How times have changed, Tom thought. Ranks of infantrymen firing muskets at each other from ranges of fifty or seventy-five yards had given way to the five-hundred-round-a-minute machine guns of the Great War. Artillery killed and maimed at impossible ranges, but at times the fighting still came down to crazed men, face to face. Stabbing and clubbing, blood flowing.

Clara sipped at her half-pint. "Tell me what you did before you enlisted."

Tom pulled his mind back to the present. "I was on my way to a career in the law, until it caught up with me."

"Now what does that mean?"

"Just that there was a mixup, and I came out of it on the wrong end."

"Will you go back to practising law?"

"Not for all the tea in China. I don't know what I'll do, but I won't do that." The words slipped out before he even thought about them. When he had dared consider his future, and the possibility of surviving the war, the question of his career had hovered at the edge of his consciousness. For a long time he had not been sure but now, suddenly, he was, and he felt as though he had floated free from a weight that was dragging him down. As far as he was concerned the law was arbitrary and lawyers were untrustworthy. He was done with it.

"So what will you do?"

"Depends on how long it takes for me to get out of this chair. How did you end up as a nurse? Are you from around here?"

"No. I was raised in Devon down on the south coast." Clara looked around the room, then back at Tom. "I was engaged to be married. He enlisted. Jeremy and I—we all thought it would be over by Christmas. He used to write something every week. Now he writes once a month, if at all. It's too depressing." She tossed her head as if to dispel her mood.

She had let her hair down from the tight bun she wore at the hospital and it was a blonde cascade that swept her shoulders, much lighter than it looked when it was confined.

Clara and Tom talked about the men in Tom's ward, keeping the conversation breezy. Tom breathed in her faint perfume, which somehow hung in the air, lingering and cutting through the thickening smoke in the room. She had taken her coat off, and he basked in the presence of a woman, the tension in his body and mind easing. He was reminded of his lunch with Ellen in the Royal Alex back in Winnipeg. Would they do that again?

Later, Clara trundled him through the quiet village in the direction of the hospital.

"Don't spare the horses," Tom said, out of the blue.

"What?"

"These cobbles are awful hard on my condition."

"Condition?"

"Condition. I drank a lot of beer and stayed stuck in this bloody chair. I appreciate the effort, but I've got to get back and find Herbert to give me a hand, quick."

"Oh, you poor man," Clara laughed, and pushed faster.

She summoned Herbert as soon as she got Tom up the ramp and into the lobby and Tom, to his intense relief, was wheeled into a washroom and assisted out of the chair. Hell of an end to the evening, he thought, his head spinning from the effects of the unaccustomed beer.

When he made it back to the ward he was happy to be greeted by snores from the ranks of his fellow wounded. Herbert helped him get out of his clothes and he collapsed, exhausted, into a dreamless sleep.

♦　♦　♦

Tom heard from his mother. The word in Winnipeg was that Ellen was engaged to a new man in town. He wished again he hadn't ripped up her last letter. Maybe he could glean from it a sliver of hope that she would not go through with this marriage—if that's what was actually happening. But he didn't have the letter, and he was left with the crucial line, which he could remember all too clearly: "I'm sorry, Tom, but you have been away so long. I feel I've waited half my life."

He chafed at his confinement, thousands of miles from home where he could have done something about Ellen. One day he would be hopeful, vowing to get back to Winnipeg, determined to obliterate all obstacles and make her his own. The next he would feel beaten down, fretting about his wounds and unsure he'd ever walk again. Hell, she might even be married by now.

He wrote to her, just this one last time, he promised himself. He vacillated about mailing the letter but finally asked Herbert to post it for him. "Hope to be home soon, as soon as I can get the docs to clear me for travel and His Majesty finds room for me on a ship."

The newspapers trumpeted Allied advances, and rumours flew around the hospital. A final push. German collapse. Heavy fighting, heavy losses. The war would be over tomorrow, the war would be over by Christmas. Tom had heard it all before and discounted most of it. Behind the stories, he knew, the fighting went on, and men died. More hospitals were being opened, existing ones expanded. Ambulances came and went. Ambulances and hearses.

Tom asked Clara to go with him for a walk around the village on her next day off, and she agreed. It was a beautiful summer Sunday, a few clouds in the sky adding to the lustre of the scene, with its blue sky, green meadows, and villagers enjoying a quiet day. Wanting to test himself, Tom had held off on his painkillers. For the first hour, as they made their way along hard-packed paths and quiet streets, he was able to propel himself, but slowly the pain in his legs forced its way into his awareness.

"I can't make the connection," he blurted irritably. "I know damn well men are getting blown up or shot to bits in France and Belgium, but you'd never think it looking around here."

"I sometimes have the same feeling. But, you know, it's not like that. People look normal, but they're all suffering. It's been four years of war. Everybody I know has lost family members."

She's right, Tom thought. I'm letting it get to me. I shouldn't be whining; I won't be fighting again. But what about Bruce, and Gordon Ferguson, and . . .

"I've overdone it," he muttered, pain crowding out his thoughts. "Can you take over?"

Clara pushed him back to the hospital, where he was happy to take the painkillers when the duty nurse came to see him.

◆　◆　◆

On their next afternoon foray, Romeo went with them. Tom was able to wheel himself along, and Clara pushed Romeo, who was propped up in his chair with pillows. At Tom's request, she had brought a bottle of rum and three glasses. They found a secluded place by the edge of the common overlooking a pond, and Tom poured them each a tot.

Romeo had progressed to where he could eat liquefied food, but he was deaf in one ear and very weak. It was obvious his soldiering days were over; as soon as he was strong enough he'd be discharged. They toasted his survival and watched ducks paddling in the still water. Buzzing insects, the quiet scene, and the rum combined to make Romeo doze off, his head tilting to rest on a pillow.

Almost by accident, it seemed to Tom, Clara kissed him. He tasted the warmth of her mouth on his, her breath sweetened by the rum.

◆　◆　◆

A new nurse named Sheila Standing appeared, a no-nonsense type with short hair and strong hands. She wheeled Tom to an exercise room where she gave him light dumbbells to exercise his arms and shoulders. His legs, though, could not be exercised, not until his grafts and open wounds had more time to heal.

He developed bedsores, open fissures in his skin caused by the pressure of his body on the bed, made worse because his circulation was impaired by damaged blood vessels in his legs. A team of doctors and students came to examine him.

"You see the problem," the chief surgeon, Smythe, pontificated. "A healthy man to start with, and we were able to beat the gas gangrene."

Sure you did, you son of a bitch, Tom growled to himself. If I had let the sawbones have their way, I wouldn't have any legs at all.

The younger doctors crowded around and stared at Tom's exposed legs, scarred and scabbed from ankles to hips, the remaining open wounds lightly dressed.

"Now, gentlemen, a new problem. Bedsores. So it's a balancing act for . . ." he glanced at the chart in his hand, ". . . Macrae here. We'll need to get him up, move him around, do what we can for circulation. Ease the pressure on the sores. But not interfere with healing."

He gestured to Nurse Standing. "Get him up every day. Gentle exercise. Ease pressure on the legs but protect the wounds."

Tom spent as many hours a day as he could out in the fresh air, in his chair, a blanket over his lap against the cooling fall air. At times he was distracted by activity in distant fields, where he saw farmers hauling hay for winter forage. He read dozens of books provided to the hospital patients by the local library. Clara went on leave to visit her parents in Devon.

Tom's mates on the ward changed. Wisecracking Romeo was discharged to a different hospital and would soon be on his way home. Sykes was gone, never having spoken again. Clara had commented it was real shame: how would his family cope with him? Tom was now one of the healthier men on the ward and he wanted out, but an officer told him he'd only be shipped home once he was healed.

Clara came back from her leave, and after a night shift she sat with Tom in a secluded corner of the hospital grounds. It was a clear, early fall morning, leaves fluttering to the ground. She was solemn and thoughtful.

"How was Devon?" Tom asked.

"Devon was fine. But it took me back to a different reality, to things outside the hospital. This time it really hit me, how many people are living a normal life out there. But I don't need that right now. I need to concentrate on my work." She thought a moment. "I've heard nothing from Jeremy for two months. He may be dead. He may be like Sykes."

Tom's heart melted. He wished he could comfort her, but he wasn't sure how. "Don't assume anything about Jeremy, Clara. There could be a hundred reasons why he hasn't written. Maybe he has, and the letters have been lost." His words sounded hollow even to him.

"Sometimes I wish we had married. I'd have something to hold on to."

Tom felt bereft, her words reflecting his own thoughts of Ellen. They sat in silence for a few minutes, then Clara stood.

Tom reached over and took her hand. "It'll work out." He certainly hoped so, for both of them.

"Good luck, Canada," she said, as she turned, slowly walking away up the path to the hospital.

◆ ◆ ◆

"All right, soldier, let's have you then." Sheila Standing, the exercise nurse, loomed over his bed. Standing. Tom was sure there was a joke there somewhere, but it eluded him for the moment. His name must have been at the top of her list of victims, because she was at his bedside each day before he had finished breakfast. She whipped back his blanket and sheet and whisked him into his chair, her sturdy frame and square, business-like hands manoeuvring his emaciated body with ease.

"They sure raise skinny kids in Canada," she snorted.

"Canadian kids aren't used to English food," Tom snapped. "And I can wheel myself."

"While I'm looking after you, I do the wheeling," Standing laughed, with a breezy shake of her head as they went flying down a hall to an elevator.

On the ground floor, she swept him into a large room with windows that looked out on a courtyard garden, all close-clipped green lawn and well-tended flower beds. "Welcome to the torture chamber. After a week here you'll be begging to be sent back to the front."

Tom doubted that.

She wheeled him up to an apparatus with assorted handgrips, and rails that ran parallel at various heights. Locking his chair in place, she guided his hands to grasp overhead bars. "Pull yourself up."

Tom tightened his grip and pulled on the bars, slowly easing himself up to a standing position, spindly legs shaking. Sheila helped him maintain his balance for a few seconds, then eased him back down.

"Not bad," she noted.

"Not bad? I thought it was excellent."

She unlocked his wheels and swung him into the open. Sitting on a low stool, she stretched out his legs, one at a time. Then, on her instructions, he bent them as far as he could while she provided gentle assistance.

Massage of feet, calves, and thighs followed. Tom had almost no feeling in much of his legs, but they did start to tingle after a half-hour of manipulation. They throbbed as her efforts went on, and by the time she ran him up to his ward again he felt drained.

The worst of Tom's bedsores improved, and the smaller ones healed, leaving discoloured patches on his battered legs. Sheila worked on him for the first hour of every day, careful not to overstretch his healing wounds. At the end of every session, she helped him to his feet, steadied him, and handed him crutches. He could stand, legs shaking with the effort, for half a minute. Then it was into his chair and back to the ward.

Clara dropped by to tell him she had requested a hospital posting closer to home. Later the same day, Matron came to see him. A short, stout woman with a commanding air, she deferred only to doctors and not always to them. She stood at the foot of Tom's bed, clipboard in hand. A faint but distinct scent of carbolic soap and disinfectant wafted Tom's way. He had developed a grudging respect for her.

"Macrae," she intoned. "I see you've been making some progress in your condition. It has also come to my attention that you've been seeing rather too much of one of my nurses. There will be no more of that foolishness."

"Yes, Your Majesty," said Tom with a grin.

"Look here, soldier. What I say goes, in this facility. Out on the battlefield you may be a hero for all I know, but here you are a patient and you'll obey the rules." She waved an admonishing finger at him. "But that's not why I'm here. We need your bed. We have wounded soldiers in more need of care than you are and I've been instructed to clear out anybody who can be treated outside the hospital. Your government wants to ship home anybody not useful to the army. And that means you. Get your things organized—transport is arranged for 1300 hours today."

The matron made a note on her list and moved away like a full-rigged clipper ship, white uniform billowing, down the row of beds, to talk to other patients.

Tom's head swirled. He would be happy to be done with the hospital, the army, and the war. But this—this was too sudden. He wanted to be recovered from his wounds before he went home. He still had open lesions, pus draining from two of them, others not totally healed. And he couldn't walk.

Then it struck him—he was going home! In one piece! His heart pounded, and he threw back his covers. He'd need help. Where was Herbert? Where was his uniform?

The matron finished her rounds and approached Tom's bed on her way out of the ward. "What—you still here?" she asked, a mock frown on her face.

"Not for long, Matron. Where have you hidden my boots and saddle?"

"Never mind your nonsense. Ambulances will take you to a hospital at Southampton. They'll look after your medications. First class all the way, Sergeant. Maybe you'll get a ride on a proper liner, back to Canada."

"That or a cattle ship, I reckon."

WINNIPEG

◆ ◆ ◆

The trip to Southampton got off to a slow start. Staff at the army hospital had the anxious patients waiting a half-hour early, but it was two hours before four ambulances turned up. Besides the drivers there were two medical assistants, one of whom was a corporal in charge of the whole show. Tom wanted to exert some authority, so he wangled his way into the noncom's vehicle. Once they cleared the hospital grounds and were on the road, he talked the corporal into letting him ride up front, jammed between the driver and the corporal, whose name was Smith. Tom's legs hurt like hell, but the nurse on the ward had given him a shot of morphine, "to send you on your way," and the edge was off the pain.

Corporal Smith was a British Columbian, a casual sort who knew how lucky he was to be ferrying wounded around England and not dragging them out of No-Man's-Land. Tom persuaded him to order a stop at a pub when it opened at 1600 hours; he collected money from his fellow patients' pay-day savings and dispatched the amiable Smitty to purchase beer for all of them, plus a few extras to stave off any drying out that might occur during the remainder of the trip.

Another stop was made for pork pies, which fortunately were available at yet another pub where they replenished the beer supply. Tom felt on top of the world, and he didn't intend to let anything get him down. Smitty napped in the ambulance as they ground southwest toward Southampton. He had a document box with him and had told Tom it held medical records for the ambulance patients.

Tom had never seen any of his own records, so he took advantage of the opportunity and pulled out his file while Smitty slept. The driver saw what he was doing, but shrugged and ignored him.

The records were hard to follow, with pages of nearly illegible handwriting and obscure abbreviations. A diagnosis of "Multiple GSW both legs" he assumed meant gunshot wounds. He leafed through the loose sheets, and came to one headed "Prognosis."

Severe dislocation and damage to blood vessels. Currently wheelchair. May ambulate with assistance for a few years, then will require ongoing surgical attention. Amputation an option. Likely ongoing wheelchair afterward, with or without radical treatment.

He sat unseeing and crumpled the page, then smoothed it and read it again. A black mood grabbed him by the throat; he thought he'd pass out. He knew his legs were bad, but this was a shock. God, he thought, maybe it's true. He remembered the agony as he was carried off the battlefield, the surgery without anaesthetic, the pain that came with Nurse Standing's ministrations. A glance down at his emaciated legs, like sticks in his uniform trousers, confirmed the medical opinion.

But his mood shifted again. The bastards. Who the hell do they think they are? What does some quack know about what Tom Macrae would or would not be able to do?

Smitty woke up on the outskirts of Southampton and guided them to their destination in the blacked-out city. When they got to the hospital, it turned out to be a segregated portion of a large freight terminal, with makeshift facilities and a harried team of nurses tending to the patients.

The Canadians were assigned beds and examined by the staff. Two nurses, one with the ever-present clipboard and the other doing the work, told Tom that he and the others would be aboard ship by morning. They removed his bandages and examined his wounds. When they finished they left his legs exposed.

"We'll have Doctor check you out," said the tall one, not smiling.

Tom didn't like the sound of that.

A pale man in a white coat with a stethoscope around his neck came and looked at Tom. He tapped his chest and listened to his heart, and paid particular attention to his legs. "You're not going anywhere," he said. "Not with that infection."

◆ ◆ ◆

Tom missed the scheduled sailing date by two weeks: two weeks of relative calm in Southampton Hospital, where civilian nurses and doctors cleaned his wounds, applied sulpha drugs, and kept him still, with only loose dressings to allow healing. He wrote letters to his family but any mail coming the other way didn't catch up with him. The Canadian army seemed to have lost track of Sergeant Tom Macrae. His wounds healed slowly and were finally pronounced acceptable for travel by the pale young doctor, so once more he was sent off, this time to a passenger terminal. Peacetime posters on the wall touted Cunard liners, urging travellers to sail the blue Atlantic to the New World.

The SS *Berkley*, a ten-thousand-ton general cargo freighter converted to carry troops, was no Cunarder. Her hull was black riveted steel, her decks rusty under peeling paint. On October 12, 1918, she slipped from her berth and proceeded from Southampton en route to Halifax, carrying a mixed complement of wounded soldiers, German prisoners of war, and military personnel on duty.

The *Berkley*'s officers and crew were a fatalistic bunch. The constant threat of German U-boats and four years of non-stop trips back and forth across the Atlantic had worn them down. The bosun told Tom he had already survived one torpedoed ship and hated to go below decks in case he was trapped there by another attack.

Tom spent his days trying to distract himself from his physical pain. Sympathetic medical staff on board were willing to help, which meant he could have morphine when he needed it, but he tried to avoid it. He stayed on the upper deck as much as possible, his wheelchair braced against the funnel, gazing out at the North Atlantic, its familiar grey tones giving the lie to the posters in Southampton. The weather alternated between windy and cold, and windy, wet, and cold. When it was bad he was forced below, carried down by medical attendants, where he was wedged into his bunk for hours at a stretch with too much time to think about how things had changed for him.

One minute he had been a warrior, untouched physically by the war, in the prime of life, strong and healthy, albeit generally hungry. He knew his job and was rewarded for it by the respect of his subordinates and commanders alike. The regiment, with all its warts, was family. Now he was crippled, down to skin and bone. No prospects, his career long gone, no Ellen, no plan. He was determined he'd get back to health, but in darker moments he acknowledged to himself that he might never be whole again.

He may have lost Ellen, but hell, if she wasn't already married, there was still hope. And he hadn't actually lost his legs; they were still there, weren't they?

Tom was on the upper deck when a lookout shouted, "Land ho!" At first he saw nothing but the grey fog that enveloped the ship. Then a dark, low band coalesced, dreamlike, as the Nova Scotia shoreline appeared and disappeared in the billowing mist. One minute it was there, the next it was gone: his first sight of home, although not the hoped-for welcoming vista.

When they got alongside, Halifax was a drizzly, cold nightmare. Able-bodied passengers rushed ashore, but medical staff insisted all others be placed on stretchers, and they waited on the open deck for hours, fog condensing on their bedding. At last it was Tom's turn to be carried, feet first and shivering in sodden blankets, down the steep gangplank. He held onto the sides of the stretcher, resisting gravity, afraid he'd be dropped into the murky water of the harbour.

The wounded were deposited in a dockside shed, where another long wait ensued. No one paid any attention to the by-now thirsty and hungry men. Tom undid the straps that secured him to the stretcher, pushed back his blankets, and laboriously swung his feet down to the rough plank floor. Shivering, he was still cold but immediately felt better, just to be sitting up. He dug out and lit a cigarette, sharing his pack with the men around him.

At last the patients were transported to yet another hospital. There was no time to settle into a routine or get proper attention—the Halifax hospitals were jammed. Tom spent three days sleeping on his stretcher in a hall, feeling as though his legs were seizing up on him through lack of use. Harried officials would appear from time to time, checking off names on clipboards, avoiding questions from the grumpy veterans.

Finally the big day arrived, and Tom and two hundred other military personnel were trundled in ambulances and trucks to the main rail station. The chaotic scene was like something out of hell, locomotives belching steam onto passenger platforms jammed with people, mostly men in uniform. Attendants transferred Tom from his stretcher to a wheelchair and then to a lower berth, inadvertently forgetting to remove the wheelchair in the pandemonium of dealing with so many wounded men. Tom commandeered two ambulatory privates to help him out of the berth and into the wheelchair while they converted the bunk back to seating configuration. He had no intention of arriving in Winnipeg as a bedridden cripple; better the wheeled vehicle. After a maddening wait the carriage lurched slowly into motion, gliding out of the terminal and into the fading light of a frustrating day.

The next morning Tom was surprised when a familiar face came into view in the train corridor and shouted a greeting. His old friend Bill Reagan from the Fort Garry Horse pounded him on the back. Bill was missing his left forearm—he had been wounded on the same day as Tom. He had been on foot in Moreuil Wood when an artillery shell exploded a few yards away and had survived only because his horse was between him and the blast.

"I'll never forget that horse," he told Tom. "He was a walleyed son of a bitch, kept trying to kick me every time I saddled him up. Had to watch him all the time. Hell, he even tried to bite our adjutant one time during an inspection. Guess he wasn't all bad." He laughed between draughts on a bottle of rum he had smuggled on board, sharing it with Tom.

"Funny, though. I swear that horse calmed down all of a sudden and for five minutes before he bought it he followed me around like a dog. Now what would make a horse do that, all of a sudden? I tied him to a tree because he was getting in the way and I didn't want him shot. Makes you wonder, doesn't it?"

Tom thought about Toby, his last mount. Maybe his last ever. They had been together only a matter of days, but in those days they had done a lifetime of fighting, and more. Toby had carried him faithfully in numerous skirmishes and up the draw to the last battle either of them would see. They had pressed home their attack, and Toby had paid the ultimate price. Then, even in death, he had protected Tom.

"Hey, I guess you were there when Flowerdew earned his Victoria Cross?" Reagan asked.

"I was there."

"Did he know he was leading you into the teeth of the Germans? Or was it a surprise?"

"Damned if I know. For sure, I didn't see them until we galloped around the corner of the wood." Tom thought a minute. "He always did want to die a hero, if it came to dying." That reminded him of another ferocious VC warrior. "Last time I saw Lieutenant Harvey, he was on foot, going into the wood to take on the Germans in there. What have you heard of him?"

"Going strong. Still with the Straths."

◆ ◆ ◆

On the last night, Tom lay wide awake in his bunk. When he was younger, the train would put him to sleep, with its hypnotic rhythms. Now, he was aware of every lurch, every switch they clicked over. For three days he had gazed as if in a dream at the unfolding countryside. The woods and rivers of the Maritimes had given way to the cities of Quebec and

Ontario, and now to the dark green forests and granite-fringed lakes of the Canadian Shield.

The dream was coming to an end; the train was only a half day short of Winnipeg, where his family would be waiting. He pictured his mother as he had last seen her, tired from the cares of a large family, worn down by the death of his brother earlier. He hoped she'd feel better once he was home. His father would be puffing on a pipe, while his younger brothers and sister would be in their best clothes to welcome him home. Maybe they'd come on board to help him off. Not that he had much to carry: duffle bag, his wheelchair, his crutches. And himself. That might be the toughest part.

And what about Ellen? He'd have to get mobile so he could go see her, reassure her. He'd win her back again, if she hadn't done anything final and was not married already.

A mournful howl from the steam whistle up front told him they were crossing yet another country road, rattling through sparse, one-horse towns on the mainline north of Lake Superior. He stared at the bottom of the berth above him, where Bill Reagan's snores waxed and waned as he tossed around. Overheated air, redolent with men's breath, cigarette smoke, and alcohol fumes drifted across his face.

After leaving the Lakehead at Fort William the train picked up speed, and with it the atmosphere cleared. Many of the veterans were due to leave the train in Winnipeg, and for those going on there would be a short layover.

Bill paced up and down the passageway, stooping often to peer out the windows and identify landmarks. Most of the returning soldiers were disabled, some of them, like Bill, missing hands or feet. When the train left Halifax they had been excited; now, as many of them neared home, they were quiet, almost fearful, it seemed.

Tom too was nervous. He didn't know what he was going to do with his life. He was still in the army but presumably not for long.

Suddenly Reagan, at an open window, let out a yell. "St. Boniface! I can see the edge of town."

Tom sat as tall as he could, peering between the shoulders of the men on their feet who crowded the windows. He had an impression of buildings, then open space as the train crossed the Red River and eased the last quarter mile into the station.

Men leaned out of the train, waving and shouting, as the railcar gave a last jerk amid the dying squeal of brakes and the distant hiss of steam. Doors at both ends of the carriage banged open and the excited men charged off. Tom watched as the compartment cleared out. Reagan was the last to leave, and then there was silence.

He was trying to figure out how to get to his wheelchair, now stowed at the forward end of the car, when there was a scuffling sound at the doorway, and Bill reappeared, a grin splitting his face. His cap was gone and there was lipstick on his cheek.

"Tom! Tom! Get up!"

"What?"

"She's here, you fool. Come on. They're all here." He waved. He had Tom's chair and pushed it to him. Tom lunged up, grabbed a seatback, and pulled himself upright on his shaking legs. The hell with the wheelchair.

"My crutches, Bill. They're under the seat."

Bill pulled out the crutches. "Never mind those," he yelled. "Come on! I'll help you out."

Tom reached for the crutches. "Stand back, old pal." He planted himself with his left hand on the back of a seat, clutched his crutches in his right and leaned on them as he struggled toward the front of the compartment. Then, with one hand on the handrail, crutches in the other, Bill hovering behind, he levered himself down the steps. Once he was on the platform he pulled himself erect, a crutch under each arm. He swayed but caught his balance, pain shooting through both legs and a trickle of sweat running down his back. He looked up, across the crowded platform, and saw his family, just as he had pictured them.

And there was Ellen, off to one side, only feet behind them, hands clasped in front of her. She was taller than he remembered, and her eyes were bluer. She wore a black suit with a white blouse, a red scarf at her throat. An uncertain smile lit up her face. She was the prettiest thing he had ever seen.

Tom's family exploded around him, laughing and talking. His mother was crying, and he thought his chest would burst open with the joy that welled up. He was home. He was alive. There were tears in his eyes, tears of relief, of happiness. And through them, as the hubbub died down, he saw Ellen, still standing alone.

He got his crutches under his armpits, his hands on the grips, and started toward her. She ran to him, and the next instant his crutches fell and she was in his arms. Somehow, they stayed on their feet.

EPILOGUE

◆　◆　◆

On October 4, 1920, a six-foot-tall, broad-shouldered man in a three-piece business suit walked carefully up the steps of the Empire Club in downtown Toronto. He never held onto railings, but he didn't take chances, either.

When he reached the portico Tom stopped and lit a cigarette, one habit he could not shake after shrugging off his uniform for the last time the year before. At least he had put on some of the weight he had lost. Funny, he was feeling out of sorts coming here on this occasion; he'd have a drink if one was offered. Absent-mindedly he reached into his inside breast pocket—the side opposite to his cigarettes—and felt the letter. Still there. He could have quoted it word for word but preferred to take it out and read it once more, the firm, no-nonsense but feminine handwriting.

Dearest Tom,

I know it has been months since I wrote you, a letter written when I was at a low ebb. Can you forgive me, Tom? I was lonely and afraid, afraid of what the future might hold. Afraid of what might happen to you, and afraid I might not be able to handle it. And it had been a long time. As I write this my brother Ned is downstairs, drinking, and Joan, his wife, is looking after the baby. It is not a happy picture. I have just heard that you have been wounded. One thing is clear to me now, Tom, and that is that you are not like my brother, and never could be like him.

It is snowing, but the sun is breaking through. The sun sparkling on the flakes as they float down reminds me of our ride in the cutter, our brief time together. I remember your pride in your family, and the way you cared for Belle after our accident. You are a good man, Tom, and I pray for your safe return. We must be together, no matter what. I love you.

Ellen

He smiled as he put the letter back in its envelope with its King George stamp and postmarks and changes of address in varying hands from what seemed like half the western world. The army post office address in France was nearly obliterated by two English postmarks that were on top of the address for Number 4 Canadian Hospital, which was stroked out and followed in turn by a Southampton post office address. From there the letter had gone to Halifax, then finally completed the circle at the Winnipeg Depot where it had reached him after the war was over. He and Ellen managed a good laugh when it finally turned up. Tom carefully refolded the letter, returning it to his jacket pocket.

He could have been on his way home by now, but he had stayed overnight out of curiosity. He wondered what two and a half years had done to Seely. Tom had heard from Bruce, while he was still in hospital, that the former statesman, politician, and brigadier-general had swallowed German gas, and his days of roaming the forward positions in person had come to an end.

Tom was not a member of the Empire Club and doubted that any former enlisted man was. A hall porter raised an eyebrow, but Tom ignored him and the man subsided into his cubbyhole, waving vaguely toward double doors leading into a ballroom.

Tom slid into the back of the room. Officials of the club seated at a head table included a sprinkling of men he recognized as former army officers. A few members of the audience were in uniform.

The introduction had just finished and Seely started to speak. "Mistah President and Membaahs of the Empaah Club of Canada . . ." His topic, he said, was "a very thrilling story—the story of your Canadian cavalry."

The general knew how to move a room. He addressed many of the former officers present in personal terms, playing to their pride in the exploits of the Canadian army, and the cavalry in particular. The general's south-of-England, drawn-out vowels and missing consonants thrust Tom back in time, the room around him blurring, out of focus. The general had survived the war, and so had Bruce Johanson, now back home in Alberta, looking down his nose at city slickers who couldn't ride, and Quartermain, glaring fiercely at new recruits to the peace-time army. Gordon Ferguson, the last he had heard, was thinking about moving to the west coast. At least they had made it safely home, as had Tom.

But he couldn't dwell too long on the past. His wounds plagued him every day and he was still unable to shut out the horrors of the war. Before he could stop himself he saw, once again, Flowerdew tumble from his saddle, the boy Longley go down in the act of raising the trumpet to his lips. Again he was alone on galloping Toby, bent low over his neck, blood lust up, sword levelled, blood spattering from his flayed legs as Toby grunted in pain. Horses screamed and men moaned for their mothers and Planck bled out on the ground. René Carbonnier insisted on a *coup de grâce* for his horse, then died in Tom's arms. Inkmann hovered, he who had long since joined his brother in whatever hell awaited them. Tom shuddered and left the hall, the general's cultured tones fading.

◆ ◆ ◆

Ellen straightened and pushed with both hands on her lower back. Any day now, and it couldn't happen too soon. She wondered again whether it was to be a boy or a girl. A daughter who would be close to her, as she had been to her mother? Or a son, to make Tom proud? But he'd be proud, either way. She poured two cups of coffee, then sat and picked up the *Free Press*.

Her mind wandered. How different things could have been, how improbable her present happiness, if she had chosen Harry. Harry had left town to return to Toronto, never having spoken to her again after she returned his ring and told him in her letter that she would wait for Tom. I wonder if Carol went with him?

Tom walked into the kitchen and bent to kiss her, holding her for a moment. He looks tired, she thought. Too long out of town on a business trip with his legs acting up. He never slept well when his legs were bad.

"I'm staying home today," he said. "I feel like this is the day."

"Since when do men have intuition about babies?" she laughed. "Besides, that's what you said last week. You go to work. Daddy is just around the corner in case I go into labour."

A headline on a small story on the front page caught her eye. "General Seely. They're quoting his speech, the one you heard in Toronto. Did you hear what General Foch had to say?"

"No, sweetheart. I think I mentioned I left early."

"General Foch—he was the French general in charge of the Allies when the Germans were defeated, wasn't he? Anyway, here's what Foch said to Seely:

> I do not forget the heroism of the valiant Canadian Cavalry Brigade. In the month of March, 1918, the war was at the gate of Amiens. It was vital to maintain at any price the close contact between our two armies, the British and French. On March 30 at Moreuil, and on April 1 at Hangard en Santerre, your brigade succeeded, by its magnificent performance and its unconquerable élan, in first checking the enemy and finally breaking down its spirit. In the highest degree, thanks to your brigade, the situation, agonizing as it had been at the opening of the battle, was restored.

"He's talking about the big picture," said Tom. "All I know is it was a bloody mess from where I saw it."

She sent him off to work, and he promised to stay close to a phone. Like many veterans, he had not gone back to his former pursuits. All thoughts of Zink—still behind bars—and the practice of law were long behind him; he was employed by Eaton's, working his way up in the hardware department.

Tom hardly ever spoke about the war, and even when he did, it was only to make casual, general comments. Nothing specific.

"Aren't you ever going to talk about it?" Ellen had once asked.

"Not now. Maybe not ever."

Maybe, she thought, it's for another generation to explore.

Her father would be over shortly to stand by in case he was needed to get her to the hospital. She gathered the breakfast dishes, and was leaning into the sink when a sharp pain wrenched her body and a cascade of water flooded down her legs.

Yes, she thought. Yes.

ACKNOWLEDGMENTS

This book is a work of fiction and as such, characters, places, and incidents are products of my imagination or are used fictitiously. That being said, I have tried, where possible, to be true to the events my father described to me and to the times in which my characters are placed.

This book would not have been possible without the great support and unerring advice I received from my wonderful wife, Patricia Sandberg, our sons, Scott and Ross, my sister Lamont, and friend Phyllis Hinz.

Comments on the manuscript were generously provided by the Rainwriters, especially Ed Griffin and Carol Tulpar, as well as all the others; early versions were reviewed by my friends Robert Smith and Cyndi Kilroe.

Historical research was accomplished with the generous assistance of Warrant Officer Donald E. MacLeod, Curator, Lord Strathcona's Horse (Royal Canadians) Museum and Archives, in Calgary.

Jean-Paul Brunel and his wife, Nicole, were our gracious hosts in Moreuil, France. Jean-Paul, after his 1986 discovery of the remains of a Canadian trooper killed in the Battle of Moreuil Wood, became a passionate and inspiring amateur historian of the activities of the Canadian Cavalry Brigade. His enthusiasm and support are most appreciated. Picardy author and local historian Marc Pilot was most helpful with translation and our tour of the area.

Finally, I must thank Ruth Linka at TouchWood Editions for her generous support and encouragement, and my accomplished and professional editor, Marlyn Horsdal, for her perseverance and dedication to the process of turning the manuscript into a book.

Robert W. Mackay's interest in military history is deep in his roots. His father was in the Canadian Cavalry in the First World War, and his brother was a career naval officer. Robert served with the Royal Canadian Navy and the British Navy until 1969. He attended the University of British Columbia and practiced law until his retirement in 2008. He lives with his wife in Surrey, BC. *Soldier of the Horse* is his first novel. Visit robertwmackay.com or follow Robert on Twitter at @RobertWMackay.